Cassie Connor lo⸱ ⸱joys weekending in Nice and takes her own champagne flute wherever she goes. She's also got a history degree and has never finished *War and Peace*. When it comes to dating, her motto is CBA - Can't Be Arsed - and has resorted to writing and inventing her own men because fictional heroes are always so much better. Hudson in her debut novel, *Love Under Contract*, proves the point perfectly.

 instagram.com/CassieConnor

Also by Cassie Connor

Love Under Contract

HOT PURSUIT

CASSIE CONNOR

One More Chapter
a division of HarperCollins*Publishers* Ltd
1 London Bridge Street
London SE1 9GF
www.harpercollins.co.uk

HarperCollins*Publishers*
Macken House, 39/40 Mayor Street Upper,
Dublin 1, D01 C9W8
This paperback edition 2024
1
First published in Great Britain in ebook format
by HarperCollins*Publishers* 2024

A catalogue record of this book is available from the British Library
ISBN: 978-0-00-866289-9

Printed and bound in the UK using 100% Renewable Electricity
by CPI Group (UK) Ltd

For, Ellie, a feisty, strong, bold and brave woman – an absolute inspiration and role model.

Chapter One

LYDIA

Flying to Barcelona for the day sounds dead glamorous, except my in-flight bag contains a hi-vis vest, hard hat and steel toe-cap boots. Today's trip hasn't started off well. At stupid o'clock at Heathrow on a Friday morning, I find out my boss Jeff Truman has bailed, some family emergency. A replacement is en route. Which is a bummer. Dependable old Jeff is happily married, with trendy, popular teenagers. They've trained him well – he's never tried to talk me into bed on a business trip or made inappropriate comments. The perfect workmate. Always a plus in my book.

When I land, my phone starts vibrating like a Rabbit on maximum setting, a flurry of texts bursting onto the screen advising me that I'll be joined by a colleague who's just joined the company, so I've not encountered him before.

Great. I always love an unknown quantity. Apparently he was on my flight, so our driver can pick us at the same time.

I indulge in a spot of people-watching as the escalator glides down to the main concourse. There are an awful lot of hot Spanish men in their forties with just the right amount of distinguished grey tinting their temples. Is that something in their collective genes?

There's a guy a few steps below. He immediately captures my attention, even from behind. His hair is cropped short at the back, neatly trimmed and leading down into a strong neck, and if you were into that sort of thing, you might fantasise about wrapping your arms around it when you're kissing him. Dark grey suit. Fitted across broad manly shoulders. Long lean legs and the sort of taut arse that makes parts of me sit up and purr. His suit jacket is rucked up by the strap on his laptop case, allowing me to totally objectify the hell out of him. I'm wondering about his haunches, that sexy muscle and tendon bit of thighs and buttocks.

Yeah, I know, a bit weird, but I've had a thing about haunches ever since the time I had the BEST sex of my life. The filthiest, full-on two-night stand that left me starry-eyed and my nerve endings throbbing for a week. Just thinking about it still creates a rosy glow between my legs. I clamp my thighs together. Don't go there, Lydie. Not now, when you're about to meet a new work colleague as well as Señor Lopez, head honcho of the sports retail company that owns the distribution centre that has just burnt down.

I avert my eyes from Sexy Suit man who, to my disappointment, takes a sharp left at the bottom of the escalator, while I turn right, following the exit signs, my eyes scanning the ranks of men bearing whiteboards, handwritten signs on A4 sheets of paper and – fancier – iPads with a variety of international names.

Although I've travelled a lot with my work, it never ceases to be a thrill that someone has come especially to collect me. Someone is here for me.

With the usual burst of happiness, I spot my name.

On. An. iPad.

'Lydia Smith' is spelled out in large white letters out of black. Proper text. For some stupid reason it makes me even happier. Someone had to make an extra bit of effort to do this. Even having to share the billing doesn't dim my delight. Beneath my name it reads 'Tom Dereborn'. This must be the name of New Guy. The surname rings a bell and I feel like there was a girl in my college at university that had that same name. Although I've not met him before, I'm not too worried about him being chucked in at the deep end as I seem to recall he's come from another well-respected loss adjuster.

I approach the driver at exactly the same time as Sexy Suit retraces his steps and comes towards me. Our eyes look at the iPad and then at each other.

Oooooh Fuuuuuck!

Some higher being on another plane is obviously bored today.

I do not sodding well believe it. Seriously?

I know this guy. Intimately. Very, very, very intimately. It's Mr BEST Sex of my Life or at least … I think it is.

There is the faintest flicker of recognition in his steel-blue-grey eyes but then, like a portcullis slamming down, it's gone. He blanks me. Completely. Now there's nothing in his bland impassive face to suggest we had sex numerous times, in numerous positions, in numerous rooms in his apartment. I could almost believe he's never met me before.

A middle-aged man steps forward from behind the driver like a referee stopping me from blurting out, 'You!'

'Señorita Smith. Señor De Reborn. I'm Guido Lopez from Consa-Calida. I thought I'd meet you here and we can go straight to the site for a survey before going into the city to our offices and for some lunch.' He holds out a hand, and as I'm closest, I hold mine out.

So does Tom Dereborn.

The client looks from one to the other of us and out of gentlemanly chivalry takes my hand and shakes it first.

'Mr Lopez,' I say. 'Nice to meet you.'

'You too, Señorita Smith.'

Lopez turns to my colleague. 'Señor De Reborn, nice to meet you.' It must be mild hysteria that makes me want to giggle at his mispronunciation of Dereborn. He repeats the same formalities while the two of us look everywhere but at each other. This cannot be happening.

As Mr Lopez and the driver turn to lead us to the car, I

leave Tom De Reborn to make small talk as I try to fathom how the hell this could have happened.

We slide into the back seat from opposite sides as our host gets into the front passenger seat and immediately turns to talk to us. We don't even look at each other but I'm so very conscious of Tom just centimetres from me. My body hums with awareness, every hair on my arms standing to attention, tiny blonde iron filings tuned to Tom Dereborn's magnetic north.

I know this man. I know exactly what he looks like naked. I know how his skin feels. Know what his dick feels like, full inside me. I know what it's like when he whispers shamelessly filthy words in my ear, to make me come, while he's finger-fucking me. For two days and two nights the man knew me inside and out, milked orgasm after orgasm from me. He grunted, groaned and ground. I can still see the tendons in his neck as he's thrusting over me, holding on for dear life, trying to prolong the race to the edge. Hear the long-drawn-out 'fuuuuck' as he comes, pumping and pulsing.

I'm damp, wet and horny. He's ruined me for anyone else and, believe me, I've tried to blot him out. I've tried to erase him. Boy, have I tried, but every sodding subsequent sexual encounter has been a big fat disappointment. So much so – I've given up. No sex, not so much as a sniff, for ages.

I glue my posture upright and forward so I'm not for

one minute tempted to look at him, catch his gaze, or even so much as acknowledge him. Thankfully he seems inclined to do exactly the same, although what else can we say in front of the extremely charming Guido Lopez, who seems to have taken a shine to me.

'Señorita Smith,' he shoots an admiring glance at my legs in heels and barely-there sheer tights, 'would you like to stay in the car? After the fire it is … not the place for a beautiful woman.'

I hear a snort come from my left. I don't blame him. I'm here to assess the scale of the loss of the contents of a warehouse which two days ago contained sixty-four thousand square feet of sports equipment. Those football shirts, it would seem, are very flammable. I'm not sure how Señor Lopez expects me to do that from the back of the car.

'Your colleague, Mr De Reborn, will, I'm sure, be able to conduct the survey on his own.'

I give the Spaniard a cool smile. It's not the first time I've been underestimated and relegated to note-taker or back-up partner. Some might say it's because I insist on presenting myself as a smart, feminine woman but why the hell not? This is who I am. It's been hard won and I'm not about to compromise for anyone. I don't have to apologise for being young and attractive or dressing how I want. I'm vain. I want to look good, so I do. But I allow for some practicality – it's common sense if you're working in the field.

When the car pulls up next to the blackened site,

buckled and twisted steel uprights testament to the former warehouse, I open my travel bag and pull out a pair of thick hiking socks, my steel toe-capped boots, my hi-vis vest and my yellow hard hat as well as what looks like a brown lab coat.

I try not to feel self-conscious taking off my shoes in the back of the car in front of Tom Dereborn. It feels intimate and far too reminiscent of him unbuckling the straps on my sky-high sandals and running his hands up and along my calves. I gulp and hurriedly pull on my thick, distinctly unsexy, wool socks.

By the time the driver has parked the car, my footwear is on and I've regained a little equilibrium as I step out onto the slightly sticky tarmac, which must have melted in the heat. Acrid smoke taints the air and there's a glow of warmth that has little to do with the local climate. I shrug the overcoat over my suit without saying a word to our host. My colleague mutters, 'Show-off,' under his breath.

Señor Lopez walks us around the site, our feet crunching on broken glass and blackened debris, indicating the warped metal struts – all that's left of the extensive racking that once lined the aisles. His face is twisted with woe and despair as he relays in that spare, hopeless way of the bereft how much has been lost. I have to stamp down on the innate sympathy and the desire to reassure him. It's always sad to see the aftermath of destruction, especially when it's someone's business.

Unfortunately, we're the bad guys sent in to determine the truth of the loss and adjust expectations back to reality. Some clients exaggerate the size of the loss – after all, who does it harm? They've paid their premiums all this time, they deserve the pay-out. But I have a responsibility to shareholders and to other insurance customers to stop out-and-out fraud and keep their premiums affordable. I might sound callous, but I don't mean to. Often we're dealing with shell-shocked, horrified people who've seen a lifetime's work snuffed out in one fell swoop. It is heartbreaking but there is a certain percentage of people who will always try it on. According to Señor Lopez, who has already provided us with extensive figures and details of the amount of stock that was held on this site, the company was holding more stock than it sold in the whole of last year. The figures didn't stack up even back when I was in London.

I know exactly what I need to see and I ask Señor Lopez to show me round the former warehouse. I ask a ton of questions that he quickly starts to get irritated by, but I want a watertight case and for my report to be incontrovertible. I'm known for being thorough.

'For fuck's sake,' mutters my colleague, when I ask Lopez to indicate exactly where the shelves were. When I ask the height of the shelving and how many shelves per unit there were, he tuts under his breath.

I ignore him. I know my job. To be honest it's a relief he's being a complete arse. Stops me remembering all the ways he was so good in bed.

'Señorita Smith. What difference does it make? Everything is gone. You have the figures.' Lopez frowns.

'Yes, Miss Smith,' replies my colleague, undeniable withering sarcasm present in every syllable.

'How wide were the aisles?' I press, pacing across the floor, trying to visualise the scene. Across on the other side of the factory is a skip full of water-soaked sports shirts.

'We couldn't salvage much,' the client says, mournfully trying to steer me away from the skip.

'I'd like to see,' I say and shrug off his restraining hand and march over to the skip. Tom Dereborn follows me, hissing in a low voice, 'For God's sake. Didn't you read the file before you got here? No way in hell did they have ten mill's worth of stock stored here. Any idiot can see that. What are you trying to prove?'

I know exactly that but…

'I'm making sure the job is done properly. I bet you ten quid that there aren't that many shirts in there and the rest have been repatriated by the company to sell on some market stall or car boot sale.'

'So what?'

I whirl on him unaccountably raising my voice. 'So what?' I put my hands on my hips and glare at him. It feels good to be mad at him, although I'm madder than I usually would be because he's done such a good job of pretending he's never met me before. I want to make him pay for that. Pay for all the other people who've pretended they don't know me because I'm not good enough.

'Yeah,' he says going toe to toe with me, his smart brogues nudging up against my scuffed leather boots.

'I don't bloody believe it.'

'Why are you making a meal of this? The company is obviously inflating the claim.'

'I know that but I'm being thorough.' The word brings back a memory. Tom Dereborn was very thorough, and I flush remembering how assiduous he was... A lick of heat touches my core at the sudden memory – the slow careful slide of his mouth up my thighs and his hot breath teasing my clit.

I suck in a quick breath, to shake loose the thoughts and focus on the specks of white-grey ash dusting the air. 'I want to be able to prove it should they appeal.'

'Our word should be good enough.' His arrogant drawl brings me back to the present.

'We're supposed to be professional. We should be meticulous. Give me a hand.' I regret my choice of words. I've had those hands over every inch of my body.

'What?'

There it is. Just a tiny tell, his left eye twitches ever so slightly.

'I want to get in the skip. Give me a leg up.'

'You are fucking joking.'

'Do I look like I'm joking? Why would you even think that?'

'Because what you want...' The pause is infinitesimal

but it's enough. *Tell me what you want.* He murmured it over and over in my ear, followed up with filthy suggestions. '... is for me to do the gentlemanly thing and volunteer to go in there. These are custom-made brogues and a Brioni suit. You going to pay my dry-cleaning bill?'

'I am more than capable of getting into the skip and some of us dressed appropriately. Who the hell wears a suit that needs dry cleaning to go on site?'

'We're representing the company,' he hisses at me. 'And this is a straightforward case. We could be doing this in an office going over the financials. I dressed to look professional.'

'And I didn't?'

He gives my skirt, with its flippy frill, a dismissive look. 'You'll do.'

'And for the record, I don't expect you to get in the skip just because you're a man and I'm a poor weak female. So if you can quit whining for five minutes and give me a leg up, I'd be grateful.'

He holds out his hands and I take great satisfaction in planting a soggy, ash-covered boot in the palm of his hand. 'For fuck's sake,' he grumbles, 'I don't know why you're bothering. We both know the client's a lying sack of shit.' With that he heaves me upwards with more testosterone-fuelled force than necessary and I tumble into the skip, my weight crashing through the pile of soggy empty boxes immediately beneath the surface layer of slithery plastic-packaged shirts. It takes me a while to wade through them and resurface, and when I finally emerge, I spot Señor Lopez scowling behind Tom's back. It's obvious he's heard every word and is less than impressed with either of us.

Somehow, I think lunch is a goner.

Chapter Two

TOM

W e're on the same flight back, though thankfully not sitting next to each other. I'm not sure I can keep up the pretence of being unaffected by Lydia. My dick seems to have developed some Pavlovian dog response to her perfume. Every time I get a whiff of that floral citrus fragrance of hers, it twitches.

Even I realise that it might have been good manners to acknowledge we had sex once … actually it was a lot more than once, but it was a one-time thing. What the hell do you say when you're unexpectedly reunited and in a work situation? *Hi, nice to see you again?* rather than the first things that sprang to mind which were, one, *It took me a while to walk straight after that weekend, how about you?* and, two, *Damn, fancy running into you when I've been doing my utmost to try and forget you.*

It doesn't help that I'm in a seriously shitty mood today.

Maybe I took it out on her because that weekend had been so fucking glorious and terrifying. My actions were completely out of character during those forty-eight hours but at the same time so in tune with the guy I'd rather be. Free, uninhibited and a little bit wild. Truth is, I hate my job. Absolutely loathe the fucker. I never wanted to be in insurance, still don't. Problem is, you do it for a while, to keep the peace, and then you get used to a salary. You rent a place, then you have rent payments and bills and you're stuck.

So maybe I took it out on Little Miss Eager Beaver. No one likes a keen bean. Especially not one who plays by the book. Normally I'm pretty good at hiding my frustration but not today. And not with her. She's supposed to be an illusion, the perfect companion that clicked with another me, one that's never existed outside that weekend. Now I have to face up to the fact that she's a living, breathing person that I can't just ignore, as well as the dissatisfaction of who I really am these days. I pull out my phone and open the email I received overnight. You'd have thought the words would be burnt into my brain I've read it so many times. I sigh, frustration and elation jostling with each other.

I throw myself back in my seat and hear a tut from behind. I can't even skive off this afternoon as there's no excuse for not going back to the office given our trip has been cut short. Lopez couldn't get us to the airport fast enough. Probably wasn't that professional to call him a lying sack of shit – even it was true – especially not when I've only just joined the company.

It's fair to say I sulk for most of the flight back to London. Not my most attractive trait but hey, we're all allowed an off day. Although I seem to have had a lot of them in recent months. Eleven months to be precise.

Rather awkwardly, Lydia and I go through passport control at the same time and end up walking together towards the Underground following the signs to the Piccadilly Line. I should have taken a cab.

We're standing waiting for the Tube when she nonchalantly asks while studying the advert opposite and not even looking at me, 'How long are you going to keep this up?'

'Keep what up?' Okay, so I'm being deliberately obtuse, but why can't she leave it? It happened. Months ago. Eleven months ago.

'Pretending that you don't know me.'

'I don't know you,' I say because if we're being pedantic about these things. I don't *know* know her. I don't know her age, and before today I didn't even know her surname, didn't know what she did, where she lives or anything about her. I don't know her heart's desires, her past, present or future.

There's a pause and I regret being such a dick but it's too late to backtrack.

To give her maximum credit, she doesn't make a thing of it, which perversely makes me like her even more. I like that she's no-nonsense, making it perfectly plain she thinks I'm a wanker in the way that she purses her lips and gives me a pitying smile.

'I take it you're going back to the office,' she says.

'Might as well. You going to write up the report?'

'I think that would be best,' she says, her voice clipped and disapproving. 'Given that I was the one actually investigating the claim.'

I wince. She's right. She was doing the job I should have been doing. Despite being made to feel in the wrong, I kind of like that she knows who she is and isn't going to compromise. Not that I'm going to show it.

'Fill your boots. The financials speak for themselves.' I sound like a petulant prick. It's not her fault I've been offered my dream and can't fund it, or that she makes me think of what a fake I am.

I sit opposite her on the Tube and covertly study her. Shoulder-length brunette hair, sensible suit. In fact, everything about her is sensible. I'm still not sure what made me move on her that night. I mean she's pretty in a non-showy way, very understated. I usually prefer more out-there women, glamorous and glossy.

There was something about the dress she wore. Black. Silk. Severe at the front, unexpectedly sexy as hell at the back. I study the navy blue suit she's wearing now. It looks expensive and plain apart from the feminine little flippy hem to the skirt. She's self-contained, like she knows her own worth, but under her clothes I know her body is...

I shut the thought down and try to concentrate on the rattle of the train hurtling through the dark tunnel. It was just sex. Good sex ... okay, amazing sex. I might even go as far as to say once-in-a-lifetime sex. At that moment I catch her eye and it all comes back. Blood starts to circulate where it shouldn't and I put a brake on those thoughts and transfer them.

Email. Film. Offer.

This morning the email came. The one I've dreamed about for years. After months of discussion, Oswater Productions have green-lighted my screenplay, with ME, yes ME, as director – this is a BFD. The biggest in my life, except I need to secure more funding to make the project happen and be able to give up my day job.

Maybe I could moonlight as a gigolo or an escort. The thought makes me scowl just as Lydia looks my way again. She stiffens, I can see it in the tightening of her jaw. She thinks my grimace is aimed at her. I look away, down at my phone, one hand rubbing against the faded fabric covering my seat. She unsettles me and I don't know why. Is it because she was completely uninhibited that weekend and so was I and it scared the shit out of me?

When the train pulls into Green Park station, I'm even more grumpy than I was getting off the plane. I need to pull myself together and put on a good show. I ought to try and make a good impression at the new company.

My parents think it's fan-fucking-tastic that I've joined Bignall Harcourt Claims Assessors, although I suspect Dad pulled a few strings to get me the job – even though I asked him specifically not to. He can't help himself. I shouldn't have let on I'd got an interview, except my sister Rosie announced over Sunday lunch she'd just had a promotion. Competitive much?

Mum and Dad are thrilled by the big fat salary increase – Mum especially. She thinks it's a 'pass go' to mortgage, matrimony and multiple babies, which apparently I owe her. The idea fills me with terror.

I follow Lydia out of the carriage and into the throng of people. She doesn't even look back at me, just strides ahead, weaving her way through the crowd with the navigational ease of an Exocet missile.

I'm in a halfway house of indecision. We're both going the same way, to the same place – it feels churlish not to talk and I don't feel like apologising or explaining but manners – thanks, Mum and Dad, you'll be proud – get the better of me.

'Hey.' I stop and tug at her arm at the top of the escalator. 'Look, I'm not in the best mood today, right. I don't always behave like this.'

She stares at me, utter indifference streaming out like a searchlight in the night sky, and shrugs. 'I don't know you.'

Touché. I'm reluctantly impressed.

'It makes no difference to me,' she continues. 'Besides it's unlikely we'll work together again. Today was a one-off.' She lifts her chin, the 'thank God' unspoken but it's there. 'I need to get the report done today, I'm away next week.'

With that she starts walking again and doesn't even pause at the glass sliding doors of the offices.

She's cool. I like that she doesn't engage in any drama.

'Hey, Danny,' she greets the security guy at reception with a broad smile. 'How was the match last night?' There's a marked difference in her attitude to him and it intrigues me to see a completely different side to her.

'Micky scored three goals.'

'Proud Grandad.' Her face softens. It makes her look much younger. Even a little vulnerable, which surprises me. She's seemed fortress-like until now.

'You bet. How was sunny Spain?' he asks. 'You're back early.'

'Complete washout,' says Lydia with a quick look my way. 'Storm clouds spoiled a perfect sky.'

'That's a shame. Never mind. You looking forward to being a TV star next week? My granddaughters love that *Sex Island* thing.'

It's the first time I've seen her look uncertain. That's interesting.

'I have to pass the audition first.'

'Rather you than me,' says the security guy. 'Although I wouldn't turn the money down.'

'You only get the cash if you get through,' says Lydia.

'They're still looking for a couple more people. Maybe I'll speak to HR, although the missus says they wouldn't want my ugly mug on screen – my granddaughters would die of embarrassment.' He guffaws. 'I wouldn't mind a shot at a hundred grand though.'

If I was an Alsatian dog my ears would be perfect triangles they're so pricked up.

Lydia nods, flashes her identity badge and walks over to the lift, I follow her and only just make it between the closing doors. I think she pressed the button to close them deliberately.

'What's this about a reality TV show?'

She suddenly looks a little shifty as her eyes don't meet mine. 'You've heard of our esteemed chairman.'

'Harcourt, yeah.'

'His production company is producing a new TV pilot series. They need guinea pigs for the first show. All the details are on the company intranet.'

I'm intrigued. 'I didn't have you down as a wannabe celeb.'

'I'm not,' she snaps.

It's fun to tug the string some more. 'A hundred grand is a lot of moolah.'

She nods as if she's too good to admit to needing filthy lucre.

'Where do I sign up?'

Her look is pure scorn. 'Yeah, because someone like you really needs the money.'

Her dismissive assumption punctures my self-composure and anger flashes through me. 'Like you said earlier, you don't know me.'

She flinches but lifts her chin again. 'No. I don't.'

The subtext beneath her words makes me regret my temper but my curiosity is up and running like a well-fuelled hamster on a wheel. I want to know more about this reality TV gig and the prize money. It's a long shot but that would be the answer to my prayers.

As soon as I get to my desk, I open up my computer and log into Newspace, the company intranet site.

Everyone's heard of Harcourt Productions, They make the cringe-inducing programme *Naked Adventures*. It features a series of people around the world bungy jumping, zip wiring, cave diving, parachuting – as the title suggests – completely in the altogether.

It's on its fourth season. Personally, I'd have thought they'd have run out of blokes prepared to have their dangly bits out at five thousand feet and above but apparently not.

Want to win £100K? reads a large heading at the top of the page.

Wouldn't that come in handy? I read the blurb, crossing my fingers that nudity is not involved.

Harcourt Productions is filming a new reality series, *Fleeing for Your Life.*

That sounds hardcore. I'm surprised Lydia has signed up.

Think Hunted *meets* The Island with Bear Grylls. *Our pilot series will pit teams of contestants against each other, making their way from the Lake District to London under their own steam while evading capture from our elite squad of hunters. The first team to arrive wins a hundred grand.*

Definitely no mention of being naked. Although fleeing for your life sounds a bit dramatic – but it's bound to be, given that this is cheap telly. I read on, feeling more hopeful than I have all day.

There are two days' induction and selection for which candidates receive ten thousand pounds, with the chance to win the main prize if they pass the audition process. The final challenge will take place over five days and may be subject to change as this is a pilot series…

How hard can it be to go on the run for a week? I was a Venture Scout back in the day.

I place a call to HR.

Chapter Three

LYDIA

It's one thing to glibly agree to a challenge a month ago in a bright sunlit office in the anonymous safety of the city but now, pulling into Oxenholme station, which looks just like something from *The Railway Children*, I'm having second, third, fourth and ninety-second thoughts. *Fleeing for Your Life* suddenly sounds terrifying, especially surrounded by open country. For the last hour there's been nothing but fields. Where are all the buildings? The people? The cars? Where the hell do you hide out here?

With a pang I think of my grandmother's home, the one she left to me. The one my parents have ravaged with their neglect over the last twenty years. I could cry when I think of the sagging roof, the broken windows and the unkempt garden, and that's just the outside. God only knows what it's like inside. I swallow a hard lump. I have to do this. I can do this. I have to restore the sad house. It symbolises the family life I experienced when my grandmother was alive, the normality and order that came with living with her. Once she died, all that disappeared. That house is so much more than a mere building to me.

I'm not going to give up at the first puny hurdle, which is that I can barely lift my suitcase down onto the platform. I shove, push and pull the outsize case, trying to get it out of the door, and when I look up for help, I see Tom bloody Dereborn is disembarking from the next carriage and watching me, his lip curling, his disdain obvious. Then, to my utter surprise, he strides over and takes it from me, lifting it and lowering it to the platform with a quick grunt.

'What the fuck have you got in there?' he says.

'What are you doing here?' I ask, horrified by the quick punch of excitement my body produces at the sight of him.

'Same as you, I'd imagine.'

He dumps my case on the ground and turns his back on me to pick up his own fancy rucksack, navy blue with dozens of straps and plastic catches in co-ordinating orange. It's a proper boys' adventure piece of kit with orange mesh pockets of varying sizes, packed with bottles of water, bananas, a book and his mobile phone.

It doesn't bother me. At school I was always the poor relation, woefully ill-equipped. Not anymore. My case might be huge, but I can guarantee I'm prepared for every eventuality.

The tiny train station is the gateway to the Lake District, where, according to the paperwork, we're being picked up and taken to 'base'. The word brings to mind military-style tents and men in combat gear. Said paperwork has been sketchy about the exact details of the next two days and what is involved as they're 'subject to change', though it had included a detailed waiver and a release form, and a loose two-day itinerary. Today we'll meet everyone during an orientation session and tomorrow there will a day's team-building audition process to assess our suitability for the programme. I'd really like to have known more to prepare a little. I have a lot riding on this.

I sneak a look at Tom's stern profile. Christ, just imagine if the production company knew we'd slept together and hadn't seen each other until last week. It would increase our chances of being picked to take part as it would make good telly. But I can't let them know. It was humiliating enough that we slept together and then the bastard couldn't wait to get rid of me afterwards.

I can remember it so clearly. As the sun started to go down on Sunday and the evening drew in, it was as if he morphed into another person. One minute he was kissing my shoulder and then the next, he was hustling me out of his apartment like his pants were on fire, and his parents were due home any second – except I'm pretty damn sure it was his place given the all-grey, tasteful and blatantly single-guy decor. I can't decide whether I'm still mad as hell with him because of the way he pulled the plug on that weekend or because he pretended he didn't know me.

I've gone over a gazillion times what I might have said

to trigger it that Sunday evening – that portcullis coming down, the warmth fizzing out of those blue eyes turning them steely grey. I saw it again when we were on site in Spain.

I met Tom Dereborn … I can't bring myself to call him Tom because while my body might know his intimately, having been expertly filled, fucked every which way by his, until the other day I never knew his full name.

Exactly eleven months ago, one Friday evening, he sat down next to me at one of those interminable industry conference dinners. From the moment his shoulder brushed mine, firing up an electric frisson-fuelled awareness, I was conscious of his every move. Even the low-pitched timbre of his voice, gravelly and smoke-filled, set off a crazy flash of lust curling and twisting through me. We barely spoke, both of us intentionally concentrating on our other neighbours as if determined to ignore the Northern Lights flare of energy dancing between us. Halfway through the main course – could have been chicken – I bent to pick up the napkin that had slipped off my lap and he bent at the same moment to gather it for me. His hand touched mine and for some stupid reason, my breath caught in my throat as I looked into his deep blue eyes.

'Do you want to get out of here?' he asked.

Without so much as a blink of hesitation, I nodded.

'Meet you in the foyer in five,' he murmured out of the corner of his mouth and got up from the table.

I remember slugging back the wine in my glass, picking

up my clutch bag and forcing myself to watch the second hand of the big grand clock above the ballroom of The Dorchester until exactly five minutes had passed. I half expected to find that he'd gone.

Shamelessly and without a second thought I followed him into the cab the concierge had called up for us. Our mouths fused the minute the door closed. I never felt such desperation to get so close to someone. It was as if a jar of fireflies had been emptied into my brain, dazzling me with sparks. Every long, slow, drugging drag of his lips over mine made them brighten, and when his tongue touched mine, they exploded, sending cascading vibrations fizzing down through my sternum.

I suspect when it came round to Sunday evening, he regretted the whole weekend.

Accepting that is like a tiny stab wound, small on the outside but it goes deep. I was good enough to fuck senseless, but nothing else. It makes me mad at him all over again as well as reinforcing that awareness that I've always carried with me that I'm somehow lacking in some way. I'm good at my job, I have friends, people like me, but there is something intrinsic, a basic essential bit of me that is wrong in some way. Over the years I thought I'd got used to it, but his rejection of me after the intimacies we shared has scored deeply.

Sometimes I wonder if I imagined the connection between us. I've replayed that weekend so many times in my head, but I'm a realist, not given to flights of fantasy and

I know it was there. I didn't imagine it. Tom chose to reject it, but it was there.

Pride stops me bringing the subject up. Fuck him.

I stagger a little with the weight of my case and almost bump into him as I try to keep up with him.

'Kitchen sink?' he asks raising a supercilious eyebrow.

'Look, why don't we call a truce?' I suggest. I'm not built for conflict. I like to fly under the radar, which is what I've tried to do for most of my life.

'A truce would suggest we've fallen out,' he says.

I frown, completely disconcerted by this statement.

'I disagreed with your approach in Barcelona but I'm adult enough to accept that colleagues will have differing opinions.'

I gape at him because I am truly flabbergasted, gabberflasted and dabbergaffled.

Before I can shout, 'What about the sex?' an exceptionally tall man, with shoulders so wide he must have to turn sideways to walk through doorways, approaches us.

'Lydia Smith, Tom Dereborn?'

Still simmering, I leave Tom to say yes.

'I'm Mark, one of the team. Welcome. Car's out front.'

The man-giant takes my case without so much as flinching at the weight and leads us to an eye-wateringly bright orange Land Rover in the car park.

'Welcome to the Jaffamobile,' says Mark when he catches me examining the colour.

'It's bright.'

'Yup. Can't lose us.'

I am pleasantly surprised when Tom asks if I'd like to go in the front, so surprised that I say yes and climb up. Most men assume that the front seat is for them.

'It's a half hour's drive to get to Mannderdale, where we're headed. It's a management training college and will be our HQ. I suggest you lean back and enjoy the scenery.' He flashes a grin before adding, 'It's probably the only chance you'll get.'

Apprehension skitters across the base of my belly. I've tried hard not to think about what the next five days hold. I'm not really an outdoorsy person, not by design or choice, just because I never had the opportunity. It's outside my experience, so I have no idea whether I'll be good or bad at it. Looking at Tom's walking trousers and Granite Gear rucksack (I'm betting it's a good brand), I can confidently predict that he was probably a Boy Scout or did a Duke of Edinburgh award.

Dry stone walls, neat and precise, line the road. We're not in London anymore. There seems to be an inordinate number of coaches cruising at snail's pace along the narrow roads and we're soon stuck behind one.

Mark, however, is patient as we trundle along. 'Local hazard. Coach trips.' I turn away from the view of the wheezing coach exhaust as we meander along and instead look at the green fields dotted with grubby sheep, heads glued to the grass, which abound in every direction. I'd expected something a bit more dramatic, so I'm relieved we've been driving through soft and gentle scenery. I had visions of hiking up mountains.

'Lake Windermere,' says Mark, a man of few words, pointing through the trees to the flat water we catch glimpses of along the drive; it looks peaceful and serene. It's the tail end of summer, early September, and the trees are still full-leaved and green.

Traffic is heavy until we turn off the main road, gradually climbing. The landscape starts to change, fewer trees, and the green is replaced by the burnt bracken and tussocky grass. Suddenly we crest the hill and I gasp. The view is magnificent and, with a visceral punch to the heart, I get what all those 'wander lonely as a cloud' poets and painters had been banging on about. Mountains in faded purples range along the horizon. The hillside falls away in front of us, another lake glistening in the distance, the road a vee between hills winding down.

'Never gets old,' says Mark, looking over at me.

I smile at him although my brain is screaming, 'Eyes on the road, eyes on the road.' 'No. I imagine not.' They are big hills. Mountains. Did I know there were mountains in England? I hope we're not going to be hiking up them. Suddenly five days on the loose seems quite a long time. They're not expecting us to walk to London, are they?

I shrink back into my seat trying to fight that familiar I'm-out-of-place feeling, which most of the time I'm able to keep on top of.

Mannerdale Hall looks like a stately home, nestled in the valley surrounded by trees, with verdant gardens swooping down a gentle swell to the shores of a lake. There's a jetty down there, around which kayaks and floats are tied up. My stomach drops. Why hadn't it occurred to me that there might be water-based activities? The Lake District might have been a clue.

'Here we are. I'll drop you at the front. Someone'll meet you and show you your rooms. You'll be sharing.'

Tom and both look at each other, startled horror etched large.

Mark guffaws. 'Not with each other. Don't worry, it's not that sort of programme.'

He's still chuckling away to himself as we traipse through the porch into the hall where we're greeted by another rugged-looking bloke. Once he's checked our names on his clipboard, he leads us towards a grand staircase that has seen better days. No lift then. There's no offer to carry my case, which is absolutely fine by me. I'm quite happy to do it and quite capable – as long as it's at my own pace. The two men lope ahead exchanging small talk.

I tune out because I need all my effort to lift, grunt, move forward and not fall. The steps are wide and shallow, which means there are a lot of the buggers.

'Here, let me.' Tom appears at my side, nudges me out of the way and picks up my case. 'Otherwise we'll be here all night. How many pairs of shoes have you got in here?' he asks, and before I can roll my eyes at the unnecessary girly pigeonholing, he adds, 'Please don't tell me you have more than one pair of those hobnail boots of yours.'

Is he actually making a joke?

'Well,' I tilt my head, 'there's the green pair, the blue pair and of course I have purple. You have to co-ordinate, you know.'

His laugh is a short, sharp bark. 'I knew I shouldn't have asked.'

'I like to be prepared.'

We reach the top of the stairs and I'm shown into my room first.

'Here you go' is all the rugged bloke says before he turns and leads Tom further down the corridor.

I walk into a beautiful bright room with three windows looking out over the lake. There are two single beds in the room, with white functional duvets. At the end of one there's a suitcase, which if anything is marginally bigger than mine.

'Hey Roomie!' A woman pops out of the bathroom. She takes one look at my suitcase and beams.

I beam back because she has one of those lovely open sunny faces that are impossible not to like.

'I'm Tansy.' She holds up her hand. 'And before you say anything, I know, I've heard it all before. Shit name but I didn't choose it. Apparently, it's a plant and also a really pretty beetle. Not sure my folks knew the latter.'

I want to laugh. She doesn't know how lucky she is.

My parents, buoyed up by my arrival, downed not one but two bottles of champagne. Consequently, on their visit to register my birth they had settled up on Taittinger as a suitable name but, at the last minute, decided it would be utterly hilarious to name me … Chlamydia. I have since discovered that registrars are prevented by law from making any comment on names. That's one law I'd campaign to change.

Of course I don't ever reveal this, so I say, as I always do to any new acquaintance, 'Hi, I'm Lydia. Lydie to my friends.'

'See, why didn't my parents give me a nice name like that? Honestly, you'd think I was some hippy child that grew up on organic home-made yoghurt and quinoa. My parents are Mr and Mrs So Normal.' She shakes her head and grins. 'You travel light too.'

I grin back at her. 'Not particularly.'

'Fancy a G&T?' She opens her case and produces a bottle of gin and a six-pack of Fever Tree tonics. 'I think we might need something to get us through this. My flatmate blackmailed me into signing up; she's on the production team. If they didn't get enough bodies on board, she was out of a job. Given she pays half my mortgage, it was a no-brainer. Besides, you got to be in it to win it. Ten grand for showing up will do nicely. And a shot at a hundred grand doesn't fall in your lap every day. How did you get conned?'

'The short story is that I inherited my gran's house and it's been trashed by … by squatters. I want to use the money to restore it.'

'That sucks. Hope you get through.' She laughs. 'If I win, my flatmate is dust. I'm going to pay off her half of the mortgage so I don't have to share with her anymore.'

While Tansy liberated a couple of tooth mugs from the bathroom, I unpacked essentials from my suitcase, careful not to expose too much of the contents.

'I have snacks,' I say, producing two packets of crisps.

She doesn't need to know there are another two packets in my case. I'm the human equivalent of a squirrel, saving now in case of lean times. It's a compulsion that I've had since I was a kid. My friends Eleanor and Olivia still tease me about the full carton of canned beans under my bed at university. But when you live in chaos, you try to bring order and prepare for any eventuality.

Why else would I have brought a dozen condoms, two packets of digestive biscuits, a pack of disposable razors, hairdressing and nail scissors, two sachets of CupaSoup, six packets of instant pasta, a full pack of Tampax even though I'm not due for another three weeks, a sewing kit, umpteen sachets of coffee, three travel bars of soap, a roll of Sellotape and various other items that I might need?

In addition I'd bought a couple of things specifically for the trip, like a waterproof and woolly hat, as we'd been sent a suggested kit list for the course. We'd also been advised that any specialist items would be supplied but I like to be over-prepared. Always.

'Here you go, chin, chin,' said Tansy handing me a mug.

'Cheers,' I reply, chinking my mug against hers.

With a companion like Tansy, things are already looking up.

Chapter Four

LYDIA

Man, who knew how hard it is to get into a wet suit? I never thought I'd relate to being swallowed whole by a boa constrictor. Thank God there isn't a camera in sight. Although, hello, people, it's no surprise that Tom is looking like the poster boy for outdoor adventure, bare-chested with the top of his wet suit hanging around his hips. Fuck, he looks good. Another heat-searing flashback nudges my hormones. For fuck's sake.

Why can't they accept I'm still fuming with the bastard for refusing to even acknowledge that night?

'Well, hello,' drawls Tansy, standing next to me. 'You lucky bitch, working with that.'

'Mm.' I'm not committing to a word about him.

Having met everyone yesterday during the afternoon, today we're congregated on the sandy shore of the lake, twelve of us in total, and we're up against two other groups of twelve that have been sent out on other activities, no doubt to see how camera-worthy they are. Another burly instructor, Jordan, dressed all in black like a ninja warrior, surveys us in grim silence. Any second now I expect him to lunge into some sort of *Matrix*-style moves.

Of the twelve contestants in our cohort, six are all from one company, GreatCorp – where Harcourt is an exec director, surprise, surprise. Judging from the catcalls and comments, they know each other well. The remaining six are made up of Tom, Tansy, two women who look as if they'd rather be having a root canal than be here, a very earnest guy, Rory, who has insisted on asking us all our names and shaking our hands, and me.

'This morning we're going to divide you into two teams and with the equipment available –' Jordan gestures towards a pile of ropes, wooden poles, large plastic drums and several oars as well as a dozen life vests '– you're going to build a raft and cross to the island under your own steam.'

'Of course we are,' says Tansy, shooting me a look of rueful resignation.

'The first team to reach the island wins.'

Everyone looks at one another with varying degrees of enthusiasm, horror and resignation. Tansy elbows me. 'Glad I didn't blow dry my hair this morning.'

And then we're back at school as he begins calling out our names and dividing us into two teams. It's not quite as bad as being on the school sports field – this lot don't know my real name and my trainer soles aren't flapping, tripping me up.

I'm in a team with Tansy – thank you, God – Rory, one of the two timid women and two men from GreatCorp. And not Tom. Thank you even more, God.

'You lot are the Sharks,' Jordan says to the other team. 'You,' to us, 'are the Jets. When I blow the whistle, you have three hours to build your raft and reach the island.'

I squint at the island. It looks a hell of a long way away over the grey flat water. The trees, which come right down to the shore of the island, are reflected in the surface of the water. It's all a bit closer to *Swallows and Amazons* than I ever thought I'd be and suddenly my childhood longings for freedom and escape don't seem quite as wonderful to me. Maybe I can be ground crew and shout encouragingly, 'Pull, pull' or whatever those little people do at the back of the boat in a boat race.

'The whole team has to get to the island, and everyone has to be transported on top of the raft.'

There's a pause as we all absorb this.

'Lydia!' He shouts my name and I think I'm going to be told off for daydreaming.

'Yes.'

'You'll be team captain of the Jets.' Everyone turns to look at me. I smile weakly. Marvellous. Great. Wonderful. Thrust into the limelight. Just what I love.

'Team captain of the Sharks … will be Tom.'

You couldn't bloody make it up. Me and Tom eye each

other. I can see the minute he decides, game on. A slow smirk that signifies he's going to pound my team's sorry arse into the ground and enjoy every minute of it. Over my dead body. I can't believe someone like him needs the money. I only have to remember his sharp suit and hand-made brogues. What? He needs more designer gear? I *need* to get through to the next stage. I *need* to win that money. Gran's house is a whole lot more than bricks and mortar to me.

After looking over our supplies, which seem to include an awful lot of blue nylon rope (all the better to tie someone up and drop them into the bottom of the lake), we separate into our teams on opposite sides of the little bay, the wooden jetty equidistant between us. Our team gather around a wooden picnic bench. The two GreatCorp men, Richard and Alastair, have already assumed control and are discussing what they think are the best tactics, while behind them Tansy is taking the piss out of their mansplaining with a lot of eye-rolling and under-her-breath comments. Timid Verity, if ever a name was suitable, keeps very quiet and keeps looking anxiously at the water as if the Loch Ness Monster might emerge at any moment.

'Right, let's sit down and make a plan,' I say. I'm not wasting the advantage of being team leader. It's an opportunity to shine even if I haven't got a clue what I'm doing.

'It's obvious what we need to do. Lash the poles

together and attach the floats.' Richard thumps his hand on the table to emphasise he knows best.

Alastair nods in agreement, rising to his feet.

'Obvious,' drawls Tansy with impatient sarcasm.

I hold up a hand. 'That's great and it is probably exactly what we need to do.'

Everyone laughs.

'However, as we've got to act like a team,' I emphasise the word with spangly jazz hands to defuse the male egos, 'it might be useful to see if anyone else has any ideas. And also, we might want to think about who does what.' I give a self-deprecating laugh. 'Anyone any good at tying knots? I can tell you now, I'm crap. Never a Brownie or a Girl Guide.'

Richard looks at me with the enthusiasm of a toddler being told he can't have ketchup on his chips.

'I was a Boy Scout,' says Rory. 'Not a very good one. I've got problems with spatial awareness, dyspraxia and a dodgy back but I do have a Swiss Army penknife.'

Alastair folds his arms in silent disgust, which immediately makes me feel sorry for Rory. I'm always a sucker for the underdog.

There's a silence and then Verity speaks, her voice louder than expected as if she's forced herself to project it beyond its usual limit. 'I crochet, so I'm quite good at knotting things.'

I smile at her warmly. 'Brilliant.'

Emboldened by this, Rory raises a hand. I nod at him.

'I just wonder if it might be a good idea to draw a plan. Sorry, I'm one of those visual learners, I need to see what something looks like.'

'I'm the same,' says Tansy, and the smile she directs at Richard and Alastair is so sickly sweet it's tooth-rotting.

'Great idea,' I say with faux enthusiasm. My team might kill each other before we even start building this bloody raft.

Alastair huffs but I give him an of-course-I-know-what-I'm-doing smile.

'Anyone got any pen and paper?' asks Rory. Richard produces a very small, stubby pencil. 'I play golf in this coat.'

'Can anyone draw?' I ask as Tansy pulls out a tattered scrap of paper.

'Me,' says Alastair. 'I used to be a draughtsman.'

'Great. Okay. Any ideas on design?'

'A square with a float on each corner,' suggests Tansy.

'They've given us six floats, so I think we should use them all,' says Richard.

He makes a good point.

We spend a few minutes discussing what shape the raft should be. I'm quite happy to let someone else take the lead on this but I guide them back to the mission every time things seem to be drifting, with a mix of cajolery and self-deprecation. It seems to work.

Alastair draws a shape and everyone chips in, tweaking

the design until we're happy with what we've got. It's surprisingly unbloody.

I look over at the other team and my heart sinks. Balls. They are well under way with their construction.

'Shit,' says Richard.

'Slow and steady wins the race,' I say with far more confidence than I'm feeling. Everyone looks at me like I'm some sort of sage. I smile and stand tall. I've never designed a sodding raft in my life, how the hell do I know what I'm doing?

There is one good outcome, because we've spent the time planning, we know exactly what each of us has to do. Verity's expertise is a godsend, and she insists that we cut the rope into lengths. 'If you have just one length of rope and it starts to untie, then the whole lot will.' She's got a point, although it takes up extra time – Richard and Alastair tut at this. Thankfully we have Rory's penknife. The other plus is that it means that more of us can work together at the same time, tying the poles together at regular intervals. She teaches the others how to knot, leaving them to lace together the base of the raft. We've gone with a long, thin design with floats at the front, the middle and the back, figuring that with three of us on each side we can paddle more quickly once we've launched the *Apollo 11*, as our craft has been named. Richard wanted to call it the *Titanic*, but he was overruled. Too much of a bad omen.

Even though we've started construction well after the other team, our raft is coming together as per the plan.

Verity is our secret weapon and those knots hold firm when we lift up the raft to attach the floats beneath.

'Shit, they're launching,' says Richard, as the other team hoist a square raft onto their shoulders and run lifeguard style towards the water's edge.

I look over doing my best to appear nonchalant. Is a square design better? 'It's fine,' I say, ignoring the stab of panic as Tom singles me out, flashing me a triumphant smile.

'Just one more float,' says Verity through gritted teeth, her tiny hand tugging hard at the nylon rope.

Richard is dancing about with barely contained impatience. Rory is handing out the life vests while Tansy and Alastair gather up the oars. Alastair is studying his drawing, his mouth drooping a little. 'Maybe we'll win a prize for the best designed raft.'

'They've still got to get to the island,' I say. 'We've got this. It's an excellent design.' What the fuck do I know?

'Okay, we're almost good to go,' says Verity still tying the final knot as the others lift up the raft and start running to the shore.

Tom is standing on the other raft and gives us a wave. The Sharks, paddling furiously, are already fifty metres ahead of us on the lake.

'Shit, they're going to win,' says Richard.

'No, they're not,' I say, feeling like a school governess reassuring her charges. Of course they bloody are.

'Hell, no,' says Tansy, ploughing into the water up to her knees.

Somehow we launch our raft with all six of us on board. Everyone starts to paddle at once.

'Wait,' I say. 'Someone needs to count.'

'I will.' Tansy starts immediately. 'One, two, one, two.'

To my secret elation the raft slides smoothly through the water, although I'm not sure we'll be able to keep up this sculling pace; I'm already puffing.

Tansy grimly keeps count, even though her face is as red as mine.

Is it my imagination or is the gap starting to close?

There's movement on the other raft. One of the floats comes free and then as we puff and pant our way towards the island, we see that their raft is fast disintegrating. We're only a little bit behind them now and the island is less than half a kilometre away.

'Keep paddling,' Tom bellows at his team. 'Faster. Come on, don't give up.'

'Fuck off, mate,' shouts one of the team. 'This is shit.'

'Why don't you paddle, you lazy bastard?' shouts the quiet woman.

'Keep going, we can do this,' yells Tom.

I'm smirking now. The rear left of their raft is below the water line and they've all had to shuffle forward. Some of the poles making up the base of the raft are starting to drift apart and the Sharks are trying to hang on to them at the same time as paddle.

We glide level with them, our raft still perfectly intact.

It's panic stations on the Sharks' raft. Everyone is shouting at each other, countermanding themselves as the poles start to detach from the main body of the raft. One of the team falls in.

'Get back on!' screams one of the women. But as the man struggles to board, another few sections of the raft separate, taking another float with them.

We're ahead of them now. Tansy has taken her foot off the gas and we're paddling in quite a leisurely manner as Tom's team all end up in the water. I give him a wave as we cruise towards the island. Victory has never tasted quite so sweet.

———

Tansy raises a glass of wine. 'Cheers to *our* team leader.'

'Thanks.' I grin and take a sip. It's actually been a fun day, although it helped that we won the morning's challenge. After that we had lunch and then went on a long hike with a couple of the Mannerdale Hall staff, which was supposed to be very amicable. However, the slightly scary, heavily musclebound staff members moved from group to group. With short buzz cuts and sharp observant eyes, they're the type that don't miss a thing and I'm horribly aware that we were being judged in some way. Tansy and I fell into conversation and spent most of the hike together, although Rory and Verity joined in frequently while

Alastair and Richard good-naturedly took the piss when I struggled to get to the top of a rocky outcrop with a shove from behind from Richard. Our team has definitely cemented.

Dinner has a slightly gala-like feel because we're all dressed up (by order) but it's also very tense because everyone knows that in a little while we'll find out if we've made the grade. The other two groups of contestants are also here, bringing home the fact that I have a one in six chance of going through. I wonder for how many of the people here the money is so important. A make-up artist has been buzzing about dabbing powder on a couple of shinier faces and for the first time there's a cameraman quietly filming us. Following a debrief about the task this morning. I'm feeling a slight hopeful glow, having been commended for my leadership skills and managing my team so well that our raft won a special prize for being the best one ever built at the centre. Surely that's a promising sign.

Somehow they got hold of Alastair's drawing, put it in a cheap plastic frame and presented it to me. I'm rather touched and more than a little bit pleased with myself. Not, of course, that I show it. Tom seems to have taken failure very personally and has barely said a word to anyone all day. I would feel a bit sorry for him but he's so bloody competitive that I can't bring myself to be magnanimous and talk to him.

'Very well done, Lydia,' says Verity.

'I think your champion knot-tying had a lot to do with our victory,' says Alastair, with a warm, admiring look at Verity. 'Although credit to Lydia, for bringing your light out from under the bushel.'

Verity blushes.

After dinner, we all move to a room, set up with rows of chairs and one of the scary guys stands up and asks us all to close our eyes. Once we do, he announces that anyone tapped on the shoulder is to get up and leave the room. The staff members all exchange serious, doom-laden looks, which is ever so slightly worrying. If you have to leave does that mean you haven't gone through, or does it mean you have? No one asks. We just look at each other, the tension vibrating in the room palpable as one by one we close our eyes.

I swallow and wipe my damp hands down the length of my skirt. This is it, make or break. Tomorrow I could be going home.

Chapter Five

LYDIA

When we're instructed to open our eyes a few minutes later, Mark, of the giant shoulders, and Jordan, the ninja man, have been joined by four equally fearsome-looking guys at the front of the room, where they stand, all in black, hands behind their backs, projecting SAS vibes. Their thin jersey tops emphasise their compact, well-sculpted bodies.

The room has thinned out and I take in the now empty seats I can see. We still have no idea if we've gone through to the next stage or not. Tom is still here, so if I've failed, so has he, which brings some small amount of consolation. (Yes, I know I'm petty.)

'Oh lord, it's the A team,' murmurs Tansy, who sits next to me and fans herself. 'If I accidentally twist an ankle, do you think one of them would sweep me up in his arms and carry me?'

'Ha! Fireman's lift, if you're lucky,' I tell her.

'You're no fun, Lydie.' She pouts then grins. 'Spoiling my He-man fantasies. Although Sharky boy had a fit upper half. Did you notice?'

'No,' I say, perhaps a bit too quickly.

She studies me. 'No love lost there then.'

'None,' I say. There's a prickle between my shoulder blades. I am so totally aware of Tom, sitting at the back of the room three rows behind us. Where he's concerned, I seemed to have developed my very own Spidey sense. I always know where he is. It's bloody irritating.

'First, the good news, you have all qualified,' Mark calls from the front of the room.

There's a cheer and we all applaud. Thank fuck for that. My shoulders sink back to their natural position.

'Tomorrow morning at O eight hundred hours, you'll be *fleeing for your lives*,' says the black-clad giant at the front of the room. The way that he emphasises the words makes them sound terrifying. I'm clearly not the only one who thinks so because there's an audible intake of breath behind me and Tansy shoots me a nervous glance.

'Do you think it's too late to change our minds?' she whispers.

Mark holds up his hand. 'It's TV, guys. Don't worry. No one's really gonna die.' He pauses and then adds with a laugh, 'Well, we hope not. We can't afford the insurance!

'Now, in a minute we'll announce the teams and

tomorrow you're going on the run.' He pauses again, with just the right amount of drama, to let this sink in.

'What the sweet mother of Mary Jane does that mean?' Tansy asks, sounding panicked. 'I thought it would be like a jailbreak or something and we had to escape. Not go on the run.'

There's another brief hum of chatter as we respond in varying degrees to this news.

After waiting a few seconds, in which the cameraman homes in on the SAS guys' menacing faces before swinging round to film us, Mark continues. 'No phones, twenty quid a head and you, your partner and your wits. You'll get a basic set of supplies including a tent, compass, map, enough food for a couple of nights and a half hour head start.'

'A tent!' says Tansy, appalled. 'I only do camping by Marriott.'

I have never camped in my life. I'm not sure I've even been within three feet of a tent. The thought of sleeping outside where anyone could happen upon you unnerves me. I remember nights curled up against the door of my bedroom wrapped in my duvet so that no one could walk in to doss down for the night.

'Any questions?' asks Marcus as everyone starts talking at once.

'Yes. Can I go home now?' mutters Tansy. I'd like to go with her but once again I remind myself about the money.

'Each team has to get as far away from here as possible and make its way to London without being caught by our crack tracking and surveillance team. Meet our elite hunters, Midge, Jonno, Scott and Teasedale, who'll be on your trail. All of them have served with the SAS and have considerable expertise in hunting down the enemy.

'The first team to reach Trafalgar Square wins the grand prize of a hundred thousand pounds each –' he pauses to let this sum sink in '– however if only one of you makes it, that figure is reduced to twenty thousand pounds. You have five days. The deadline is 8pm on Saturday. Today is Monday. If no one makes it to London, the team that gets furthest from here in five days without being caught gets the second prize of twenty grand. If you're caught, you're immediately disqualified.'

I feel slightly sick.

'You'll need a combination of wits, guile and team-working. And expect the unexpected,' is the final helpful sign-off.

Marvellous. I am so not good with unexpected. I've rebuilt my life since leaving home by imposing order and control on everything. That night with Tom was the first time I'd ever given in to instinct and let myself go – maybe that's why it hurts so much that it meant so little to him.

'What if we decide not to take part?' asks Rory.

Mark shrugs. 'You lose the first payment. Today, just by turning up, you can earn 10K. Easy money.'

He has a point and it's better than going home empty-handed.

'We'll be filming but you'll also each be issued with a

GoPro camera and spare SD cards. You need to record footage every day of yourself in action and some talking to camera about how you're feeling. There's guidance in the packs.' He indicates a plastic wallet on the table behind him. 'Remember, we want drama, folks.'

Yet again I remind myself. Money. It's all about the money.

Then the pairings are read out. Oh dear God, please no. I have a horrible feeing I know what's coming. My neck and shoulders are so tense as they work through the names, I'm worried my head might pop off, squeezed out from the pressure exerted by my shoulder blades.

'Lydia...' I look up, my pelvic floor and stomach muscles clenched tight. My Pilates teacher would be proper proud. 'You'll be with... T...' I close my eyes. 'Tansy.'

I open them and turn to her as she raises a hand for a high five. Result. I allow myself a relieved breath. That is good news.

'You do know we are going to be crap at this,' she whispers and starts giggling. 'Do you think they'll let me pack my gin? You can carry the tonic.'

'It's a deal,' I say, with a smile that hides my apprehension. Oh dear God, the two of us in a tent. I'm not sure I've got the motivation to carry Tansy through. We'll have a laugh but is she as desperate as me for the money?

The rest of the session is spent picking up our rucksacks and supplies, and divvying them up with our partners.

Tansy will carry the tent, the map and compass (and the

gin). I will take the groundsheet, sleeping bags, food, enamel mugs, plates and cutlery (and the tonic). We'll be allowed to add to the rucksack our clothes and whatever else we can carry.

Verity asks if she can take her crochet hook – is she planning to crochet herself a hammock? Rory wants to know if it's okay if he takes his Swiss penknife. Personally I would not have owned up to that one in case they said no. Apparently we can take any personal items we feel will be useful.

'What happens to our stuff we leave behind?' asks Richard. 'Our phones, wallets and I brought an iPad and a laptop.'

'I can guarantee that a percentage of you won't get very far.' Mark grins with malicious glee. 'It's highly likely you'll be back here within a day or so. Should any of you get further or even get to London, everything will be returned to you.'

'Do you anticipate many people getting to London?' asks a voice I know well.

Mark looks at Tom, his eyes narrowing in contemplation. 'No.' He looks back at the wall of black-clad men behind him and grins. 'But you can try.'

'What if there's an emergency?' someone asks.

'Good point,' replies Mark. 'Each team gets one of these.' He holds up a basic Nokia phone, about as unsmart as you can get. 'I advise you to keep it switched off unless absolutely necessary to preserve the battery.'

There are lots more questions, but I tune out. None of the answers fill me with optimism.

'Enjoy your last night of civilisation, folks. From tomorrow you're going to be in the wild and on your own.' With that we're told that breakfast is at O seven hundred hours and to be ready to leave and in the foyer at O eight hundred hours sharp the next morning. Then we're dismissed, free to commiserate with those that didn't make the grade.

'I need a drink,' says Tansy. She's not the only one and we all end up in the bar.

I find myself next to Tom. 'You'll be leaving most of the contents of your suitcase behind, I'm thinking. Regret bringing all those shoes now?'

'Very funny,' I say although inside my heart is beating double time. I'm going to have a tough time leaving anything. I'm already worrying about leaving behind something I might need. 'Who are you paired with?' I ask, as if I don't know. I was listening avidly for his name when the teams were read out.

'Rory.' He scowls. 'Why have they paired me with him? We're like chalk and cheese.'

'I think that's the whole point,' I say sweetly, happily pointing out the bleeding obvious. 'He's a *nice* person.' Tom scowls at the inference. 'It makes better television.' Although to be fair, gentle and sweet as he was, Rory was quite hopeless apart from his Swiss Army knife.

Tom sighs. 'I'm sure he is but he doesn't strike me as the outdoors, physical type. I suspect I'll be carrying him.'

Even though knowing Rory's propensity to trip over his own feet, I can't resist saying, 'Cocky, much?'

For some crazy, crazy, complete brain aberration reason I look down at his crotch.

He blinks and catches my eye. We stare at each other for what feels like a full minute. And then he swallows, an urgent gulp, the tendons in his neck hard and proud.

I can't help myself. I glance down again. He turns away quickly to hide a burgeoning erection and presses himself against the bar. Apparently those neck tendons are not the only thing that's hard.

'Do you want a drink?' he asks, his voice gruff.

I'm a bit nonplussed. What the hell's the etiquette in this situation? A dozen questions rocket through my mind. Do I want a drink? What am I saying to him if I say yes?

'It's not fucking *Mastermind*,' he snaps. 'Yes or no?'

'Er, yes. White wine. Please.'

He orders the drinks and hands me the glass of white wine, taking care to keep me at arm's length.

'Well, the good news,' I say, 'is that you don't have to spend any more time with me after this evening.'

'There is that. Not sure Rory is preferable though.'

'You really are a miserable bastard, aren't you?'

He chokes on his pint and then starts to laugh.

'No one can ever accuse you of pulling any punches, can they, Lydia?'

'Do you know, I think that's the first time you've ever used my name.'

'Is it?' he says with blasé dismissal, which tells me he's fully, fully aware of that fact.

I tilt my head and study him. Has he been adopting the same tactic as me? My mental labelling him with his full name has been a deliberate way of separating him from the passionate, sexy and, yes, caring, man that I had amazing sex with. Has he been doing the same in reverse? Trying to block memories of me from his mind? And if so, why?

'Hey, roomie.' Tansy drapes an arm around my neck.

'Hey, Tansy.'

'Bad luck on the challenge today,' she says to Tom.

He gives her some sort of grimace, which I think is supposed to be a facsimile of a smile, but for once there's a hint of real emotion in those steely grey eyes of his. I can't quite fathom what it is. Hurt? Resignation? Angst? Fear? And then it's gone, as fleeting as the phosphorus blaze of a match.

'Tom's teamed up with Rory,' I say helpfully.

'Oh, you mean dodgy-back-trips-over-his-own-feet Rory? What a shame,' says Tansy with a grin. 'He's lovely though.'

Tom glowers at both of us.

'Thanks for filling me with confidence,' says Tom, his mouth firming in resignation, which once again draws my attention to it. Something – possibly my heart – flutters beneath my ribs. He *can* do wonderful things with that mouth.

'Never mind.' Tansy wrinkles her face in false sympathy. Can she not feel the charge of electricity that hovers above my skin at his very proximity? Is this all in my imagination? All I can say is thank Christ I won't be seeing him for a while. I am starting to fear for my sanity.

Chapter Six

LYDIA

When Mark places a blindfold on me and guides me out to one of the waiting Land Rovers the following morning, my breakfast starts to churn in my stomach like a brick in a tumble dryer. Apprehension sizzles along my nerves. Suddenly this is horribly real and not a game.

In the back of the Land Rover, I can hear other people breathing and I'm sitting sandwiched between two other bodies. No one is speaking. I think being blindfolded does that to you. Makes you feel insular. In the dark it's like being a kid again, not sure of the rules and fearful that everyone else knows what they're doing and I don't. I clutch my rucksack protectively to me, as if it's a life vest. It has my things in there and, try as hard as I could last night and this morning, I couldn't bring myself to ditch everything. It might be a bit heavy, but I will carry everything in it to the ends of the earth.

The engine chugs into life and the radio on the dashboard blares into life, ironically with REM's 'It's the End of the World As We Know It'. Nervous laughter titters in the back as off we go. Reliant on my sense of hearing, I strain my ears to listen for anything over and above the engine. I clench my fists on my knees, my eyes closed behind the blindfold. I have to take deep, even breaths because I want to snatch that fucker off my face. The muscles in my back are bunched as if I might spring into action like a leopard on its prey. I hate this. Absolutely hate it. Being at the mercy of someone else. I want to get out of the Land Rover. Right now. Panic is creeping over me, strangling ivy, wrapping its way around me with insidious tendrils of self-doubt.

I hold in a sob, but it shakes my body.

'Lydia?' It's Tom's voice. He's right beside me. 'You okay?' he whispers.

'Mm.' My voice, tight with tension is croaky. 'Don't like the blindfold,' I murmur back, sounding childlike.

I feel his hand fumble across my thigh to take mine. 'Shame,' he murmurs in a smoky voice full of sex and sin. 'I've heard it can be a lot of fun.'

Despite his words, his hand gives mine a reassuring squeeze and I splutter out a laugh. 'I don't believe you just said that.'

'Took your mind off things, didn't it? They should

provide silk blindfolds, holds a better association than kidnap victim. What do you reckon?'

'That you have a dirty mind,' I say.

'Filthy,' he agrees somewhere near my ear at a volume that only I can hear. 'But you already knew that.'

My heart thunks in my chest. It makes me feel odd and extremely grateful that we can't see each other. And that in another hour we won't see each other again until ... who knows. Back at work? Back at Mannerdale Hall?

I don't say anything, but I relax back into the seat, grateful for the reassuring presence of his hand around mine.

A little while later, the Land Rover has clearly come off road and we're bumping along a very uneven track. The engine whines and the gears crunch as they're taken down.

'Right, first stop. Everyone get out. If we touch you on the shoulder you're to stay put. This is your team drop-off.'

We scramble awkwardly out. My legs are a little shaky and I can't decide if I'm dreading or looking forward to the touch on the arm. Tansy has been strangely quiet throughout the journey but she's probably as nervous as I am. I'm glad that I've been teamed up with someone I feel so comfortable with.

Five minutes later, we're told to get back into the car. There's a little more space now and I've no idea who I'm sitting next to but it's not Tom. I don't know how I know that, but I do. I seem to have some kind of ESP where he's concerned. Maybe he was one of the ones we've just dropped off.

We make another drop and then the third drop is mine. I feel my rucksack dumped next to me. I put a hand on it to reassure myself.

'Wait until you can't hear the engine any longer and then take the blindfolds off,' instructs Mark. 'The clock starts ticking now. You've got an hour and a half before the hunters set off. They don't have your precise location, just a radius of fifteen miles. Best of luck. You're going to need it.'

The door slams and the Land Rover rumbles away. It's a relief to be out in the fresh air, released from the tense atmosphere inside the four-wheel-drive.

The sound of the engine dies away and I rip off my blindfold, blinking into watery daylight. It's a cloudy day with ominous black clouds gathering. I turn round to find that Tansy has grown half a foot and is now looking disturbingly masculine.

He takes off his blindfold and we stare at each other.

He has a filthy mind and I already know that is all that goes through my head.

'Lydia.' Tom looks round as if there might be someone else but no, there's just the two of us. 'Where's Rory?'

'I've got a horrible feeling he's with Tansy.'

He looks down the track in the direction we assume the Land Rover left. 'Do you think they'll come back when they realise they've made a mistake?'

'Can we afford to wait and find out?' I ask. 'Expect the unexpected.'

'You think?'

I shrug. 'No idea but … if we need to get out of here in an hour and a half, we can't waste time.'

'You're right.'

'I think that's the first thing we've ever agreed on,' I say.

He gives me a you're-kidding-me look. And I remember quite a few things we agreed on.

'Since then,' I say tartly. 'And you're finally remembering that, are you?'

'Which way?' he asks, ignoring my question. 'Have you got the compass?'

'No. Tansy's got that. I've got the map.'

'Not much good if we don't know where we are,' he says. 'Please tell me you have the emergency phone.'

'Check,' I say. I hitch my rucksack onto my back. The phone is in the top pocket, within easy reach.

'I guess we can worry about where we are later. We need to make a move otherwise it'll be over before it starts.'

'Right. Which way?' I say, echoing his question back to him.

I stand still and listen. The wind is whipping through the pine forest beside us. There's no way I want to set foot in there, too dark and sinister. The other way is open moorland and its downhill. We're being hunted by super-fit humans and I am not super-fit.

'That way,' I point. 'Easier and quicker.'

'And more obvious. For those very reasons.'

'What do you suggest then?'

'That way.' He points to the slope and the trees. 'Harder to spot us than if we're out in the open.'

He has a point, although going uphill is going to slow us down but then so is arguing, so I start plodding towards the trees. We walk in silence, the eerie quiet of the pine forest disquieting. The layer of needles deadens our footsteps as we tramp up the hill. My rucksack is already cutting into my shoulders and I wonder if we should have abandoned any of our duplicate gear. Too late now; it would leave a clue as to which direction we've taken.

The wind whispers around us, high above, branches rubbing against each other with the occasional crack and screech. It's like all those flipping horror films. Spooked, I keep glancing back over my shoulder.

It takes an hour and a half to reach the top of the hill and when we look back it doesn't seem as if we've come very far. The landscape has opened out and there are miles after miles of drystone walls, spotted with lichen and moss, skirting and bisecting rolling green fields. I guess they have them all over the country, apart from the part of Essex I grew up in. I find them comforting, a sign of civilisation, proof that this place isn't entirely uninhabited, although the only buildings I can see are derelict, with sagging roofs and scattered stones around the crumbling walls.

I'm used to cars, roads and houses everywhere. Not this open, sweeping, dramatic countryside. Except, in some ways, it does feel familiar. As a child I was a voracious reader, inhaling the fictional adventures of other children who escaped adult influence. I lost myself in the worlds of *Swallows and Amazons*, *The Lion, the Witch and the Wardrobe* and *The House at World's End* – the ancient classics were the only books in the house. They lived in a box in the spare room containing the remnants of the life of my grandmother. My heart hurts just a little as I think of her and the sad remains of what was once her home. It reminds me that's why I'm here. I heft the rucksack higher, the straps feeling like they're grinding their way into my shoulders and wearing away the bones.

I focus on my surroundings to take my mind off the increasing weight on my back. In some places barbed wire stretches along parallel to the walls, tufted with wool fibres like spring blossom. For some reason I collect some and stuff it into my pocket. You never know when things will come in useful. My pockets are always full of potential rainy day necessities. As a child I collected things to take them out and pore over them later, perhaps because I had so little to call my own.

There's a path that we can follow that offers a magnificent view down through the whole valley. It's also a bit easier going, after the earlier constant weaving through trees. Fear keeps me turning my head and looking back the way we've come.

'Shit. Look!' Tom points down the valley and far, far in the distance, moving at speed along a road sandwiched between drystone walls, is one of the familiar orange Land Rovers.

It's miles away but even so my legs turn into pudding. I've lost the ability to lift one after the other. Visceral fear pinches my lungs, making my breath shallow and ineffectual. I am full-on terrified. My heart is racing so fast I can feel it pounding in my ears and I'm worried they might explode. Tom is already striding ahead, picking up the pace. He's leaving me. Fight or flight. I always thought I'd put up a fight. I'm horrified by how pathetic I've turned out to be. I'm not even capable of flight.

'Fuck's sake, Lydia. What are you doing?' Tom shouts over his shoulder at me. 'They probably have no idea we're here but if they've got binoculars we don't want them spotting us straightaway.'

I stare at him, my mouth opening and closing as I try to frame words – anything, sensible or stupid. Nothing comes out.

'Jesus.' He stops, gives me a you-must-be-fucking-kidding glare and then stomps towards me.

He waves a hand in front of my face. 'We have to move.' I nod with all the animation of a zombie. 'Now!' he barks in frustration, before cupping my elbow and frogmarching me along. 'Don't look back.'

I nod dumbly.

'Once we get over the top, they won't be able to see us.'

'Unuh.' My panicked brain is full of images of slavering dogs pulling at choker chains barely held back by their handlers, chasing us down.

'Come on.' The peremptory order cuts through my fog and I snap back into sense. My heart is still thudding like the hooves of a racehorse on the turf at Epsom but I've regained control of my limbs.

Breathless, we breach the top of the hill. The pain in my chest, spreading from rib to rib, eases at the sight below us. Civilization or something close to. There's a viewing point car park about quarter of a mile ahead with several tour buses, and what looks like a café and a bus stop.

We both stop to catch our breath and relax a little, now that we're at least out of view. With a groan I lower my rucksack from my aching back. I'm exhausted already.

'What are the chances of a local bus coming in the next hour?' asks Tom, his mouth twisting cynically.

I look hopefully down at the ribbon of road curling around the hillside. 'Good?'

He gives me a withering look. 'Seriously? You've never lived in the country, have you?'

I stiffen. So I don't know stuff like this. So what? Just as I'm about to tell him where to go, I'm distracted by an unfamiliar buzzing noise. After his last comment I'm not going to mention it, the sound probably belongs to some giant *country* wasp I'm not aware of, but it's getting louder.

One of those tinny irritating sounds that after a while drills through your head. The sound carries across the big open field.

'Fuck!' says Tom. 'They're using a bloody drone.' He grabs my arm. 'Run before they see us.'

Chapter Seven

TOM

The small black drone with a blur of propellers starts to move in our direction. I have no idea if it's spotted us yet, some of those fuckers have incredible range, but I'm not taking any chances and I take off at a run before realising that Lydia has frozen to the spot. Again.

'Come on!' I yell. For fuck's sake. She's a liability. It takes a couple of seconds scrambling about before she scoops up her rucksack and, clutching it to her chest as if it's a personal lifebuoy, she begins to lumber down the hill like an overburdened donkey.

I look up as the drone, which has ascended to a higher altitude. I wonder if it's sending Lydia's wide-eyed, panicked expression back to our faceless hunters on the other side of the hill. Oddly I want to protect her from being exposed that way. I run back to her, losing valuable seconds and help her put her rucksack back on.

'Christ, Lydia, what the fuck have you got in here? It weighs a ton!'

'Stuff,' she pants at me, looking fearfully up at the drone.

Then, as quickly as it appeared, the drone inexplicably flies away.

'It's gone,' says Lydia, slowing down.

I shake my head. 'No, it's flown back to base. They can move faster in the car now they know where we are. We need to get away and hide out of sight. They'll be coming to cut us off.'

Lydia tuts. 'That's cheating,' she says, and I want to laugh at the disgust on her face as I see her usual impervious spirit reasserting itself.

'Expect the unexpected,' I say, tamping down my amusement, irritated by my loss of focus. We have to get away. I can't fail on day one. I pick up the pace. I am not going to let her slow us down.

'Maybe we can hitch a lift before they get here,' she says, pointing down at the busy car park with its parallel lines of tourist coaches. 'We could scrounge a ride on one of the coaches.'

Christ, I'm with fucking Pollyanna. This isn't a game to me, I really want to win that money. 'You think they're going to let you do that? Just waltz on? "Hey, guys, of course you can hitch a lift. These fare-paying folk won't mind." Unless...' I pause and hold up an index finger, adding with unnecessary sarcasm in a silly, cosy voice. 'We bribe the friendly coach driver with our combined forty quid.'

With a pitying look, which I almost admire, she says, 'Who says we're going to ask?'

'Lydia, we're probably a third of the age of most people on those tours. I think they're going to notice us sneaking on board.'

'Not if we go in the luggage compartment.'

'What?'

'Look, that one has its doors open. All we have to do is loiter nearby and then when no one's looking jump in.'

I stare at her a little stunned by the brilliance of the idea. 'I can't decide if you're mad or an absolute genius.'

Tom's stunned praise – he's obviously already forgotten who won the challenge yesterday – boosts my confidence. Imminent rescue gives us wings and we hurry down to the car park, crossing the road curving around the contour of the hill. I'm so focused on the coach that I don't even glance at the view that everyone has stopped for. My fingers are crossed tight on both hands, as I pray that the driver doesn't close the luggage compartment before we get there. Terror has me constantly checking behind us, almost tripping each time. Tom keeps me upright, for which I ought to be grateful, but it just irritates me because it reminds me of my failings and the fact that he's so in command of himself.

We slow down as we clamber over a grassy bank into the car park. Tom, still calm and measured, dammit, takes my hand.

'We're just a couple of hikers on holiday,' he mutters. 'We don't want to draw attention to ourselves.' His fingers clasp over my crossed ones and he gives my hand a little shake.

'Just hikers. Holiday,' I repeat, my heart thundering, as we saunter over towards the coach. A woman is standing by the door, and like a jaunty air hostess she's wearing a navy jacket and a yellow neck scarf with tiny little logos dotted over it. 'How was that, Fred?'

'Awesome. I can't believe we're really here,' replies an elderly man in Shrek-green trousers, thick-soled trainers and a flat cap. His drawl is transatlantic.

'He says that every day, don't you, honey?' adds another voice.

'I'm glad you're having such a good holiday,' the hostess says in a smooth English accent.

We circle to the opposite side of the bus and slide down the side, wriggling out of our rucksacks.

'Are you sure about this?' asks Tom.

'No,' I reply, catching my lip between my teeth. We could end up stuck in there for hours. And there isn't a huge amount of room. The first and second compartments are completely full, the third half full. 'Maybe we should wait for a bus. We've got some money.'

'A bus?'

I nod.

'You do know we're not in London anymore, right? Places like this have a couple of buses a day – if you're lucky.'

'I knew that,' I say. Clearly, I didn't. How the hell does anyone get anywhere if that's true?

Just then two things happen: one, there's the hydraulic hiss as the door of the first luggage compartment starts to close, and two, we both glimpse a flash of orange on the road above the car park.

Tom grabs my rucksack, chucks it in and then bundles me in with him following. A second later the doors close, sealing us into the dark. Immediately the sense of relief lifts all the stranglehold of tension gripping the muscles in my shoulders. We've got away. The flood of elation makes me relax back against Tom's side.

'We did it,' I whisper.

'We did, partner.' He looks at his watch, which lights up in the dark. It's five past eleven.

Sitting in the dark, closed in, we're safe. No one knows we're here.

'Wonder where we're headed,' Tom muses, his breath close to my ear.

'No idea but they might stop again soon.' I pause as a comforting thought strikes me. 'Don't old people need to pee a lot?'

Tom half laughs in the dark. It's comforting. We're in this together. Who knows, we might pull together yet.

We can hear footsteps overhead but there's no sign of the coach moving off.

'George, if you try that again, I swear I'll cut your balls off.' The low indignant voice is right outside on the other side of the door and I have to stuff my hand in my mouth to stop a gale of laughter.

'What happened to the days of al fresco quickies?' asked a plaintive male voice.

'Lumbago and arthritis, you daft sod. What were you thinking? We'll have a nice comfy hotel bed in a couple of hours. Honestly, you…' grumbles the female voice before drifting away out of earshot.

I giggle very quietly.

'Fair play to the old guy,' whispers Tom. 'Life in the old chap yet.' There's a thread of laughter in his voice, which is interrupted by the sudden, distinct rumble of his stomach.

'Hungry?' I ask.

'Starving. Unfortunately the food they gave us is that regurgitated stuff that needs hot water adding to it.'

'You mean dehydrated,' I tease, still on a high from our escape, and pull something from the pocket of my rucksack and hand it to him.

'Here's something I prepared earlier,' I say, feeling just a little bit smug.

'What is it?' I can hear him unfurling the tin foil.

'Bacon butty. I made them at breakfast.'

'You made them at breakfast?' He laughs.

'I didn't know when we'd next get fed and there was

loads there this morning.' I don't like to tell him that previous necessity has created a habit that has me stockpiling food whenever I can. It still seems slightly shameful. I also snaffled a couple of mini packs of Coco Pops and Sugar Puffs from breakfast.

The silence between as we chew cold bacon is very nearly companionable and it's not half bad.

I'm just about to fish out the Sugar Puffs, figuring they'll make an excellent dessert, when I hear a familiar gruff voice.

'No sign of them.'

I tense, I swear the food going down my oesophagus stalls, suddenly an indigestible lump. It's Mark from Mannderdale Hall.

'The drone clearly saw them up top. They're here somewhere. Besides, where else would they go? People always head to civilisation, first sight of it. Let's have another look, you take that side of the car park and check the path down.'

We're both rigid with tension.

'I'll check this side and the path up. They won't have got far.'

'Kay. See you back at the Landy.'

When the engine starts up minutes later with a loud diesel rumble, I sag with relief, even though it's like being in the belly of a dragon. A heavy thrum vibrates through the floor rattling my seat bones and the crunch of the tyres on gravel highlights how close to the ground we are. Every judder and shake jars my body as the coach lumbers out of the car park. This might just be the stupidest idea I've ever had but we've got away just in the nick of time.

Once we're on the road, it's a little smoother but very noisy; there's nothing soft down here to absorb the sound of the guttural chug of the engine and the hiss of wheels on tarmac. Tom's watch has tiny fluorescent green dots that become a tiny beacon of light in what is now oppressive darkness each time he moves. The absence of my phone has never been felt more keenly. It's become universal insulation from conversation and lack of conversation.

We know each time the bus goes up a hill because, one, we start to slide backwards against the pile of cases behind us and, two, the whine of the engine and the judder of the gears are exponentially more noticeable.

Every twist and turn of the road engages muscles I didn't know I had as I try to maintain purchase on the floor. Apology after apology trips from my tongue as I keep lurching against Tom.

'You okay?' asks Tom as I try to haul myself upright after being pitched up against him for what feels like the nine hundred and ninety-fifth time.

'Not really. I'm not sure I thought this through.'

He laughs. 'Lydia. It's not supposed to be comfortable. That's what they want. Putting up with adversity and triumphing for the TV cameras. We're probably supposed to be wading through bogs, hiding in caves and being generally wet and miserable. That's what the audience wants to see. At least we're dry and out of danger of being captured.'

'I suppose so,' I say, grudgingly accepting his point, although I'm feeling slightly sick with the diesel fumes.

'Here.' He fiddles with something and his torch light comes on and I realise he's switched on the GoPro.

'Day one and we've hitched a ride.' He makes a wide sweep of the belly of the coach, holding the torch and GoPro in one hand, lighting up all the suitcases herded in one side of the compartment like livestock at market. 'Not sure where we're headed but hopefully it's a good distance away from the immediate vicinity and the hunters. We've had a near miss with them, but we got away in the nick of time.'

The light has lit up an empty corner and he tugs on my sleeve for me to follow. I crawl next to him. This is better, there's a proper wall for us to lean against but it's a narrow space, and the two of us can just squeeze in together. To make it easier, he puts an arm around my shoulders and pulls me closer so that we're wedged side by side.

The journey varies, stopping, starting, slowing and speeding, and I remember Mark picking us up from the station and being stuck behind the coach. Being able to visualise the coach's progress is reassuring as my stomach is turning slow somersaults. Please, please don't let me be sick. Closing my eyes makes no difference, not that I thought it would.

I grit my teeth. I just to need to endure this. I'm plenty practiced at enduring things.

There's a series of rapid gear changes and suddenly the going is much smoother. Faster too. We can also hear the rumble of other traffic, whooshing past us.

'I think we might be on a motorway,' I say.

'Sounds like it,' agrees Tom. 'Which is good news. It's taking us that much further away from the hunters.' I can't see him, but I can tell from his voice that he's grimly satisfied.

The motion and the dark make me drowsy and droopy. My eyes close and I start awake as my head lands on Tom's chest. He slides his arm down around my back, pulling me in to him. 'Go to sleep.'

Miraculously, I do just that.

Chapter Eight

TOM

I must have dozed off. Disorientated, I wake as the coach slows to a stop, the engine still running. Feeling stiff, I twist my neck, conscious of Lydia's soft breathing, her head resting on my chest. She must be asleep.

I wriggle carefully so as not to wake her, stretching a little, my muscles protesting at the stiffness holding my legs to ransom.

'What time is it?' Her voice sounds loud in the dark belly of the coach and I feel bad that I must have disturbed her. I also miss the warmth of her body as she moves away.

'It's five to one.' I do a quick mental calculation. The coach has been travelling for an hour and fifty minutes. Say an average of thirty miles an hour at a very cautious estimate which means we must have travelled sixty miles. Well out of reach of drones. I heave a silent sigh of relief.

'So we must be a good way from where we started,' she says, with that ever present spark of positivity in her voice.

'Yeah, though we're stuck in traffic now.' Every now and then the coach lurches forward for a few seconds and then stops again. Somewhere around us, there's a vehicle with very screechy brakes that squeal a few seconds ahead of us each time we stop. It doesn't take long for the sound to get irritating. I tune it out and think about how I'm going to make my film. I've already got the opening scene in my head. I'm going to go in close on the lead actor to show his emotions. His wife is leaving him. I've got no idea how that feels. I've never done commitment in my life. My last girlfriend, Natalie, accused me of being emotionally unavailable. What the fuck does that even mean? I was always clear with her from the outset. We were exclusive. For me, that was enough. Realising I'm straying into stuff I don't want to think about, I stop and go back to figuring out camera angles.

Another half hour passes of the interminable stop, start. The oily diesel fumes intensify to the point where I can almost taste them in my mouth and my jaw tightens along with the slow roil in my stomach. I take a couple of deep breaths but they really don't help the queasiness that has taken hold.

Beside me Lydia starts wriggling. Why can't she just keep still?

'What's wrong?' I snap. I hate feeling weak like this.

'I want something out of my rucksack. Do you think you could put the torch light on again?'

For Christ's sake. 'I'm trying to keep the battery going as long as possible,' I say, but I turn on the light anyway and the tiny glow lights up the blackness. Lydia shuffles over to where the rucksacks are. I can see the dayglo orange straps of my pack and watch as she rummages in her bag. There's a heavy thunk as she drops something. What is she doing?

'Aha!' she says but the light is too dim to see what she's retrieved. I hope it's worth it. My stomach rolls again. I'm not going to be sick. Mind over matter.

She sits down next to me again.

'Would you like a mint?' she asks as if we're in the cinema on a date or something. 'Take away the taste of the diesel. And I've got some water. It's probably a bit warm but better than nothing.'

'Thanks.'

She hands the pack over and my fingers close over hers. They're freezing.

'You're cold.'

'Just a bit. My bum's the worst.'

I know the feeling. 'Do you want a fleece? I've got a spare in my rucksack,' I offer.

'Thanks but I've got one.' I smile a little in the darkness. She's certainly independent. I think of Natalie again. She always expected me to do gentlemanly things for her – no doubt she'd have insisted I strip off and hand over my jumper.

I hear the rattle of pans as Lydia fights her way into her rucksack again. What does she have in there? We need to ditch some of her load. I can't carry her on this trip.

'Here,' she says and I feel a lightweight sleeping bag dumped on my lap. 'We can sit on this, insulate our arses.'

'Good call.'

'I am so glad I was born in the age of electricity,' Lydia says. 'Getting dressed in the dark with all those buttons must have been a nightmare.'

I burst out laughing. It's so typical of her. I barely know the woman but she's consistent.

'What's wrong with that?' she asks.

'Nothing. It's you. You always manage to find a positive. Most people I know would have complained.'

'You haven't,' she points out.

'True.'

'Wow, something we have in common. We're both stoics.'

'Who knew?' I say.

'Anyway, there's no point complaining about something I can't do anything about.' I can feel her shrugging her shoulders. 'What's the point. You just have to get on with it.'

'Not everyone thinks like that. Some are big on complaining.' I think of Natalie, who was always telling me I wasn't doing things right. My parents are the same.

'Are you speaking from experience?' Of course Lydia is straight in there with the questions. Normally I wouldn't answer but what the hell, we're buried in the bowels of a bus, nothing's normal.

'I was thinking of my mother … and my ex-girlfriend. But mainly my mother. She complains a lot. I'm late. I'm early. I'm not wearing the right suit—'

'Don't tell me she doesn't love your Brioni suit?'

I laugh. 'In the right circumstances, yes, but if I turn up to Sunday lunch in the wrong sort of trousers—'

'No!' says Lydia with mock horror. 'There are wrong sorts of trousers? Why didn't I know this?'

When she says it like that, I realise how ridiculous it is. 'My mother notices that sort of thing. Apparently it's disrespectful not to be correctly attired when someone has invited you to lunch.' I pause and add, 'She just has high standards.'

And suddenly I'm defending my mum and I've no idea why. It's bugged me for most of my life that she and my dad have this perverse snobbery and narrow, self-defined expectation of how you should behave.

'So what sort of trousers are wrong for Sunday lunch? Not that I'm expecting an invite.'

'You know…'

'No, I don't know. I have no idea.'

'If its lunch in the garden then chinos might be acceptable but not shorts. Not at lunch.'

'Right and if lunch is in the house?'

'If it's in the dining room, then trousers with a shirt.'

'With a shirt. You don't go topless then? Or is that if you eat in the kitchen?'

I laugh out loud. Her teasing makes me forget the fuss that Mum and Dad can make if you don't do things the way they should be done. They're really good at laying on the emotional blackmail.

'We never eat in the kitchen. Always the dining room.' I put on a slightly snotty scandalised tone, the sort my mother would use. I wait for Lydia to take the piss. Our short acquaintance is enough for me to know that she is not one to hold back. To my surprise though, she doesn't say a word. The silence makes me think that she's digesting this fact and I wonder what she's thinking.

'You said your ex-girlfriend complained a lot. Is that why she's an ex?'

'No,' I say, surprised by the change in direction of the conversation. 'I'm used to complaints. I'm good at ignoring them.' Which is a lie. I'm just good at avoiding them and working out which ones I can put up with.

'How long were you with her?'

Shit. Easy question. Difficult answer. I shift a little, conscious that my bum is a bit numb. I do a quick count. How do I sum it up? The time we dated, or do I include the last part where we were just friends but benefits crept in?

'Are you counting on your fingers?'

It might have been nine months if I count the booty calls – which she made too, to be fair. I go with 'Seven or eight months.'

'Seven or eight. You're not sure?'

Now I shift uncomfortably and it's nothing to do with the numbness in my backside. 'I thought it was over, but she didn't get the memo.'

'You sent her a memo?' Lydia sounds half amused and half appalled. 'I've heard of break-ups by text but not by memo.'

'No, of course I didn't.' There's another one of those guilty pauses. 'I might have given her mixed messages.'

Lydia's straight onto it. 'Let me guess, the classic "I don't want to see you anymore but I'm happy to keep having sex with you"?'

How does she know? But it was mutual ... or so I thought. I found out later I was very wrong about that.

'I didn't lead her on. I made it clear. But she...' Am I really going to say this out loud? 'She said I was emotionally unavailable.' I can't believe I just admitted that. It's been going round and round in my head for weeks. I guess a female perspective on it might be useful. God knows my mates, Griff and Rob, have no insight. They just take the piss and use the phrase on every possible occasion.

'Hmm, is that what emotionally unavailable means? Making it clear in word but not in action?'

I'm not sure what she means. It's like I'm high up on the trapeze without a safety net.

'Although to be fair,' she continues, 'you're good at making things very clear.'

'What's that supposed to mean?' I ask even though I probably shouldn't.

'You're very good at switching off your emotions. I've seen you do it. The portcullis comes down. Your eyes go blank.'

'When have I done that?' I try to say it casually, but it comes out defensive because I know I do it... Shit. I've walked right into no man's land. The thing that we've both been skirting around since the day we met in Barcelona.

'You don't remember?'

'Don't know what you're talking about.' Or rather, I know exactly what she's talking about and I don't want to go there. It will involve peeking under the covers to see what's really there. I want to ignore what happened.

'Tom! Get real. You know exactly what I'm talking about. We had sex. A ton of it.'

In the dark I wince. Sex in the bedroom. Sex in the bathroom. The kitchen. Even the hall. The recollection of the pure heaven of sliding into her the very first time, that absolute sensation of relief, of being whole, stiffens my cock.

'You do remember that?'

'Yes.' The word is sullen and clipped but how can I not remember it? Those two nights are embedded in my memory like ferocious ticks clinging on for dear life. I don't want to remember how easy she was to be with. How undemanding. It was just sex. Good sex. That's all. If I tell myself often enough it will be true.

'Just yes?' she queries and I get the impression she's fed up with having to prod and poke for every response, but I don't owe her anything. I never lied to her that weekend. We never made promises and neither of us so much as indicated that there'd ever be a repeat performance.

'What do you want me to say? I'm not going to apologise. We both had a good time, you didn't complain—'

Of course, once again I walk right into that one as she can't resist chipping in. 'I don't complain, remember?'

Now I'm getting pissed off. What does she want from me? It was a two-night stand.

'Unless you're one hell of an actress, you had a pretty good time. I particularly remember one point when I had my head between your thighs...' Okay, low blow, but she's making me feel annoyed and guilty and defensive and ... I just want her to stop talking about it.

'You don't need to embarrass me.' As soon as she says that, I feel like a shit. Because that's one thing she shouldn't be. The sex was amazing, unconstrained, natural. I want to reassure her.

'Why would you be embarrassed? Like I said, we had a good time.'

'Yeah,' she agrees but she's still pushing. 'We had good sex and then you shut down. Closed yourself off.'

Of course I fucking did. I was terrified. There, I've admitted it ... to myself, at any road. I was absolutely fucking terrified of the way I felt. That connection ... Christ, listen to me. Connection? Whatever it was scared the shit out of me. Things like that don't really exist. It's a con. One-sided for sure. It ties you to people and you lose the control. That Sunday night was like standing on a precipice – one foot wrong and I'd be straight over to an uncertain … what, I didn't know, but I wasn't going to risk it. There'd be conditions, she'd want something from me and I'd be putting myself out on the line.

I push those thoughts back in the box marked 'never to be looked at again' and man up again.

'It was a one-night stand. Hell, I didn't even remember your surname until Barcelona. I thought you knew the rules. It was Sunday night. A school night. Time to go home.' I say it so matter-of-factly, I almost believe it.

Chapter Nine

TOM

It's a relief when the coach comes to a stop. Lydia and I have been sitting in silence for the last twenty minutes, during which time the coach has picked up speed again and the road seems bumpier. We're turning more frequently and there are fewer cars passing outside.

The engine is turned off and we both jump as light filters through the gaps in the doors as they start to rise. I nudge Lydia. I reckon we're far enough away for us to jump out here and we need to be quick before anyone spots us. If they're opening the storage compartments, I'm guessing we've arrived at a hotel or something.

Fumbling for our rucksacks we both scramble out of the compartment, dropping to the floor beside the coach. Dusting off my trousers I move away from the coach, hauling Lydia to her feet just in time as the coach driver appears. We're in a layby in the middle of nowhere. As I gulp in fresh air, the nausea in my stomach suddenly deciding to make a comeback, I can't decide if this is a good or a bad thing.

'Where did you two come from?' The short, stumpy coach driver with the bandiest legs I've ever seen puts his hands on his hips.

Lydia – she's a quick study – follows my lead and we lean against the barrier at the edge of the layby, doing that nothing-to-see-here thing as if we're a couple of hikers stopping for a breather. My heart is suffering from another adrenaline overload but I have to admit it feels good. We got this far and I reckon we can talk our way of this.

I coolly indicate back there with my thumb over my shoulder to the open rugged landscape. The coach driver doesn't even look.

'I fucking hate driving pensioners,' he grumbles, talking more to himself than us. 'There's always some bugger who packs his bloody medication and then needs it urgently.'

I'm bloody glad I'm not an octogenarian on his bus. I have a sneaking sympathy for the poor sod who's in dire medical need. It's hard living your life trying not to inconvenience other people.

'Gotcha. Mr fucking Leighton.' The coach driver grabs a case and stomps off. Seconds later the compartment doors close and the bus pulls out with a sharp jerk. I see a blur of faces trapped behind the windows and I'm very glad that I'm outside under my own steam and not at someone else's mercy. Although now I have a chance to look around, I realise we are the middle of nowhere. There isn't a house or building in sight. Not a single telegraph pole, electricity pylon or road sign.

'Where do you think we might be?' asks Lydia.

'No idea.' There are no obvious landmarks or large handy signs saying 'you are now in Lancashire' or 'Lower Beckington is ten miles away'. I do a quick calculation. 'We were on the coach for three and half hours, and some of that felt like good roads.' I up my previous average. 'If the coach averaged say fifty miles an hour – at a guess I'd say we've travelled at least a hundred and fifty miles from the Lake District.'

'So we're near London?'

Is she taking the piss? I goggle at her. 'We might have gone north.'

'Geography's not my strong point,' she admits. 'Born and bred in Essex, until I moved to London. Not really been anywhere else. And I don't drive.'

I don't stare, that would be rude, but seriously. She's what, twenty-nine, thirty, doesn't drive and has never been anywhere. I can't imagine that. My parents regularly packed me, my brother and sister into their Mercedes estate for educational days out the length and breadth of the country.

'I'm guessing we're in Yorkshire or Derbyshire.'

'At least we're a long way from an orange Land Rover,' she says with a wry smile.

'I'd say we're well out of range.'

'Now all we have to do is get to London,' she says.

'Yup,' I say with sudden determination. We're over the first hurdle and we've put quite a distance between ourselves and our would-be captors.

I suggest we get our bearings and then make a plan. 'If we walk to the nearest road sign or village, we can work out where we are and then try and hitch our way to London.'

'Okay,' she agrees, and I like that she's happy to leave the decision-making to me.

'Which way?'

I look up and down the empty road, then up at the sun and then at my watch. 'If the sun rises in the east and it's past midday... South is that way. London is south.' Unfortunately, the road is unhelpfully east to west. 'This way,' I suggest, and we head west.

We set off, walking in single file. The landscape is beautiful in a bleak, uninhabited way but the distinctive stone boundaries running along the contours of the hills worry me and I can't quite put my finger on why.

We walk in silence for ten minutes. There's not a single signpost. I stop to survey the area and realise that Lydia is lagging some way behind. I've been so lost in thought I'd not been aware of the growing distance between us.

I wait for her and, when she catches up, she's red-faced and panting, tugging at the straps of her rucksack as if it's uncomfortable. I ought to apologise for setting the pace at my speed, but I'm irritated with her. Why didn't she have the sense to pack light?

'You okay?' I ask and I can't help the clipped tone, which doesn't invite an honest answer. I already know she's struggling. Although fair play to her, she doesn't complain or give me any grief.

'Fine,' she says and keeps on walking past me, doggedly putting one foot in front of the other. I fall in behind her, letting her walk at her own pace. Part of me admires her silent determination but another part of me wonders how much she's going to hold me up. Potentially there's a lot of walking ahead of us. Now we're far enough away from Mannerdale Hall, we can head to the nearest motorway and then hitch a lift to London. I suspect we've done the hardest part of the challenge, getting out of range of the hunters. Tonight we'll have to sleep rough and who knows how far we're going to have to walk to reach a major highway. Our combined cash won't pay for accommodation, although it will pay for a hot meal and a cup of coffee. I could murder a flat white. Now my ten quid a day coffee habit seems a ridiculous extravagance.

It's a huge relief when we spot an old-fashioned cast-iron white signpost with black lettering at a junction with a much smaller road leading off to the left.

Skelwith Bridge 4 miles.

I weigh up our options. The road is barely a track and four miles is not too far. If we stay on this road we've more chance of seeing a bus or hitching a lift, not that we've seen much traffic so far, but we have no idea where the next settlement might be. Going on the smaller road will mean just over an hour's walk ahead of us. If I was on my own, it would probably take three quarters of an hour.

'Ever heard of Skelwith Bridge?' Lydia interrupts my thoughts as if I'm some geographic guru. 'Do you know where it is in the country?'

'No but we can ask someone when we get there.' And that makes my mind up. Better to go for the finite distance than keep walking endlessly without any clear indication of what's ahead. Lydia follows me, which I'm glad about because I don't want to have to discuss my reasoning.

We set off in silence but after less than half an hour she's lagging behind again. I stop and wait for her. At this rate it will be dark before we reach the village.

'You're going to have to dump some stuff,' I say. 'Your rucksack weighs too much. We want to get there before dark.' It's early September and already the nights are starting to close in.

'It's fine,' she replies, a tight line of mutiny forming on her lips.

'You're slowing us down.'

She lifts her chin and looks straight at me. 'Tough,' she says.

I stare. She's been so compliant since we left the layby that I'd got used to it.

She does that shrug that I'm rapidly realising is her

equivalent of saying 'go fuck yourself'. 'You can go on ahead and wait for me in the village but I'm not taking anything out of my rucksack.'

'You're just being stubborn now.'

'No, I'm not.' She sounds so reasonable. 'I'm compromising.'

'How do you figure that?' I rasp in frustration.

'I'm not insisting you walk at my pace, am I?'

I huff out a long sigh. I can't dispute her logic and I'm kind of impressed by her cool dismissal of the argument. Her refusal to engage is admirable. My dad could take a few lessons.

Forty minutes later, we finally trudge, together, into Skelwith Bridge, passing the village sign.

'Looks very pretty,' Lydia observes but I'm distracted and all I can manage is 'mmm'.

Something isn't right. The village is picture perfect, with stone-built houses with dark slate roofs and weathered porches, but something is niggling at the back of my brain. I can't put my finger on what is worrying me. Maybe I'm feeling a touch of paranoia.

There's a café across the road called Chester's Bread and Take Away. My stomach rumbles, reminding me that we haven't eaten since our bacon butty. A man and his dog are coming towards us. Shit. There's no way of avoiding him. I look at his face trying to assess whether he's friend or foe. Even Lydia, next to me, has stiffened. The elderly golden Labrador immediately approaches us and starts sniffing my hand. I relax a little. The man's expression is benign and the Lab doesn't strike me as much of a tracker dog.

'Excuse me, I wonder if you can help—'

'You looking for the Force, it's that way.' The man's smile is friendly and his immediate assumption gives me the impression that, one, he's safe and, two, he's given directions more times than he can count.

'The Force?'

'The waterfall, Skelwith Force.'

'Er, no. We were wondering what county we were in.'

The man takes off his hat and pleats the tweed between his fingers for a moment. 'Cumbria, lad.'

'Cumbria.' I flash a quick wary look at Lydia. Those niggles are starting to make sense now. The scenery hasn't changed that much. The landscape is the same.

'Aye.'

'And what's the nearest town?' I hardly dare ask.

'Are you lost?'

'Yes,' I say, impatient for his answer.

'We're about three miles from Ambleside, seven to Windermere and about fifteen to Kendal.' He's a mine of useful information and without pausing for breath, he adds, 'If you want to you can get the bus, the 516 – be here soon – goes to Kendal via Ambleside and Windermere.'

'We're in the Lake District?' I ask as my spirits drop to the soles of my shoes. Seriously?

'What, were you beamed in by aliens?' asks the man, scratching his head. 'You youngsters.'

'We hitched a lift,' Lydia says helpfully as if she's aware that I've seized into one massive ball of tension.

'You want to be careful doing that, missy. But then you've got your big strapping boyfriend, I reckon he can look after you.'

She nods. I'm still trying to process the fact that we're probably closer to Mannerdale Hall now than when we were dropped off this morning.

'Have a good day now. Come on, Tiger.' He tugs at the lead and the docile Labrador trots along after him. Lydia looks as if she's about to giggle at the dog's name. Mentally I almost dare her. It will give me the excuse I want to explode but it appears I don't need one.

'I don't fucking believe it,' I burst out. 'How could we have been driving round the Lakes for over three fucking hours?' I glare at her. Fucking tour bus. That's what we were on. Trundling through the fucking Lake District.

'Don't blame me, you bundled me in.'

'You suggested it.'

'If I suggested calling a client a lying sack of shit to their face, would you do it?'

'Are you ever going to let that go?'

She folds her arms and glares back at me. 'No. I like winding you up.' At least she's honest about it.

We're so busy arguing with each other that we don't see the bus arrive at the bus stop. The first we see of it, is as it trails past heading out of the village.

'Fuck's sake,' I say as the bloody thing lumbers away in

a cloud of diesel smoke. I march over to the bus stop and look at the timetable tacked up there. 'Fucking brilliant, the next one isn't until 8:15 tomorrow morning.'

'It's probably for the best,' she says.

'How do you figure that?'

'Remember. Mark said people always head for civilisation. That's where everyone will head. We've got a tent. We can camp and stay off the grid for a couple of days.'

I stare at her. Does she even know what staying off the grid actually entails?

She continues in that blithe way as if she has the first clue about what she's talking about. 'Now we know where we are, we can look at the map and maybe hike for a couple of days towards a main road and then we can perhaps try to thumb a lift.'

I'm irritated she's telling me my own plan. 'That would have been fine if we'd moved any great distance from where we started. But given we're virtually back where we began, don't you think that they'll be monitoring those routes?'

She smiles at me as if she's got all the answers. I have to hand it to her, she doesn't stay down for very long and she doesn't dwell on an argument or sulk. 'Not if we go north first. They'll be expecting us to go south. Do what everyone does. We could walk north, then pick up a main road. They can't monitor every road, can they?'

Once again, I'm reluctantly impressed. She's a smart cookie and I like her thinking.

'Okay.' I nod my head. 'Better get moving. We need to get out of here and a good distance away. The sun will go down before too long and we don't want to be wandering about in the dark. We need to find somewhere to set up camp.'

'I supposed we'd better do some filming as well,' suggests Lydia.

I get out the GoPro and do a quick selfie of us both. 'Currently still in the Lake District, in a village called Skelwith Bridge. We're heading into open countryside to find a spot to camp for the night. Over and out from Tom and Lydia.'

'That was impressive. Very smooth,' says Lydia. 'You could almost be a TV presenter.'

'Thanks.' I don't tell her that I've been making my own documentaries since I was a kid and it really is second nature to me.

The High Street is a bit too public, so we head down a footpath alongside the back of a barn and consult the map, deciding to follow one of the streams so that we'll have access to water. I wonder if Lydia has any idea how to put up her tent. I regret giving the tent to Rory now. I'm going to have to share with Lydia tonight. I just hope she doesn't want to have any deep conversations again. I hope she doesn't snore. I hope … I can sleep and not lie next to her remembering the last time we shared bedspace.

We walk for another hour, until we're well away from Skelwith Bridge and out in the open countryside. There are pockets of trees, and uneven lumps and bumps of grassy banks. I'm not sure of the legal situation but I'm pretty sure you're not supposed to wild camp in England, as opposed to Scotland where it is permissible. I don't bother raising it, there doesn't seem much point.

I hand the camera to Lydia. 'Just film me in conversation and then we can put this thing away for the evening.'

I look into the camera lens. 'This looks promising. We'll be hidden by the trees and it's not so exposed.' I look round at the grassy clearing with a small stream at one side. At another time, it might be quite idyllic but now it just feels unfamiliar and slightly menacing. Anyone could be watching us from the trees or a drone could fly overhead at any time.

'They don't have wolves in England anymore, do they?' Lydia asks.

I smirk. She's being funny, isn't she? For the camera. It eases my tension but then I see the way she's gnawing at her lip. Surely she's not being serious. I decide to tease her. 'Have you ever been out of a town before?'

'Yes, plenty of times,' she says but I see her straightening her back and that familiar lift of her chin. Archetypal defensive body language. I should know, I've employed it on plenty of occasions. I decide not to make the comment, 'You must have had a deprived childhood,' because it sounds a bit superior and judgy. Not everyone's parents are as pushy as mine or insist on taking their children on educational holidays all the time.

'Do you want to put the tent up, while I collect some firewood?' I suggest, panning round with the camera. I plan to have a bit of a scout about, check there's no one nearby and work out an exit strategy if we need one. Yeah, I've probably watched too many films, but I want to win that money and I reckon I've got a good chance.

'Sure,' she says with so much confidence I dismiss the slight concern at her lack of camping experience. These days, two-man tents are pretty simple to erect.

'Okay.' I ease my rucksack from my back and lean it against a tree. I can see the relief on her face as she lowers hers to the floor and rubs her shoulders.

What does she have in there? The tents are those lightweight ones so it's not that that's weighing her down. 'I'll leave you to it.' I start to walk off.

'I need the tent,' she says.

I stop dead and look at her and then at her rucksack. 'What do you mean?' I switch the camera off with a sense of foreboding. No need to film this.

'Tansy took our tent to carry…' Her voice trails off as it dawns on both of us. 'Rory's got yours?'

'Yup.'

Fuck, double fuck and fuckity fuck. I look up at the sky, which, did I mention, has started to darken. Black, water-laden clouds are threatening.

I exhale heavily. I do not fucking believe this.

'It's not my fault,' she protests.

'Didn't say it was.'

'But you thought it.'

'I'm just hacked off, that's all.'

'The plus side is that we don't have to share a tent,' she points out in that typically helpful Lydia way.

'That's certainly a big plus in the scheme of not having a tent.' My voice is full of snarky sarcasm. 'So, what have we got?'

Chapter Ten

LYDIA

When Tom and I examine our kit, it turns out that between us we have two groundsheets, a couple of bungy cords, one sleeping bag (in our hurry to get off the coach we left the other one behind), one bag of tent pegs, two enamel billycans with enamel mugs, four plates, four knives, four forks, two thermos flasks – both empty – four packs of unidentified dehydrated meals, a handful of energy bars, water sterilisation tablets, two first-aid kits, two microfibre towels and two identical maps. He doesn't need to know about my squirrel hoard, although I might break open the digestives later.

There's also one glaring omission. Shit, the phone. It must have fallen out on the coach. I decide that now is not the time to confess this to Tom, given that he's already irritated by the lack of tent, although that is hardly my fault.

Instead I focus on the first rule of survival, which I know

from prodigious reading and reality TV shows is to build a shelter and get a fire going. When I point this out, Tom growls, 'No shit, Sherlock. You're not the only one who's watched *The Island with Bear Grylls.*'

'Fine. You sort the fire out and I'll make a start on a shelter.' Gosh I sound as if I know what I'm doing. Ha! As if I had the first clue but I'm hoping if he buggers off and leaves me to it, I can work something out.

'I hate to point this out, but I don't have the tin with the matches and the firelighters. Do you?'

'No, but there's plenty of sheep's wool. There are enough of them about.'

'Sheep's wool. Fuck me, you're not expecting me to rub two sticks together to make fire, are you? I'm not a bloody Boy Scout.'

'Shocker, I'd have thought you were.'

'I was about ten years ago. However I'm not any longer and nor do I carry my dib dib dib dob dob dob kit around with me.'

'You surprise me.' I say before pulling out the bundle of wool fibre from my pocket and holding it aloft. 'Will this help?'

He scowls at me. 'Great, aren't you a smartarse? Have you also got a handy magnifying glass in your other pocket?' he asks with a theatrical squint up at the rapidly greying sky.

'No, but I do have this.' From my other pocket I produce a blue plastic cigarette lighter.

'You smoke?'

I shake my head.

'But you just happen to have a lighter on you.' He looks suspicious.

I shrug.

'I'll go and collect some firewood,' he says and stomps off.

I lick my finger and strike it through the air. One point to me. I'm not going to lie, the feeling of superiority warms me right through. I'm bossing this outdoor lark. Teamwork, not so much. We still hate each other.

Who knew watching so much TV and reading *Swallows and Amazons* so many times would come in this useful? In no time at all I've gathered armful after armful of sweet-smelling brown bracken and piled it up between two rocks. I figure we can lie on the bracken, use one of the ground sheets as a cover and the other as shelter. See? This outdoor stuff is a breeze.

The rain holds off although darkness has fallen, bringing with it an autumnal chill, but it's okay as we're sitting in front of a fire, tucking into extremely welcome foil bags of rehydrated spaghetti bolognese. It's almost cosy apart from the company.

'Enjoying that?' Tom asks, poking his fork at the brown mix and munching with barely concealed disgust.

I shrug even as I'm wolfing mine down. It's food. It's hot.

'It's okay.'

'Okay? Do you own any tastebuds? It's rank.' His whole face scrunches up as he pulls a 'yuk' expression.

I glare at him. 'You ought to finish it.'

'I'd rather eat my own shoes than this crap.'

When he tosses the pack aside my fingers tense around the fork I'm holding. I will not stab him. I will not stab him. But it's bloody tempting.

He catches sight of my face and throws the pack my way. 'Fill your boots, love.'

I hate him at that moment. So much that a ferocious, sharp pierce of hot, white rage burns through me.

Adept at hiding my feelings after years of practice when I was a kid, I pick up the pack and with a calm casualness that belies my inner fury, I shake the contents into my own foil sachet while he watches, trying to work out if I'm taking the piss. His hand makes a slight grabby move as if he now regrets the action. All we've had since breakfast is one cold bacon roll.

Too late. I carefully take slow mouthful after mouthful until it's all gone. It's a point of principle. I never leave or waste food. He watches every bite, the scowl on his face deepening and then when I finish and crumple up the pack, a sneer twists his lips and he looks down his nose.

'You must be one hell of a cheap date.'

My anger is sucked out, as fiercely as life through an

open window in a pressurised plane, humiliation rushing in, dousing me in utter shame. I'm a child again, out of my depth, mocked by someone with far more refinement than I'll ever have. I am nothing. A no one. I want to curl into a ball and hide from him except I don't do that anymore. I fight back because I'm a grown up.

'Screw you,' I say and march down to the water's edge to refill the billycan purely for something to do. Anything to stop me feeling powerless again. I swallow the angry tears. I'm angry at myself for allowing him to affect me. I've built a carefully constructed persona since I gained my independence. I don't expect anything from anyone. I don't allow myself to be humiliated or looked down upon and I don't rely on anyone but myself. Yet, like a bloody tick, Tom has managed to work his way under my skin. I gave too much of myself away that weekend and I'm annoyed. It takes a few minutes of staring at the black water and watching tiny ripples pooling on the edge of the little sandy beach, before I feel my emotions calming.

We sit in silence watching the flames of the fire. In another world it would be companionable, even romantic. But I'm brooding, revisiting past slights, and all in all having a complete pity party, which actually isn't like me. For the most part, I've put my past behind me. I'm an adult now, with my own money and my own home. I can make my own decisions, protect myself and decide who I let in. Eleven months ago, I made a terrible mistake believing that Tom Dereborn came to care for me in that brief forty-eight hour period. What on earth possessed me? I've been careful with my heart my whole life. I know people let you down. They can't be relied upon, so why on God's earth did I, for one stupid stinking minute, think that in this case it would be any different? But for some reason, it *had* felt different. I let my guard down. I let myself believe that we had something special between us, that the chemistry was something more. That the tender care he gave me meant something. More fool me. It was just a bloody good shag fest. Excellent sex for both of us.

Spite makes me bring it up because I know he'd rather do anything but talk about it.

'Do you ever think about that weekend?' I ask, idly looking up at the pine tree above us. The birds have fallen silent and the only sound around us is the lap of the water and the fierce pop and crackle of the flames of the fire.

'What?' He might as well have added 'the fuck' because it echoes in the words. I'm not going to let up, not going to give him an inch. We've danced around it since Barcelona and earlier in the coach all he could admit to was having a good time, but now I'm fed up, pissy and want to make him squirm. Did it really not mean anything to him?

'That weekend. When we had sex?'

There's a pause and I can see him thinking, which is sad because all he can come up with is a very lame, 'We had sex. We had a good time. End of.'

A small part of me dies. He's sticking to that story. Deep, deep inside of me, I'd nurtured and caressed this stupid fantasy that it had been as mind-blowing for him as for me. Obviously not. I want to howl at him. Good time? Good? Just good? It was the most amazing sexual experience of my entire life. I have never exposed myself to anyone the way that I did for that brief weekend. I've lost my train of thought and it takes me a moment to arrange the carriages back on the track. Tom is very good at avoiding things he doesn't want to talk about. He's a champion derailer. But I'm not about to be diverted.

'Really? You must have a lot of good sex.'

'What?' He looks over at me, brows crinkling as if he has absolutely no idea what I'm talking about and is perhaps oblivious to the unintentional compliment. But I plough on, determined, it seems, to make a dick of myself.

'It was good sex.' I'm not going to stroke his ego and tell him it was really good sex, that would be stupid. Telling him it was the best ever, even stupider. 'If you ever think about a career change, maybe you could consider the gigolo business.'

I'm pleased to see his mouth drops open before he gathers himself. 'Thanks. I'll keep it in mind. I'm sure my parents would be thrilled.'

This is a complete curve ball. Like his parents would care?

'They might be,' I say, for the sake of saying something, but it appears I've touched a nerve.

'I can assure you, my parents would be horrified. As far as my father is concerned, insurance is the only viable career. Gigolo, even if I wanted to be one, would be out of the question.' Then, with the most surprising and rather charming, self-deprecating frown, he asks with a quick laugh, 'I have wondered, what, precisely, does being a gigolo entail?'

'I think it's being a paid companion to a woman, providing her with sexual services as well as escort duties.'

'Sounds very much like my parents' marriage except it's the other way round.'

'Civilised,' I observe.

'Very. Although I think they're happy enough with the status quo. The don't row. In fact, the only people my dad gets hacked off with are me and my brother and sister.' He gives a mirthless laugh, but I see the tightening of his jaw on one side.

'My parents used to thrive on rows,' I muse. The bigger, the better. Drama and passion fuelled by alcohol and the occasional recreational drug.

'Used to? Are they dead?'

I shake my head. 'Not as far as I know.'

'You don't know?'

'I lost touch with them a long time ago.'

'You lost touch with your parents?' The incredulity in his voice pinches at me. 'How does that even happen?'

Is he for real? I can't believe he's even asking this.

'Yes,' I say. 'It happens.'

'How come? Did they throw you out or something?'

Now it's my turn to laugh without humour. 'No, I got a job and left home.'

Why does everyone assume I was despatched from the nest? After I figured there was no Fairy Godmother waiting for me in the wings and learned there was no point complaining to my parents about not having the right uniform or the right shoes, or picking fights with the school about attendance, I began working on my independence. As soon as I could, I got a paper round so that I could buy the right colour school skirt, blue instead of black – so I didn't keep getting detention – and I learned to forge my parents' signatures on letters and lied about their whereabouts on parents' evenings. It wasn't like they beat me or each other. They weren't bad people. Just self-absorbed, uninterested in me and hooked on booze. As soon as I saved enough from my job – they thought I was still going to school otherwise I wouldn't have seen a bean – I upped and left.

Since then, I've been on my own.

'But you don't keep in touch with them?'

'No.' What else is there to say?

He tilts his head to one side, considering. 'I'd love to divorce my parents. Just imagine, no more nagging texts, complaining about what I've forgotten or haven't done, or those helpful reminder ones, which assume I'm going to forget and won't do something. Oh, for a quiet life. Lucky you.'

I give him a tight smile. Sounds like his parents at least give a shit.

We both stare reflectively into the fire and I fail to stifle a yawn and a shiver. I'm knackered and it's definitely getting colder. There's dampness in the air and if I'm not mistaken the odd rain drop. My body is aching from all the exercise and my back is killing me.

'What time is it?' he asks. His watch has long since died.

'Quarter to nine.'

We both glance back at the makeshift tent-cum-shelter than I've built. Bear Grylls would be proud of me. One end of one groundsheet is stretched across two rocks and secured to them with the bungy cords and the other end slopes down to the floor to create a roof over sheltering the small dip between the rocks, anchored with tent pegs through the reinforced metal holes. I'm rather proud of it.

Of course, we haven't discussed sleeping arrangements. There's one sleeping bag between us and another groundsheet, which I thought we could lay over the bracken mattress to keep the creepy-crawlies at bay.

Another raindrop lands on my face followed in quick succession by a few more.

'It's raining,' says Tom.

'It is.'

'Time for bed.'

'Yes.'

Neither of us want to address the fact that we're going to have to share sleeping space as we crawl hurriedly into the shelter. There is literally just room for both of us side by side and, at the tallest bit, immediately in front of the rocks, space for our rucksacks.

'You can have the sleeping bag,' he says as we rustle our way across the groundsheet-covered bracken.

'Don't be silly. If we open it up, we can share it.'

The rain starts to patter on the roof, insistent drops that hammer on the plastic groundsheet.

The glow of the fire starts to die away and before long we're in total darkness.

I wrestle with the sleeping bag and undo the zip and spread it out.

'Have you got a hat?' asks Tom.

'Yes.'

'I'd put it on. It'll help keep you warm in the night. You lose most of your body heat from your head.'

'Right.' I pull the woolly pom-pom hat from the front pocket of my rucksack. It's got silver sparkly thread running through it, which makes it a bit scratchy, but I put it on.

After a bit of shifting and fidgeting, both of us finally lie down. The plastic groundsheet is cold beneath my back but hopefully it will warm up soon. Tom is beside me. I can hear him breathing. I'm glad he's there but only because he's better than nothing. I'd hate to be here on my own.

The sleeping bag only just covers me, partly because I'm trying to keep as much distance from Tom as possible, making sure I'm not touching any part of him.

'Lydia. I'm not going to bite and we have slept together before.'

'Yes. So you said. "We had sex. End of," I seem to recall.'

'Are you miffed about that?' He turns on his side to face me, bringing the warmth of his body closer. 'It was a one-night stand. Neither of us made any promises.' His voice rises dismissively.

I turn to face him, my head lying on the crook of my arm. I can't see much in the dark gloom of the shelter, but I know his face is a matter of inches from mine. I remember waking at one point that weekend and watching him sleep for a little while, the dark pinpricks of bristles dusting his chin, the long lashes curving against his cheek, the serenity of sleep across his face.

The sleeping bag settles around us, cocooning us in, and I feel warmer already.

'Not miffed at all. Like you said, it was a one-night stand. Although technically it was two.'

'Whatever.'

I sigh and then realise I'm so close he could probably feel the hot breath on his face.

The rain continues to hammer down but it's actually quite snug in here. Cosy almost. I close my eyes.

'Night, Lydia.' His words surprise me.

'Night, Tom.'

My aching body settles into the bracken base. I wouldn't say it's that comfortable but it's better than the hard ground and I'm quite good at sleeping anywhere. I've had years of practice.

But falling asleep isn't that easy. I'm conscious of Tom and I keep getting flashbacks of that first night. I wonder if he does too. Doubtful. He refuses to talk about it, so I'm guessing he's completely deleted that weekend from his memory banks, like a computer.

I close my eyes and try not to wriggle. My usual bedtime routine is to burrow in my covers and savour the contentment of being in my own bed under a feather duvet and crisp cotton sheets. I treat myself to nice things because I can. I feel slightly homesick for my little flat and imagine the double bed, the streetlight streaming through the window. I sigh again, wishing I was there. My bolthole.

'Go to sleep, Lydia,' grumbles Tom. 'I can hear you thinking. Your virtue is safe with me.'

'I never thought otherwise.' I can't resist the quip. 'If nothing else, you were quite the gentleman.' Although he was filthy, talking dirty and telling me what he wanted to do to me, he did constantly check that I was okay with everything, and I mean every damn thing.

I remember him murmuring against my thigh, 'Is this all right? Do you want me to carry on?' before he sucked my clit so thoroughly I thought I might pass out. Then, as he was circling my nipple with his tongue, urging me in between licks and nips to 'Tell me what you want.' And before that first thrust inside me, with his dick rock-hard at my entrance, nudging and teasing, asking between heavy breaths, 'Do you want me to fuck you?'

In my head I can hear my incoherent cries urging him on, begging him for more. Those quiet questions, him in command, were as much a turn-on as his mouth and fingers, which played my body like a conductor in charge of an orchestra playing an entire symphony.

And why am I torturing myself like this?

'Gentleman? I fucked you seven ways to heaven,' he says a couple of seconds later with a disbelieving snort.

'Did I complain?'

He lets out a breathy laugh. 'No. You were fucking amazing. The most responsive woman I've ever sl… fucked. There, I've said it now. Are you happy?'

Yeah. I'm delirious. Now, of all times, he admits it was more than just a good time. Great. Now I'm warm and wet. I squirm, the seam of my trousers rubbing against me. But his words are a timely reminder. Fucked. *It was just sex.* Not some great sexual epiphany that might morph into feeling. Just chemistry, pure and simple.

'Go to sleep, Tom,' I snap, irritated as much with myself as him.

Chapter Eleven

LYDIA

A loud scream jolts me awake. It's pitch-black in the shelter and I lie there for a moment, my heart pounding like a jackhammer. Have I imagined it? I listen intently. Then I hear it again. An unearthly scream. Someone is being murdered. But that's crazy, we're in the middle of nowhere. The scream comes again. I freeze. Next to me, Tom sleeps on. Oh God, I have to go and investigate, like all those dumb girls in the horror films, but I can't just lie here even though I'm actually really warm and cosy. I wriggle free of the sleeping bag, the groundsheet rustling beneath me. I glance towards Tom even though I can't actually see him. From the even breathing I can tell he's still asleep. My torch is by my rucksack and I grab it as I ease my way to the end of the shelter, horribly conscious of the creak and crunch of plastic with each move.

The scream comes again and I freeze.

Tom's torch snaps on as he sits up. The thin beam of light cuts through the darkness but I can't see his face. 'What the fuck are you doing?'

Is he in the SAS or something? He's immediately awake and alert.

'There's someone out there. I think they're in dang—' Another horrible shrill cry splits the air and I cringe but Tom … Tom starts to fucking laugh. A snigger at first but then it seems he can't help himself and it turns into an uproarious belly laugh.

My stomach shrivels as I feel that familiar sense of humiliation, the feeling that I'm not in the know. I'm outside and not privy to things that other people take for granted.

'What?' I snap, grateful that the dim light hides the hot flush of embarrassment racing up across my chest and up my neck.

'It's … it's a…' He can't get the words out because he's too fucking busy clutching his stomach, bent double at the waist. He just gets a grip and then starts laughing again.

I'm not sure what to do. Braining him with the torch seems the most enticing option right now but I button my mouth, determined not to make any more of a fool of myself, and shuffle back into position and lie down, pulling the sleeping bag back into place with a sharp tug. I turn my back on him. I'm in the school playground again, and everyone's laughing because I'm totally unaware that my new 'Mike' school bag is a knock-off.

Tom's wheezing has stopped now. 'Lydia?' There's puzzlement in his voice.

I ignore him, squeezing my eyes shut and burrowing into the sleeping bag.

'Lydia. Are you okay?'

'Fine.'

There's a silence but he doesn't lie down. He taps me on the shoulder. 'Lydia?'

I swallow a sniff but I'm not as successful as I'd hoped. If I could, without giving myself away, I'd curl into a ball right now, as defensive as a hedgehog trying to protect itself. Instead, I lie stiff and tense.

Tom's hand settles on my shoulder, his fingers cupping the bone around my thick jumper, and his voice softens. 'Lydia. I'm sorry.' He pauses and I swallow, oddly touched by his apology. 'It's a fox. I'm used to them, there are loads where I grew up, but if you're not used to the sound, it does sound pretty bloody awful.'

A fox! A bloody fox. Now I really do feel stupid.

'It does sound like someone being murdered. Why the hell didn't you wake me? Were you really going to go out there and face down some knife-wielding maniac?'

I shrug, not quite able to bring myself to speak. What has happened to all my carefully constructed defences? I've been in charge of my emotions and rebuilt my life. I've faked it to make it and, if I say so myself, I've done a pretty good job. What is it about Tom fucking Dereborn that makes me feel so vulnerable all of a sudden?

'I'm sorry. Can't decide if I'm impressed that you were brave enough to go out there and confront a potential murder or horrified that you'd put yourself in danger.'

'I wasn't in danger though, was I?' I retort, trying to save face.

'You didn't know that,' he counters, perfectly reasonably. 'You could have woken me, you know.'

'I didn't like to,' I mutter.

'You know we're in this together. You can ask for help.'

'Thanks,' I say. Like that's ever going to happen.

He laughs softly in the dark.

'What?' Suspicion shades my voice.

'You've got no intention of ever asking me for help, do you? You're far too self-contained. That's what struck me that first night I met you.'

I'm so surprised by his words that I relax and roll onto my back.

Why is it that the only proper conversations Tom and I have are in the dark?

'You were so cool and uninterested over dinner…' He pauses. 'And all I wanted to know was what your face would be like when you came.'

My involuntary gasp pierces the air. His words are hardly tender, but they melt me. It's his brutal honesty that gets to me. That night he wanted me, and he didn't hold back from showing or telling me.

'And now you know,' I murmur, trying to ignore the hot, wet spurt of desire between my legs. I'm turned on, damp and a little bit squirmy. Can he hear my hips pressing into the plastic ground sheet, my mound chafing at the seam of my jeans?

'Shame it's so dark now,' he says.

'Mmmm.' My voice is strangled.

'I'd like to make you come again,' he says, his breath hot against my ear.

I close my eyes, even though it's pitch-black, and swallow, unable to say a word. He hasn't touched me, but I think my body may go up in flames at any moment.

'May I?'

Oh God. My clit is hot and swollen. No. No. No. Yes. Yes. Yes. My body is at war with my brain. I can't open up to him again, I can't. But when he asks again…

'May I, Lydia?'

The polite request is a reminder of how careful he was with me that weekend, attentive and in tune with my needs, dirty-mouthed and respectful at the same time. The needy, neglected part inside me wants to be showered with that focused attention once more. I hate being this weak but I crave feeling like that again.

'Yes.' My voice is a breathy squeak. What am I doing? I'm making a mistake but I can't seem to say no.

His hand moves under the sleeping bag, skimming my stomach, sliding over the zip of my jeans and down to the fabric between my legs. 'Do you like this?' he asks as he runs a finger along the seam of my jeans. My hips buck in response. I want more, so much more. 'Yes.' All the tension leaks out of me and anticipation shoots through my veins like meteor showers.

He presses a kiss behind my ear. 'Are you going to come for me?' he asks in a husky whisper that makes my heart contract. 'Are you?' His hand rubs insistently. I can't think straight, my body is a blur of sensation all focused on the hot needy core of my being.

When he undoes my jeans and slides his hands inside my pants, my hips lift to meet his touch. I'm wet and slick, ready and greedy for him. He's kissing my neck, murmuring encouragement and it's sweet and filthy at the same time. His finger glides and smooths its way over my clit, the touch scorching. It's the sweetest torture and I pant as the rising tide of orgasm begins to swell but he doesn't let it break. I hear myself whimper. I can't help it. He teases and touches, relentless and gentle, and all I can feel is the hot sweetness of sensation. I want more but he's not giving it. Not yet. He's content to torment me, over and over. There's a thrill in knowing he's watching me, even though he can't possibly see my face in the dark.

Just when I'm starting to despair and the word 'please' hovers on my lips, he slides two fingers into me and with a couple of slow, firm drives over tender flesh, the orgasm explodes, pulsing with white-hot sparks of pleasure bursting like fireworks, fierce and bright in a black sky.

I'm left weak and breathless, my body limp and my brain scrambled. He moves his hand to my waist and it rests there under my T-shirt on my bare skin. His fully clothed body is warm next to mine.

Sated and sleepy, I turn my head as he kisses my neck again but he draws back, although his hand tightens on my waist reassuringly. 'Go to sleep, Lydia. Go to sleep.'

With a last sigh, I do just that.

***

Her skin beneath my fingers is soft and warm and I can't bring myself to remove my hand. I can feel how peaceful she is, as supine as a fireside cat, as if all the tension in her has been smoothed away. It relaxes me, especially as she hasn't said anything – no digging into my motivations and meaning. She accepts what I've given almost as if she knows I'm not really sure why I did it.

Somehow in the dark it's easier to give in to that low burning ember of longing for Lydia. She's the least needy person I've ever met, which for some perverse reason makes me want to look after her. Her voice when talking about her parents was so bleak, so barren of hope. She seems so alone and self-sufficient, it makes me want to ease her loneliness, which is laughable because I'm the last person to offer succour to anyone.

Emotional detachment is my super-power. I don't want, or want to need, anyone. Nor do I want the responsibility of their emotions or of ultimately disappointing them. Being loved is a heavy burden; it comes with too many strings attached. I prefer to watch life from the sideline and stay in control but I've been fighting the unwelcome attraction to Lydia since I laid eyes on her in Barcelona.

Her isolation makes things so much easier – she neither expects nor demands anything. Maybe I'm taking advantage of that to make myself feel a little better about my own failings. In the dark it's okay, I can justify myself, pretend detachment, even though those soft breathy sighs of hers made me ache with a longing to pull her close and bury myself inside her. I can close those down in the morning, leave them in the dark where they belong. Tomorrow we'll go back to being two work colleagues on a task. I close my eyes and listen to her gentle breathing beside me and hold on tight to the pleasure I gave her. For once I do feel better about myself.

———————

When I wake, Lydia is still sound asleep, her sparkly bobble hat poking out of the top of the sleeping bag. She's curled up away from me, her spine curved against my side. For a moment I lie there savouring the peace but the weight of my dick, desperate to break free of the confines of my boxers, bothers me. There's no way I can jerk off and ease the throbbing insistence for quick release when I'm lying next to Lydia, not on this rustle-fest of a groundsheet. The memory of last night crowds in, almost suffocating me with the realisation I've made a mistake. Daylight is a salutary reminder of the realities of life. Despite having great sex that weekend, I am not going back for a return visit, despite last night's weakness. I felt sorry for Lydia, that's all – at least that's what I'm telling myself. I'm not sure what to do with this little black hole in my chest when I think about her.

With a quick glance to check she's still asleep I wriggle out of the tent and wade through the heavy, wet grass down to the lakeside. Ripples race across the surface pushed by the brisk breeze but aside from the rush of the water across the small gravel beach and the distant cries of a couple of hawks wheeling across the sky, there's no other sound. The space and sense of being out of reach harden my resolve. Today's a fresh start. Lydia and I are teammates, nothing more. I can't afford to take my eye off the prize. Instead I close one eye and imagine how I'd film this scene, the lighting I'd use to capture the palette of greys crowding the sky with ominous intent. My growling stomach distracts me. After last night's lacklustre offering I'm starving and desperate for coffee. Time to get my Boy Scout pants on and go and hunt out some firewood, although after last night's deluge I'm not that hopeful of finding anything dry enough to burn. The thought of nothing for breakfast urges me on, despite my pessimism.

***

When I wake up I'm in smurf world with daylight spilling through the blue plastic sheeting above me. It's early and outside the birds are in full orchestral manoeuvres, trilling and singing in the round, like a professional choir. There's no sign of Tom apart from his rucksack, which, for some reason, is a gut-wrenching relief.

Oh God, I've got to face him this morning. Why the hell did I let myself give in? I know exactly why, because in the dark, it's easier to pretend that things are different. I sit up and roll my tight shoulders, trying to ease the stiffness out of my back. The morning air is dank and damp when I emerge from the makeshift tent into fine drizzle and a pewter-grey sky. Last night's fire looks pitiful, black charcoal pieces and white ash smeared by the rain, which has doused the pile of unused kindling and wood next to its remains. They're damp and useless. My stomach rumbles, hunger gnawing at it, leaving a dull ache. No chance of a hot sachet of anything this morning. I walk through rain-soaked grass down to the water's edge to give my face a hasty wash in the freezing water and my teeth a quick clean.

I study the glade, wondering where Tom is, and almost as if I've conjured him up, he appears, coming through the woods with an armful of branches and twigs.

'Morning,' I say, as brightly as I can, hiding sheepish

concern about how last night is going to affect things in the stone-grey daylight.

Any worry vanishes when he gives a polite but dismissive nod. 'Morning.'

So that's how we're going to play it. Pretend it didn't happen. Again. Fine by me.

He walks up to the stone circle we'd built the fire in the night before and rakes away the soggy ashes with the heel of his boot. 'I've got a bit of dry wood. Thought I'd try and get the fire going,' he says.

'Right. I'll fill the billycan. If we can get hot water we can have something to eat, whatever it is.'

'Great,' he says without enthusiasm. 'I could murder a flat white.'

'I have coffee.'

'Sorry?'

I go into the tent and retrieve a couple of sachets of instant Nescafé from one of the pockets in my rucksack.

'Here you go,' I say and pop them on one of the stones.

'You just happened to have these on you?'

I shrug. 'I picked them up in a hotel, thought they might come in handy.' Before he can say anything else or ask about my hoarding habit, I grab the billycan and stride down to the water's edge to fill it.

The water is flat and grey and I can barely see the hillside on the opposite side. It feels as if we're the only people in the world and it makes me uneasy. Very uneasy. I want to get back to crowded pavements, other people, electricity and knowing where I am, where I'm going and what I'm doing. Being in the great outdoors is like being trapped in a void.

When I return, Tom is desperately trying to fan a smoking heap of twigs into life. After a lot of effort, the flames take hold and I pour half the water away as it will take for ever to heat.

'What about the bracken from the tent?' I ask. 'It'll be dry and there's plenty of it.'

He gives me a cool look. 'We could try.'

Despite this lacklustre assent, I hurry off and grab an armful of the flattened bracken and feed it into the fire while he holds the billycan over the flames with a long stick like a makeshift fishing rod.

Dry bracken, it turns out, burns fiercely and far too quickly, but as we've got so much of it, Tom risks putting a couple of the drier logs on the fire while I run back and forth to what was our bed and bring more each time the last lot burns out.

It feels like a losing battle and the fine mist is seeping into my clothes on the outside while on the inside I'm building up a sweat with the workout.

Unlike last night, when the fire was our friend, this morning it's the enemy determined to outwit us. A voracious thing that refuses to be fed. The water in the billycan isn't even steaming yet but I refuse to give up. One of the logs begins to burn ... well, smoke, really. Thin wispy tendrils of grey rise up from it and then give up the ghost in the fine wet drizzle.

My hands are cold and the scratches from yesterday, when I gathered the bracken, are sore.

'This isn't going to work,' says Tom, when I'm down to the last armful.

'That log is starting to burn.'

'It's too wet.'

'Look, it's red, there are embers.'

He gives me a hard look. 'It's never going to heat the water. We might as well give up.'

I put frond after frond of bracken one at a time into the fire, praying it will catch properly, but they curl up in an instant flame that quickly burns itself out.

Tom sighs. 'You really know how to flog a dead horse, don't you?'

'And you know how to give up without trying.'

'Don't be ridiculous. I defy anyone to get a fire going with wet wood. We did our best.'

He lowers the billycan into the smouldering ashes next to the wooden branch that isn't smoking anymore. I dunk a finger in the water. Not even tepid.

'If we leave it to sit in the warm ashes it might heat up.'

Tom gives me a dry look. 'Yeah and look at that – a whole heap of pigs flying by.'

'You're such a defeatist.'

'And you're such a deluded optimist. You just don't know when to give up. It's like when we were in Barcelona. It was a cut and dry case. Visiting the site was a formality but you had to go poking about, winding the guy up.'

'I was following protocol,' I snap at him. 'Making sure there would be no comeback. It's called being thorough. It's called doing a job properly.'

'Are you saying I don't know how to do a job properly?' He drops his voice into a husky purr, damn him, and his eyes lock on mine.

Oh shit. A familiar curl of heat coils between my legs. I glare at him. Bastard. I have no comeback. If we're talking orgasms, then he bloody well does know.

I snatch up the coffee sachets. 'We won't be needing these this morning.' Childish, I know, but he brings out the worst in me. I march back to the tent and kneel on the floor, stuffing them back into my rucksack in exactly the same pocket as they came out of. Tom Dereborn will not be laying another hand on me ever again.

Chapter Twelve

LYDIA

'Lydia! Lydia!' His urgent call sends adrenaline flooding through my system. Oh my God, have they found us?

I scramble out of the shelter and find him crouched on the floor beckoning me. What?

'Come see this,' he says, his words insistent and fast.

I cross to him and get down on my knees to peer at the patch of ground.

'Start scraping the soil away as if you've found something,' he says leaning forward to speak very quietly into my ear.

I have no idea what is going on but he's no fool, there must be some reason for his insistence, so I do as I'm told. He has that coiled spring tension about him, it's vibrating from him in waves. I scrabble in the dirt for a full minute and I'm aware of his watchfulness. Every bit of him is alert, as if he's ready to spring into action.

'Keeping doing that.' He stands up and moves away, head down as if he's looking for something. Suddenly he grabs something and hurls it over my head. It's too high to hit me but what the... It does hit something, and that something comes crashing down nearby.

'Got it,' says Tom with satisfaction.

I realise it's a drone and my stomach cramps in fear. I hadn't heard it over the sound of the rain and the rushing water.

'They found us.' He grabs my hand and hauls me to my feet. 'We've got to go.'

I pull away and run to the shelter, grabbing his rucksack and pushing it towards him, along with the sleeping bag.

'Fuck's sake, we've got to go,' he shouts. 'Leave the rucksack.'

'No!' I shout back as I frantically wriggle into the straps and pull it onto my back.

'Fuck's sake,' he repeats, but he copies me.

'This way.' He yanks my arm and I follow as he leads me into the trees. We run under the low branches. The canopy above is thick. Clever Tom. If they have another drone can't see us in here. But they know where we are.

My heart is pounding so hard I can hardly catch my breath, but I keep running. Tom is holding my hand and pulling me along, guiding me around logs and tugging me over tree roots. I stumble multiple times but manage to stay upright. I don't even ask where we're going, he seems to know what he's doing. In a rare moment of insight, I realise I trust him. He will look after me. Despite my comments yesterday, he didn't leave me behind, he walked at my pace. And last night, hell, he definitely looked after me.

We come out of the trees onto a small, single-track lane, the houses of the village just ahead of us.

'This way,' says Tom. And we run down the middle of the lane.

'Is this … a … good … idea,' I pant. 'More lik…ely to catch us … on road.'

'They've got to get the drone first. That's eleven grand's worth of kit. They'll not leave it behind. But they'll come after us, as soon as they've picked it up. They could be anywhere up to eight kilometres away.'

'What's that in real distance?' I manage to puff out.

'Around five miles. I guess it depends on vehicle access and they'll want to be high up to fly it without too many obstructions.'

He looks at my puce face. I think I might be sick any second. I'm not a natural athlete and I've never run this far or for as long in my life. Amazing what adrenaline can do.

Thankfully, he slows the pace to a fast walk, although I'm still struggling to breathe.

'H-how … can you be sure?'

'Because they found us pretty easily … they knew where we were. I didn't spot the drone at first and then when I did, it was quite high up, that's why we didn't hear it.'

'So you pretended there was something on the ground so that it would come lower.' Wow, that is smart thinking. 'How did you even come up with that?'

'They're trying to film a TV series. I just thought like the director.'

'Obviously,' I say.

His mouth tugs at one corner. 'It's what I ... want to do. Make films. I've been making short films for a while. Come on, we need to pick up the pace again.' And then, contrarily, he stops dead.

'What?'

'They know where we are.'

'Well duh!'

He looks up at the sky and I follow his gaze but there are no black specks in the sky. Just a couple of birds freewheeling on the thermals.

'I wonder. How did they know where we were? They need footage to create drama. They can't leave it to chance, not if they're filming a pilot. They need to get it right.' He frowns, still talking to himself. 'What would I do, to manage things?' He looks at me. 'I think they might have put a tracker on us.'

'That's... Really?' Isn't that cheating?'

He snorts out a laugh. 'It's reality TV, anything is possible. They're only interested in making engaging TV programmes. Viewers want to see us hunted down, *fleeing for our lives*. That's where the drama comes in. But if they don't know where we are and we don't have any near misses, it's not much of a programme.' He pauses as if going through it all in his head.

'They have to be tracking us somehow. How else did they find us so quickly?'

My skin crawls with the thought that there's a tracking device somewhere and they've known all night where we were. They could have been watching us the whole time.

'Question is, where would they put it? They wouldn't want to risk us finding it or losing it or ditching it. And it would have to be something…' He looks at me again. 'I've just had an idea. I wondered why they'd changed the teams at the last minute. As a team, you and Tansy would have made good eye candy.'

'Is that a back-handed compliment?' I ask, but he ignores me.

'What's the one thing you wouldn't leave behind?'

'My rucksack,' I say without hesitation.

'Bingo. And me and Rory brought our own. That's why they split us up. So that they could track you and Tansy, who are both using rucksacks they gave you.'

He spins me round and yanks my rucksack from my back.

'Oy,' I protest but he's already running his fingers over the fabric. As I'm grateful for the rest, I leave him to it.

'The sneaky bastards.' He points at a little silver rivet attached to the waterproof fabric and picks at it with his fingernails. 'Bugger. It's not coming off anytime soon.'

I have a go but the innocent little disc is stuck fast. In the meantime, he's picked up a stone from beside the wall.

'We can disable it,' he says and he's about to smash the rock down onto the tracker, when I yank the rucksack out of reach.

'What!' he screeches.

After the mad panic of the morning my brain has decided to go back online.

'I've got a better idea. I've got some scissors. I'll cut it off.'

I elbow him out of the way and dig into my rucksack and produce a pair of sharp tipped scissors.

'Bloody hell, Lydia. I thought you meant a pair of nail scissors, not bloody shears.'

'I've got those too,' I say flippantly, as I carefully cut around the tiny device. 'What if we use them to send the hunters on a false trail? They bloody deserve it.'

He stares at me in stunned admiration. At least that's what I'd like to think it is. It could be bafflement.

'What time is it?'

'Just after eight.'

'Come on,' I say, pocketing the tracker and feeling a spurt of happiness. I feel back in control instead of blindly having to follow Tom because all of this outdoor, countryside stuff is so alien. Turns out *Swallows and Amazons* hasn't equipped me as well as I might have hoped. 'We need to get a move on. There's a bus in ten minutes.'

Now there is definite admiration on his face. I really rather like it.

We charge into the village heading straight for the bus stop and, miracle of miracles, the bus is on time.

I hop on and ask the driver, 'Where's the next stop?'

He isn't fazed by the question, I guess he's used to tourists.

'Clappersgate.'

'Two singles to Clappersgate.' I hand over one of our precious tenners.

He huffs. 'Got nothing smaller.'

'Sorry, no.'

'I haven't got change now. Usually walkers get on at next stop. They might have some change. Get theeselves on.'

We settle into seats in the middle of the bus where we can sink below the window out of sight. Both of us are glancing round as the bus idles. My hands are clenched tight in my pocket. We sit for an anxious minute. God, is this is a terrible mistake?

'Come on, come on,' mutters Tom, his left leg jittering up and down. 'Maybe we should have already ditched the trackers.'

'Then they'd know we'd found them. This way if we leave them on the bus, they might go all the way to Kendal. Probably follow the bus before they realise we're not on board.'

'Unless they catch us first,' says Tom through tightly

clenched jaws. 'We're sitting ducks right now. I think we should get off. Leave the trackers.'

'No.' I need to rest but I can't bear to admit it to Tom. We haven't eaten this morning and the adrenaline crash is making me feel very shaky.

'Lydia, don't be ridiculous. They could catch us at any minute. If we leave the tracker here, we can hide in the village and they'll follow the bus.'

I'm just about to agree when glory be, the bus engine fires up with a rumble, the windows rattling in their frames as we finally trundle out of the village at surprising speed.

We exchange looks.

'We're not out of the woods yet, you know,' says Tom, still obviously annoyed with me. 'They could still catch us.'

'We managed a whole day yesterday,' I say, trying to be positive and take my mind off the thought of being caught.

'Some of us are taking this seriously,' Tom snaps. 'I want to win the hundred grand. Thanks to me, we got away this morning.'

'You?'

'Yes, you were fannying about worrying about sleeping bags and rucksacks.'

'Which turned out to be a smart move because we found the tracker,' I snap back.

'Which is still on us – so we're not home and dry just yet. They could catch up with us at any moment.'

God, he's such a fucking smart arse.

A few bends later and I'm wondering if the driver once

had Formula 1 ambitions. He's throwing the bus about and I'm hanging on to the metal seat rail in front of us for grim death. I should have asked how far the stop was.

Tom's knuckles are white as he clenches the rail too, occasionally turning round and checking behind us.

It's more nerve-racking than I could have thought possible.

I look out of the windows again. Sweat is pooling between my shoulders and trickling down my back.

Suddenly the bus lurches to an abrupt halt.

'Clappersgate.'

'Thank fuck for that.' Tom pushes me down the front of the bus. 'Hurry up.'

Jeez, he's cranky.

I realise there's no one at the stop and I pause by the driver digging in my pocket for my ten pound note. Tom digs me sharply in the ribs. 'Your lucky day. Enjoy,' says the driver cheerfully and the doors open with a bang.

'You don't want us to p—'

Before I can finish Tom chips in, 'Thanks, mate,' and hustles me off the bus. With a wave the driver closes the doors, rams the poor old bus into gear and it sways right out into the middle of the road before disappearing around the bend, taking our little friend with it.

'That was a bit rude,' I say.

'Fuck's sake Lydia. We need to get off the road,' he snarls.

I glare at him but he's already hurrying across the road. He turns. 'Get a move on.'

I follow him, seething, as he ducks beneath a public footpath sign and climbs over a stile. He doesn't stop to wait for me. I only just make it over the wooden step and almost over balance. I catch my footing but he's already gone, walking at speed down a track sandwiched between two stone walls.

'Bastard,' I mutter to myself and pick up my pace but there's no way I can keep up with Tom. Today my rucksack feels even heavier than it did yesterday, despite the fact we're down a groundsheet and a couple of cooking utensils, which were abandoned in our haste to leave our campsite.

Ahead of me, every now and then I can see the bus dipping in and out of view as it careers along with the same breakneck recklessness that got us here. I feel a slight fondness for the driver and his need for speed. Hopefully he'll lead our hunters all the way to Kendal and I'll be vindicated – not that I'll know, but it would be so nice to be able to say 'Told you so' to Tom right now.

Chapter Thirteen

LYDIA

Trudging along with sodden feet, rain running down the inside of your useless raincoat and your trousers plastered to your freezing thighs, has to be up there in the top three of the nine circles of hell. After the initial burst of euphoria that we'd outwitted our hunter friends, it's official, my usual optimism has been washed away, but I'm not going to admit it, not to Tom. Stoicism is my best friend and always has been. We've been keeping to footpaths and taking the occasional peek at the map, desperately trying to keep it dry. We've not succeeded and it's now so soggy, it's almost impossible to handle. Lucky we have a back-up map, then.

'I reckon we're here,' says Tom, stabbing his finger on the bunched square of paper.

When we set off from Clappersgate, we actually agreed on a plan. Although I have to leave that bit to him as I do know my limitations. Map reading is not in my skill set. I'm of the Never Eat Shredded Wheat brigade – that's the only way I know the compass points.

We're heading east, across country, to try and pick up the slip road of the M6 going south at Tebay at Junction 38 – Tom's words not mine. Apparently this is a slightly longer route than to the junction below but it's his suggestion on the basis that that's where you'd expect the hunters to be watching. When he tells me it's about twenty-six miles, I catch my lip between my teeth. It sounds a long way until he points out it's the same as a marathon and people run that in a few hours.

Sadly we're not running, the weather is grim and the terrain is mountainous, or at least it feels it, and one of my hiking boots is rubbing a blister on my heel. After walking three hours, the 'here' that Tom indicates on the map looks no closer to our destination than it did when we set off.

I peer at it obligingly. 'If you say so. I haven't got a clue.'

'Let's take a break.' He points to a ruined structure ahead, which has half a roof and one wall. 'We could shelter there. Have a drink and one of those energy bars they so thoughtfully provided us with. Do you think they're expecting us to catch rabbits to eat or something?'

'They did say they didn't expect anyone to get very far,' I point out, grateful that I'd managed to fill both thermos flasks with cold water this morning before our hapless flight.

'That was to keep us keen. Reverse psychology.

Although I wonder if they plan to starve us into submission, that or caffeine deprivation. Oh for a coffee shop.'

We plough our way up the steep incline towards the rough shelter. It's little more than a shack. The rucksacks are dumped in unison and we slide down the walls to sit under the narrow overhang of crumbling tiles that offers some respite from the rain.

The energy bar tastes wonderful, as does the water I wash it down with. Not sure I feel any more energetic though. The thought of walking for several more hours is deeply depressing, especially in silence watching Tom plodding ahead of me.

I take off one shoe and sock to examine the inch wide blister that has burst and is bleeding.

'Shit, Lydia. That looks nasty.'

I shrug and dig into my rucksack to pull out the first-aid kit.

'Why didn't you say anything before?' he asks as I take out a plaster. 'We could have stopped.'

'It's fine,' I say, even though now the open sore is exposed, it's all I can do to stop wincing from the pain.

'No, it's not,' snaps Tom. 'And that's not going to help.' He takes the plaster from me with an impatient swipe. 'It's already burst. You need to protect it to prevent further damage otherwise you won't be able to walk.'

'Yeah, wouldn't want me to slow you down,' I snap back.

'Fuck's sake.' He shuffles forward and takes my foot in his hand, holding it up to the light. His fingers are freezing but hold it in a strong grip as if he knows I want to wrench it away.

'We need to sort this out properly.'

'Don't worry, I'm not going to hold you up,' I repeat. Sniping at him is the only way I know how to deal with this.

He shoots me a glare and rests my foot on his thigh. Ignoring me, he opens the first-aid kit and spreads the contents on the stone floor, his face screwed up in thought like a surgeon about to make the first cut.

'It's okay. A plaster will do,' I say, a little embarrassed. I'm used to sorting things out for myself.

'No, Lydia. A plaster will not do.'

He tears open a sachet and with gentle fingers he applies an antiseptic wipe. I watch him while trying not to flinch. It stings like buggery but I'm fascinated by his face. He's completely absorbed in his task, methodical and careful. Next, he cuts a square from the corner of one of the sealed dressings, keeping the remainder in the pack – 'for later' – and covers the wound with it, his touch so soft as he smooths the edges, brushing my skin. For some stupid reason I want to cry. I can't remember when anyone has taken such pains with me. Finally, he uses micropore tape to strap it all up.

'That should hold. What about the other foot?'

'Thanks,' I say, my voice gruff because I might give

myself away at any moment, but he's already tugging the other sock off to check my foot.

'Lydia!' The gentle exasperation almost finishes me off and there's a foolish flutter in my heart, but he doesn't say any more, just takes the biggest plaster he can find and applies it to the red, angry patch on the heel.

Then he looks at me intently. 'Do you have another pair of socks? I'd suggest wearing two pairs. Stops the rubbing.'

I slide my gaze away, worried he might see something in my eyes that I really don't want him to see. 'Yes. I'll put them on.'

I know he's only thinking about winning the challenge, but he doesn't have to be kind with it. I just don't know how to deal with that.

We plod on in the rain for another few hours like a pair of worn down donkeys. I don't even bother to keep track of time, I just put one foot in front of the other. Tom's rain-slicked back is etched into my vision as I peer out of the hood that is pulled drawstring-tight around my face, restricting my peripheral vision. I now know how a Minion feels as I turn, this way and that, to see any direction but ahead.

Tom stops and waits for me to catch him up. 'How are you feeling? How are your feet?'

I wipe the rain from my cheeks. 'They're fine, thank you. Much better.'

He studies my face as if he's checking I'm telling the truth. Fine drops of water fleck his face, dotting the bristles on his chin and his eyelashes. Our eyes meet and hold. I can't look away and it appears neither can he. With a flash of heat, I vividly remember him staring down at me as he was inside me, a bright starburst moment of connection before we both pitched over the edge of orgasm. I watch as his Adam's apple dips and then, finally, when the silence between is stretched to breaking point, he is the first to drop his gaze.

'Good,' he says in peremptory fashion. 'Let me know if you want a break.' We've barely spoken to one another and I don't know if he's been as lost in his own thoughts as I have.

'Yeah, thanks.'

'This is so fucking miserable,' he says, walking alongside me. It's the most we've spoken since we left the shelter.

Tom heaves a heavy sigh and tugs on the shoulder straps of his rucksack.

We travel on in silence, but it feels a bit more companionable as we're side by side, walking in tandem. The straps of my rucksack feel like they're trying to separate my shoulders from my neck and I keep fidgeting surreptitiously with them to try and get more comfortable.

'Do you want to stop for a while?' Tom asks.

'No.' I swivel around to view the landscape, which is a wasted effort. It feels as if we're inside the raincloud, visibility is so poor. 'There's nowhere to stop. We might as well keep going.'

'Are you sure? How are the feet?'

'They're fine,' I say.

He smiles a grim smile. 'And you wouldn't say otherwise. Honestly, Lydia, you are … something else.' He shakes his head. 'I don't want you to be in pain.'

The simple statement lances through all my defences. My heart does an unfamiliar bunny hop in my chest and I stare at him. This is beyond my experience and I have no idea what to do with it. I swallow a lump which has crept into my throat, sneaky bugger. 'I'm fine.'

'Okay. If you say so. Then I suggest we head for those trees up ahead.'

I can just about make out a cluster of trunks in the gloom.

'Maybe it'll be a bit dryer and we can make a shelter for the night,' he adds.

It seems churlish to ask him, what with? Especially when he's been so … so what? Kind, lovely, caring, considerate. It shakes me up inside. I'm not used to people being concerned for my welfare.

As we near the forest, he nudges me and points to a field in a valley to the left. 'Look.'

Through the misty mizzle I can just make out a structure. At this distance it isn't obvious what it is, but it has part of a roof and it looks like shelter.

We both pick up speed and after a boggy trek across the lumpy field strewn with boulders, we reach a gate and what was once a cottage. Half the roof is open to the sky, the exposed beams blackened from what was obviously a catastrophic fire, but one part still retains some slates. Ancient, tattered net curtains, sodden with rain, slap half-heartedly in the wind against the rotten window frames of the second floor like ghouls.

The front door is solid but when we reach it, there's a heavy padlock securing it.

'Fuck,' says Tom. 'There must be a way inside.'

We ditch the rucksacks and circle the building. The windows on the ground floor have all been boarded up. Tom tries to peel his fingers under one of the rough hardwood sheets but they've been well and truly nailed down.

A broken gutter sends a splashy cascade down the side of the building where a green slimy mould stains the wall and soaks the wooden board, but despite that it holds firm.

'Shit,' he says after another attempt when he comes away with a bloody finger.

I'll give him an A plus for persistence. He keeps trying and looking for a way in and I'm his faithful supporter. We find rocks to try and bash the wood in, use sticks as levers to try and lift the boards away. Nothing works.

We return to the front door and Tom gives into his frustration and kicks the heavy door a couple of times.

'Fuck. Fuck. Fuck.'

He goes back for one last kick and as he does something falls to the ground from the lintel above. He's too busy venting to notice and I crouch down and pick up the small silver key with a quick grin.

'Er, Tom,' I say but he's still busy, kicking the door and swearing at it.

So I take the key, push him out of the way and insert it in the padlock. Smooth as proverbial silk, it turns and the hasp pops open.

Tom stops and stares as I turn back to him.

'How did you do that?'

I hold up the key and nod towards the lintel where it had obviously been stored.

'I don't fucking believe it. Lydia, you're a genius.'

I'm more than happy to take credit where it's not due, so I grin at him. Whereupon he throws his arms around me and hugs me. Then he steps back as if surprised by this uncharacteristic demonstration of elation, confusion evident in his eyes, but I'm still grinning up at him. He grins back and for a second we stand there smiling at each other like complete fools. He sweeps a hand in front of him. 'After you, madam.'

My trusty torch flickers over what was once a kitchen, the only room in the house with a ceiling. The rest of the space is unsheltered, those burnt rafters like black skeletal fingers against the darkening sky. Across the hall, there's a drawing room, the walls crumbling around a chimney breast. In this room, a scar on one wall attests to the spot where there once would have been a range, but all that's left now is a crumbling 1960s kitchen dresser, a broken table and several chairs which I wouldn't trust with my weight. I also suspect we might be sharing the floorspace with sundry rodents but I'm not sure I care overmuch. It's dry, and at this moment in time that is all that matters.

'What a dump,' says Tom, surveying the room.

I peel off my wet coat and shiver a little but I hang it up on a hook on the back of the door before starting to explore. I open a door to what was once the pantry, shining my torch into the black void. There are dilapidated floor-to-ceiling shelves, home to few unsightly, rusty tins as well as a couple of assorted flabby grey cardboard boxes, which have been nibbled at the corners. I nudge one of them with curious wariness.

'Candles!' I shout, as the box collapses and several wax candles roll out. I make a grab at them, suddenly grinning.

'Marvellous,' says Tom from over my shoulder. 'Now we can clearly see what a shithole we're in.'

I examine the other boxes. More candles. Sadly, no handy firelighters or anything vaguely useful. I don't think thirty-year-old gravy salt, which is an indeterminate grey, is going to get us very far.

I light a candle, drip some wax on the table and put it down before lighting a couple more and putting them around the room. Now the room is bouncing with shadows as the flames flicker.

'Well, would you look at that?' Tom points to an alcove filled with wooden logs next to where the stove would have been. 'I've got an idea.' He disappears and minutes later I hear the sound of metal being dragged across the floor towards the kitchen door. He appears in the doorway pulling a metal grate that he's obviously rescued from the old fireplace in the lounge.

'We can build a fire and use the flue where the old stove was,' he says. 'There's enough stuff in here to burn to get a fire going.'

The thought of being warm, and drying my clothes, and being able to heat water is heaven.

'But what about if they're looking for us and they see the smoke?'

'It's going to be dark soon. Besides, I doubt anyone could see it in this weather. Hopefully they're scratching their heads in Kendal at the moment and trying to repair a very expensive drone.'

He sets about building a fire, breaking up one of the chairs for kindling, which takes very little effort.

'Don't suppose you've got any more wool in your pockets?'

I shake my head.

He takes one of the candles and tries to light one of the pieces of kindling, but as soon as it catches light, it bursts into flame and dies quickly before setting fire to the other pieces of wood. After several attempts he puts down the candle. I'm starting to shiver. He tries again but to no avail.

'Bugger. This isn't working. I need something to get it going.'

I have a lightbulb moment and rescue my toilet bag. I hand him a tampon.

'What?'

'It's made of cotton wool. Packed down tight. If you open it up, I think it will burn.'

He takes it from me, between finger and thumb as if it's a fucking hand grenade.

'Oh for fuck's sake.' I laugh at his squeamishness and snatch it from him, rip off the paper, hand it back to him along with the carboard tube before tugging at the white cotton tampon to expand it.

'Sorry,' he says, slightly shame-faced as he sets it on the grate and builds a pyramid of the kindling around it. The wooden logs, which have been in the cottage for so long, are so dry that they catch almost immediately.

He raises a hand and we high-five each other.

Unfortunately, seconds later, my eyes start to water as the room begins to fill with smoke.

'Quick, open the door,' says Tom.

'The door?' What's he on about.

'To draw the fire up the chimney. It's too cold. Go on, quick.'

I have no idea what any of this means but his imperative tone sends me scurrying to the door, which I open. Surely this will just let out all the heat?

But miraculously it does the trick and the smoke starts to dissipate. After a couple of minutes there's a roaring fire in the grate and Tom tells me I can close the door. The heat is delicious and I creep towards it, hands outstretched. It's only then I realise just how chilled I am and how cold my fingers are, as they tingle with my circulation returning.

I really want to take my wet clothes off but decide we need to get organised first. Besides I need to go back outside. Grabbing my coat, I start to shoulder my way into it.

'Where the hell are you going?'

'To get some water. I can fill the billycan from the gutter and we can have a hot drink and some food.' I bet he won't be complaining about the quality of the food this evening.

I end up filling both billycans and both thermos flasks because I don't want to have to come out here again tonight. I also take advantage of the privacy for a quick pee.

When I re-emerge from the undergrowth he is at the front of the house with the GoPro.

'We ought to shoot some footage.'

'Do we have to?' I just want to get on and set up camp for the night.

'We don't want to give the fuckers any excuse for reneging on the ten grand they owe us. They might have something in the small print. I wouldn't put it past them.'

He has a point. I stand with him as he takes a selfie of the pair of us, then films a video, breaking into yet another eloquent commentary. 'This is our accommodation for day two of being on the run.' He pans the camera around the room. 'Not the most salubrious and we probably need to catch a couple of rabbits to knock up a tasty stew but for now we've got astronaut rations in silver foil packets, which will have to do. We've also got fire and shelter, so it's over and out for the evening from Team Tomdia.'

'Did you just say Tomdia? Please don't ever say that again.' I shudder as he gives me an unrepentant grin.

'Okay, how about Lydom? Although, come to think of it, both sound a bit like an STD.'

I glare at him. I would know. Let's hope he never finds out what Lydia is really short for, I'm sure he'd find it amusing.

An hour later, Tom lifts his enamel cup, toasting me, and then takes a deep, appreciative sniff. 'Cheers, Lydia. You're a lifesaver.'

I toast him back and take a sip of the black coffee, basking in his praise.

'That is bloody marvellous,' he says with a sigh.

'It's not bad,' I reply. Amazing the difference being warm and dry can make.

The room is now quite cosy, even with our drying clothes draped over two of the chairs in front of the fire, and we're both sitting on our folded travel towels, a barrier against the cold of the floor.

I tear open the silver sachets of dehydrated food and tip in some of the hot water from the billy, my hand wrapped in a jumper, which is the next best thing to an oven glove.

'What do you reckon it is?' asks Tom as I hand him one.

'No idea and I don't actually care.'

'Me neither.'

He takes a mouthful. 'I think it's dried mouse bollocks, which have had a passing acquaintance with a teaspoon of tomato puree.'

I snort out a laugh and take a taste. 'I think it's supposed to be chilli con carne and rice.'

'I think the manufacturers should be taken out and shot. But I'm so bloody hungry I don't care. I guess the manufacturers are relying on that to save them.'

'I've tasted worse,' I say glibly but I realise I've made a mistake when in the candlelight I can see Tom studying me.

'Have you?' he asks. 'Really?' He watches me as I lift another forkful into my mouth.

I shrug my shoulders, really not wanting to talk about how I cobbled together some pretty strange combinations when I was younger.

I duck my head and the crackle of the fire fills the silence. I watch the flames leap in a mesmerising dance, primeval and reassuring, grateful for the heat.

'If you could eat anything right now, what would you choose?' he asks, swallowing down another mouthful of his food.

'Smoked salmon and a cream cheese bagel,' I say without hesitation. Ever since I first had one, they've been my idea of absolute luxury. When I'm feeling flush I treat myself to a pack of smoked salmon and a tub of Philadelphia and have it for breakfast.

'Nice and simple,' he observes.

'That's me,' I reply. 'Cheap date.'

'You don't complain, do you?' he says suddenly.

'What?'

'You don't complain. Not at all. I said it the other day but we hadn't been through much hardship, but today … I've not heard you moan or whine once. Not about the weather conditions, or your foot, which obviously hurts, or being hungry or cold. Nothing.'

I don't like the direction of this conversation. It's sounds like he's making a virtue out of something I'm not comfortable with. Talking about it will expose too much of me. The me I keep hidden.

I shrug again.

'You do that a lot, too,' he says.

This time I roll my eyes. 'Maybe I just don't want to talk about things. Same as you.'

'I talk about things.'

'Yeah, right.'

'You're talking about the sex thing again.'

'I wasn't, but now you bring it up, why did you pretend you didn't know who I was in Barcelona?'

Now it's his turn to be silent. I wait it out.

'I don't know. It was a shock to see you. It's not like it meant anything. It was a one-off.'

'Given it happened nearly a year ago, I think I got that.'

'But I'm sorry about that day. I was in a shitty mood and I took it out on you and the dickhead we insured.'

'The lying sack of shit?'

'Fuck. Yes, not my finest hour.'

'I think we were both in shitty moods.' I'm not about to confess why my mood was so shitty. That I'd been fantasising for months about meeting him again and it had been a big fat disappointment.

'Although,' I add, 'you could have apologised to Mr Lopez.'

'Why?'

'Because it made you look unprofessional. Weren't you embarrassed that he heard you?'

'You think I care what he thought?'

I stare at him. That genuinely hadn't occurred to me. I'd have been mortified.

'You don't like other people much, do you?' I ask.

Now it's his turn to shrug. 'They're all right.'

I laugh. '"They're all right." That's hardly fulsome praise. What about the people you work with? Your team.'

'They're just people I work with. I don't really think about them. Everyone wants something from you.'

'You do have friends, don't you?' I ask.

'Of course I have friends. Just not at work.' He purses his mouth. 'I choose my friends carefully.'

In that we're the same. 'Me too,' I say.

'Bet you're friends with all your team. I'm sure they all love you – the security guy, Danny, definitely does.'

I smile. 'Yeah, they do.' I pause and then say in a louder voice, 'Because I'm *nice* to them. You should try it some time.'

'I prefer to keep myself to myself.'

'So what do you do with these carefully chosen friends when you're not at work?'

He lifts an eyebrow.

'Yes, Tom, we're having a conversation. We might as well, given that there's sod all else to do. What about we make a pact, whatever you tell me on tour stays on tour?'

His mouth quirks into a begrudging smile. 'You're very direct.'

'Mate, I've got nothing to lose. Look where we are.'

'You have a point.' He crosses his legs and winces. It's not that comfortable on the floor even with the towels. 'I play five-a-side football with mates a couple of times a week. I'm a Marvel and *Star Wars* fan so I like going to the cinema. I like reading true crime fiction and listening to politics podcasts while I'm out running. I make films and I'm still in close contact with my uni friends and we socialise a lot together. Dinner, going out for drinks, all that malarkey. And Sunday lunch with the folks once a week with my brother and sister. Pretty standard stuff. What about you?'

'Similar. I've got two really good friends from uni. We go out together a lot and I socialise after work once a week with my team, because as you said, they love me … and newsflash, I like them too.'

'What about hobbies, interests?'

I'm about to shrug and then think better of it. 'Is cleaning a hobby?' I muse out loud.

'Er, no.'

'That's a bit sad, isn't it,' I joke. My flat is spotless. I don't think I've got a compulsive disorder, but I like things to be tidy.

'No. I noticed as you set up the camp last night and tonight, you had to get things into an order and sorted. You like to be organised. There's no crime in that. I shared a flat with a guy once and he lived in chaos, it did my head in. I couldn't stand it. I moved out after a couple of months. I certainly don't describe myself as a neat freak but he was...' Tom shakes his head. 'All over the place, you know.'

I give a tight smile. Yeah, I know. Only too well.

'I've never seen a *Stars Wars* film,' I volunteer as much for a change of subject as anything else because I know this always elicits howls of disbelief and wide-eyed horror. I'm pleased to see that Tom is no different and reacts with outraged predictability.

'What! You're kidding me.'

I hold up a hand. 'Nope. I've never seen Princess Leia in *that* scene with Jabba the Hutt, or Han Solo frozen in Carbonite or when Darth Vader tells Luke,' I put on the appropriate voice, 'I am your father.'

Tom bursts out laughing. 'For someone who's never seen one of the films, you seem to know a lot about them.'

'That's because people always say the same thing about them. Every. Single. Time.'

'Please tell me you've seen a Marvel film.'

'Yes, my friend Eleanor has a slight obsession with Thor.'

'Chris Hemsworth. Why do all the women fancy him?'

'Might be something to do with those twinkly eyes, that smile or the fact that he's just plain hot,' I quip lightly. 'But actually it's the real Thor, as in the Viking god. She sits through the films complaining about the license they've taken with Norse mythology. She works in a bug farm.'

'Sorry?'

I've added the latter for entertainment value and perhaps to make me sound a bit more interesting, because, hey, look, I have interesting friends. 'She works for a company that is conducting research into how black flies can be farmed as an alternative food source.'

'Seriously?' Tom looks appalled. Okay, so maybe not that interesting.

'Yup. Right in the centre of London. It's fascinating.'

'I'll take your word for it.' He shakes his head. 'I still can't believe you've never seen *Star Wars*. You must have had a deprived childhood.'

If only he knew.

'Very funny,' I say with all the sarcasm I can muster. Before I can say anything else he continues.

'I usually judge people on who their favourite character is.'

'Han Solo.'

He's surprised by my alacrity. 'But you've never seen it.'

'It's Harrison Ford. What's not to like?'

He rolls his eyes.

'Who's your favourite character then?'

'Obi-wan Kenobi, Leia Organa, Bobo Fett.'

'That's three.'

'Obi watched the man that trained and raised him be killed in front of him and still managed to avenge him despite Darth Maul being way more powerful. He was forced to kill the man he called a brother for the greater good, and gave up the love of his life for the Jedi. He's selfless to the end and still a master of the force. Princess Leia was willing to die and be tortured before giving up rebel secrets. Watched her home planet destroyed in front of her, and then despite no war experience stepped up to become a general in the rebel alliance. She never once let being a woman stand in her way, despite being surrounded by men who doubted her. Held her own in the Battle of Endor without proper combat experience. Never once complained that her brother inherited the force and was painted as the one who brought all the balance, despite all that she did. And Boba Fett, well ... he had cool armour.'

I burst out laughing at the serious expression on his face, although his answer gives a lot away about his character and his values. I'm particularly impressed by his choice and description of Leia. I'm coming to realise there's a lot more depth to Tom Dereborn than I'd originally given him credit for.

'So?' I ask, still pondering his heartfelt response.

'So, what?'

'How would you judge me?'

He smirks. 'Actually, you'd get okay marks for Han Solo. He's cool and has the best quips.'

'Well, that is a relief,' I tease. 'I'd hate to have got it wrong.'

'Do you get things wrong?' he asks, and it doesn't sound like an idle question.

'I try not to,' I say because it's the truth.

'Me too, but it doesn't always work out.' His mouth twists in wry resignation and I suddenly want to reach out and reassure him, but I have no idea what to say.

Chapter Fourteen

LYDIA

Despite the heat of the fire, it's a long, uncomfortable night. Tom tried to insist that I had the sleeping bag, but in the end we both lie on top of it, a good distance apart.

I doze, off and on, but we're both constantly on fire duty, getting up to add a log whenever it dies right back. Despite being physically exhausted, I can't get comfortable on the hard floor, no matter which way I turn. When daylight starts to filter around the edge of the boarded-up windows, I finally give up and sit upright. In the gloom, the kitchen with its layer of grime, shaggy cobwebs and debris is far more depressing than it was by candlelight. Tom groans and winces as he sits up. The fire has died down to embers but quickly roars back into life when he tosses one of the logs from the dwindling pile onto it.

I get up and busy myself boiling water and gathering up the clothes that are now dry.

'What are you doing?' asks Tom, catching me stashing candles in my rucksack.

'In case we need them again.'

'Good thought, although I hope to fuck we get to the motorway today. Not sure I can stand another night like this.' He gestures around the room and suddenly I really want to get out of the squalid surroundings.

'I need to get some fresh air,' I mutter, leaving him to sort out making coffee. I've fought too hard to escape this, and I don't like the memories it's bringing back.

Outside the contrast to the previous day is almost unbelievable. A brisk wind lifts and tosses my hair across my face and I lift a hand to hold it back to take in the view. The bright, glorious morning is full of sunshine and hope. It's a million miles from yesterday's dank, grey hours of unrelenting misery. I take a deep breath, relief flooding through me, although I can't contain a shudder. I would kill for a shower and to be clean.

I hear Tom's footsteps. He hands me a cup of coffee and we both lean on the wall in front of the cottage, taking in the wide sweep and rise of majestic hills, crowned with outcrops of grey crags and sliced by verdant valleys. There's not a soul in sight and the only sound is the distant call of a bird, a lonely echo across the field.

'Cheers,' he says lifting his cup and taking an enthusiastic sip. 'Heaven in a cup. I'll never knock instant coffee again. Thank God that you're a cheapskate and pinched a load from the hotel.'

'I call it thrifty.'

'Whatever. I'm extremely grateful for your forethought.'

I'm quietly satisfied by the praise but I revert to inanities because I don't know what else to say.

'It's a gorgeous morning.'

'Thank fuck. There was a point yesterday where if I'd seen one of those bloody orange Land Rovers, I'd have run towards it begging them to capture us.'

'Good job we didn't then. I'm a great believer in tomorrow's another day. Things can only get better.'

He gives me a thoughtful look and nods before returning his gaze to the view.

Our silence for once is companionable.

'Well,' he says decisively. 'We're almost home and dry. I reckon another six or seven miles this morning – we can do that in a couple of hours. It's seven now. Once we get to the slip road, we can hitch a ride and potentially be back in civilisation by this evening if we're lucky.'

He swigs his coffee.

'I need a wazz.'

'Right. I'll go tidy up and get ready.' Reluctantly I leave the daylight and the clean air and go back into the kitchen, where I quickly chuck another log on the fire and put some more water onto boil.

By the time Tom returns, I've rolled up the sleeping bag, tucked it back in its waterproof sack and I'm waiting for the water to heat.

'What are you doing?' he asks impatiently, doing up the

clips on his rucksack. 'We need to get moving.'

'Just making some more coffee for the thermos flasks.'

'What the fuck for?'

'In case we need it on the journey.'

'Jesus, Lydia,' he snaps with obvious irritation. 'We're only walking for two hours, tops.'

'We might be glad of it,' I insist, my fingers clenching at my side. This is a hill I'll happily die on.

'Water's fine. Once we get a lift, hopefully whoever it is will stop at a service station. We can get a coffee then. Don't forget we've got twenty quid each.'

'That's for emergencies.'

Tom glares at me, his eyes narrowing in a what-sort-of-idiot-are-you expression.

'And what sort of emergency do you think we're going to have? We've managed pretty well for two nights without any cash. I think we can treat ourselves to a bit of food. I tell you, if we get anywhere near a KFC or a McDonalds, I'll be blowing some of my cash on a burger and fries.' He pauses and takes a deep sniff as if he can smell them right now.

This profligacy fills me with horror but I'm not backing down.

'Fine, you don't have to have any but I'm not leaving until I've made coffee.'

I hear him mutter, 'Fuck's sake' under his breath.

'It'll take an extra ten minutes,' I snap and turn my back on him.

'I'll wait for you outside,' he says and stomps off.

I eye the second thermos flask, tempted not to fill it but I can't bring myself not to. Just in case.

When I finally emerge from the cottage, offering Tom the second flask, he snatches it from me with a roll of his eyes and stashes it in one of his rucksack pockets and marches off at a pace he knows I can't keep up with. Ungrateful git.

The brisk wind that toyed with my hair earlier has whipped dark-edged clouds up from nowhere, and after only an hour of walking the light has closed in. It's amazing how quickly the weather has done a complete about-turn. I wouldn't have believed it possible. Scowling up at the sky, I remove my rucksack and retrieve my raincoat as well as stop for a sneaky rest. We're on quite a steep path and I'm nowhere near as fit as Tom, who strides ahead as I struggle into the coat, the wind determined to wrest it from my fingers. Before I've managed to shrug the bloody thing on, the first heavy drop plops down the back of my neck. Like a turtle I hunch into it and swing my pack onto my back. Ahead of me Tom whips out his fancy pac-a-mac, like a sodding matador cape, and puts it on with all the panache of someone on one of those *Dancing with the Stars* shows doing the paso doble without breaking a stride. And then he puts the GoPro on his head with the supplied strap.

Bloody marvellous, he's going to film us walking into the hideous weather conditions. He has an eye for drama – I'll give him that.

Fascinated by the sudden storm, I watch the rain sheeting across the valley, coming straight towards us, and the cloud which has dropped to surround us. I hurry after Tom, my legs struggling on the challenging incline. Shit, I really should go to the gym more often but then again I'm not normally charging about with a ten-tonne weight on my back, which is the killer. In a matter of minutes, the rain hits in earnest and I can barely see, it's so fierce in my face. I duck my head and look at my feet, battling forward. When I squint upwards there's no sign of Tom because he's rounded the bend ahead. The increasingly muddy path is getting narrower by the second and is full of trip hazards with sharp rocks protruding here and there. I hadn't realised we were quite so high up and I'm sure the view must be amazing but all I can see is the mist of the cloud that has descended around us and not Tom. The bastard has left me behind. At least there'll be no footage of my struggle up the path.

With a heavy sigh I tuck my hands into the straps of my backpack and pick up my pace. God, it's hard going. 'Come on, you can do this,' I mutter to myself, forcing my aching leg muscles into action and ignoring the irate protests they're firing off to my brain. I round the corner straight into the oncoming wind and spot Tom a little way ahead. I sway for a minute, blinking the rain out of my eyes. To my relief the path has levelled out and … my toe catches a rock and I start to pitch forward, my feet stumbling as I desperately try to regain my balance. I just manage to sink to one knee, sending a shower of scree cascading down the hill, catching myself. Tom looks round and then my foot slips and the weight of the rucksack topples me over and I roll right over the edge of the path.

There's a flash of rocks, grass, plus a mouthful of said grass as I go bump, bump, bump down the hill, so fast there's no way I can stop myself. Everything is a blur, pain punching into my head, my arms, my legs as I tumble over and over and just when I think it's never going to end, my body slams into something. Shock and pain radiate through every part of me as I lie there looking up at the sky, much like a tortoise with my arms and legs dangling from the rucksack on my back. Dazed, I'm too stunned and shaken to do anything but look up, the rain spattering my face with cold wet slaps.

When, at last, I try to move I realise my rucksack is wedged fast between some rocks and until I wriggle out of the straps, I'm as stuck as a beetle on its back. In fact, more stuck; at least they can go round in circles. This irrelevant thought makes me wonder how hard I've hit my head, and then reflect that if I can think like that, I can't have done any serious damage, even though trying to extricate my arms from the straps is very uncomfortable.

'Oh my God, are you all right?' Tom comes half running, half stumbling down the hill and vaults the last few feet off one of the rocks above me. It's like watching the hero of a film swinging into action and makes me feel even more stupid for my clumsiness.

I try lever myself to my feet but it's a bit too hard to draw breath in at the moment. My back took one heck of a whack when I landed and it's knocked the wind, the stuffing and everything else out of me. I try again. Lying here like a useless jellyfish, even though I think I might have turned into one, it isn't an option. I can't hold Tom back.

'Fuck's sake, Lydia. Stay still,' Tom shouts at me and I blink up at him. What's he so angry about? Because we've lost time? I make another effort to stand up. I'm not going to be a handicap.

'I'm fine.' Bugger, there's a bit of a give-away wobble in my voice. I try again and this time sound more in command of myself. 'Honestly. Just give me a second.'

'Lydia –' his voice is gentler this time '– you're not fine. Don't move. What hurts?'

I look up at him, the concern in his eyes, the way he reaches to touch me and then pauses as if I'm a delicate thing that might break.

I stare at him mutely, microscopically aware of the darker blue around his irises, the tiny water droplets clinging to the dark hairs of his arched eyebrows and the softening of the lines on his rain-misted face.

'Lydia? Just take a minute. I think you might be in shock.' Then he hisses in a breath and says, 'Shit.'

I look down to where his gaze has landed. The bottom of my trousers is shiny with blood. He's pulling off his rucksack and throwing things out until he gets to the first-aid kit. It's a bit déjà vu; we've been here before. It's like having my own personal doctor.

He rolls up my trouser leg and I watch. That's a lot of blood and now I'm looking at it, pain roars in, ripping across the surface of my skin with sharp teeth, bringing tears to my eyes. I grit my teeth.

Tom's tossing things out of the green box and then he grabs something back again. 'Sling,' he mutters. 'That'll do.' Unfolding it, he immediately starts mopping up the blood with it. I kind of wish he hadn't because now neither of us can unsee the jagged gash slicing down my shin, which hurts like buggery.

'Shit, Lydia.' He grips my hand. 'Don't look.'

'It's okay,' I say. 'I'm not dying.'

'You're not dying but...' His voice trails away. 'I need to bandage it up and we need to get some help. And don't you dare say you're fine.'

'I'm sure I'll be able to walk on it, once it's bandaged. It's just a cut.'

He sits back on his heels. 'And what about the rest of you?' Now I realise his face is white, those dark brows and three-day stubble accentuated by the pallor. 'God, when you went over...' He closes his eyes. He's as shaken up as I am.

I turn my hand in his and give it a squeeze. 'I'll live.'

'Jesus, Lydia. You're something else.' He shakes his head and then lifts his hand to touch my face. 'You're going to have a hell of a bruise there,' he says skimming my cheekbone. 'How does it feel?'

I'm about to do my usual shrug and brush his words

away but instead, I give him a grim smile. 'Like I've done a dozen rounds with Anthony Joshua before going head to head with a herd of bulls.'

'Can you move your arms?'

I bite my lip. It's almost as if his words have taken the lid off the pain. My right arm is excruciating and when I lift it, I cry out.

'Probably just a bruise,' I say, nestling it protectively into my body.

His mouth tightens but he turns his attention back to my leg and takes out another big dressing and puts it over the wound before winding a bandage tightly round it and pulling my trouser leg back down again. The rain is bouncing on the fabric, sending blood spatters onto the surrounding rocks.

'We need to try and find you some shelter and then I'll call for help.'

I catch sight of the GoPro. 'Please tell me you're not still filming.'

His hand snaps up to the camera. 'Shit. Sorry.' In a quick fluid move, he tugs it off his head and switches it off. 'We can always delete it later.'

He stands up and surveys the area, although you can hardly see through the gloomy flat grey light.

'First I'm going to see if there's any shelter nearby. I'll be right back.'

I nod. What else can I do?

I watch as he strides off down the hill. Despite my

difficult childhood, I'm not sure I've ever felt quite so cold, wet and miserable. The pain shooting round my body like a random pinball isn't helping. It would be easy to feel sorry for myself but I grit my teeth. For all his faults I know that Tom is totally reliable. He will do everything he can to resolve this situation.

He *is* right back, for which I'm very grateful.

'There's an overhang of rock just below us. It's not quite a cave but it's shelter.'

When he tries to help me to my feet, I wince as I try to straighten one leg. I shake my head. 'Give me a sec.'

It takes me a whole minute to stand up. Every bit of me hurts. He takes my rucksack and guides me down the hill. It's slow progress, one foot in front of another, until we reach the overhang. It's very shallow and neither of us can stand in there, but once I'm sitting it's okay. It's dry. When he's arranged me in a heap, he props up my rucksack and goes into his.

'I think, on this occasion, you're quite entitled to tell me, "I told you so."' He holds up the thermos flask.

I give him a prim look. 'Wouldn't dream of it.'

'Here.' He pours me a cup of coffee and produces two paracetamol. 'I think you're going to need these.'

'Good job we have two first-aid kits,' I say. 'Who knew they'd come in so useful?'

The coffee is pure indulgence and I'm grateful for every single mouthful. When he retrieves my flask it's somewhat dented but functional. After drinking a small cup, he puts the first flask within my reach. 'Where's the bat phone? I think we need to call in the cavalry.'

'How much did you appreciate that coffee?'

The reminder immediately makes him suspicious. He just looks steadily at me. I wince and it's nothing to do with the pain settling on every bit of my body. 'The phone…'

'Lydia,' he prompts when I falter.

'I-left-it-behind-on-the-coach.' The words run together because I spit them out so quickly, like I'm ripping a plaster off a wound.

His mouth purses but to give him credit, he simply nods, admittedly several times like one of those plastic dogs you see in the back of cars, as if it's a distraction technique to stop him yelling.

'Sorry. It must have dropped out of my rucksack and I didn't notice 'til much later.' I'd sort of been hoping we'd never need it. 'But I'm fine,' I insist. 'I just need to rest. We can't give up now. We're not that far from the motorway, surely. As soon as we reach the slip road, like you said, we can hitch a lift and we'll be in London in no time. We stand a good chance of winning that prize money. You want to win it don't you?'

He scowls. 'Yes.'

'Well, so do I.' There's no way I'm letting my parents' desecration stand; I *will* reclaim and restore Gran's house.

A series of expressions cross his face, one after another. Irritation, exasperation and finally resignation. I smile because I like getting to Tom. The real Tom. The mask is off and I'm starting to know him again. The person that I connected with so briefly.

'I don't like leaving you but I'll be as quick as I can. Are you going to be okay on your own?' He catches his lip between his teeth and looks torn.

'I'm a big girl. I'll be—'

He frowns and real anger blazes in his eyes. 'For God's sake, Lydia, don't you dare say "fine".'

'I'll be all right,' I say, a little cowed by his forceful snap.

His voice gentles and it almost finishes me off when he touches my face, lifting my chin to the light and studying what I'm sure is swollen flesh. 'Sure?' His eyes crinkle with concern and I hear the hitch in his breath.

'Yes. Go,' I say, desperate for him to leave. 'The sooner you go, the sooner you can come back. And I'm toasty and dry here with coffee.' I lift the cup in an almost cheeky salute but it's a challenge.

As soon as he's gone, I close my eyes and let my head rest against the rock, tears leaking out of my tightly shut eyelids – the traitorous bastards. Fuck, I hurt all over. I've bitten the inside of my mouth and my tongue can't stop playing with the ragged flesh of my cheek. Usually it's easy to be by myself and cope on my own but now I'm praying that Tom won't be long. It's just the cold and wet, I tell myself, but I know it's a little bit more than that. He's kind. To me. And I'm worried I could get used to it.

Chapter Fifteen

TOM

I stride down the hill heading towards a thin ribbon of a track, which I can just about make out on the other side of the valley, through the driving rain. A vicious wind has picked up and is swirling around me, battling with my waterproof hood as if trying to rip it away. Nervous energy is all that it is powering me at the moment. That and fear. I don't think I've ever been as scared in my life as when I saw Lydia go rolling and rolling and bouncing and bouncing down that hill, her ragdoll limbs flailing limp and loose. It's at times like that when you realise how frail the human body is. My stomach practically turned inside out as I watched, utterly powerless, as her lifeless body slumped to a stop. When I ploughed down after her, it was instinctive, but as I neared the bottom, the fear and worry coalesced into selfish concern about what I might find.

She's so pale and her eyes have that glassy, shocked cast. It's a bloody miracle she didn't break any bones, although, even though she hasn't mentioned it, I could see she's favouring one arm and I'm not convinced there isn't more damage than she's letting on. But as I've quickly learned with Lydia, she sure doesn't like making a fuss. Leaving her on her own under the overhang of the rock doesn't feel right but she can't stay outside in this weather. I need to find her warmth and shelter and a doctor. And quickly.

I'm grateful for the shot of hot coffee in my stomach even though her insisting on making it this morning really pissed me off. Despite the water leaking down my neck, my sodden feet and my aching back, I laugh at the memory of her face when I gave her permission to say, 'I told you so.' Even having fallen down a mountain, I knew she was dying to. I've never known another woman so good at putting me in my place with such good humour.

I like spending time with her. There's so much I admire about her, which is weird because it's never been a factor in my relationships with women. I can imagine being friends with her. Okay, more than friends. The sex was amazing but now I'm getting to know her, there's something about her that is starting to get to me. I really like her. Perhaps a bit too much.

I need to be focusing on finding help rather than on useless introspection. As I come round a bend, I see a stone house about a mile away, perched halfway up the opposite hill with a long drive leading up to it. Relieved, I push my pace, even though my legs are complaining.

My hope dims the closer I get. The place looks deserted.

Ten minutes later I'm standing in the mercifully dry porch easing off my rucksack, my shoulders screaming their gratitude. Sadly, in the way of all good anticlimaxes, there is zero sign of life here. No cars. No lights. No sound apart from the rain gushing like a geyser over the side of one of the gutters. I bang half-heartedly at the door just in case. There's a key box tucked just to the right. Putting my rucksack down, I push off my hood and swipe away the drips running into my eyes.

I look at the numbers and memorise what's there to start with and then move a couple of the numbers – in case the last person that used it was lazy enough to leave the numbers almost the same. No joy. I know there could be a million combinations but I'm not going to give up, just yet.

I try a few obvious – too-easy-to-guess sets of numbers, 0000, 1234, 4321, 4567, 5678, 6789.

I could be here the rest of the day but each time I try I hope with that little, tiny spark of it-just-might-work. It doesn't.

I finally have to admit defeat. I'm wasting too much time. Lydia's lying there, cold, wet and alone.

Fuck. Now what? Do I push on in the hope of finding somewhere elsewhere? With one last bang on the door, I vent my frustration more than anything else. I need to get back to her. What if she's passed out? Losing blood? My stomach cramps with sudden anxiety. I need to get her somewhere warm. This is the nearest option. There must be a way inside.

I skirt the building, cricking my neck as I examine the first floor for open windows. What? I'm a cat burglar now? I peer through the solid bi-fold doors at the back of a big open kitchen and give them a hopeful jiggle just in case someone forgot to look them. They didn't. All my furtive prowl ascertains is that it's a very nice-looking house with a very cosy, comfortable-looking interior, which is firmly closed to me. The noticeable thing is that there are no proud parent photographs, which makes me think the house probably sees the most action as an Airbnb. My parents' house has a table full of silver framed pictures of me and my brother and sister in our finest moments – graduations, twenty-first birthdays, my sister's wedding (which, from my observation, was definitely not something to be celebrated) and my brother when his team won Actuarial Team of the Year (which he's never let me forget).

Time is ticking. There are a couple of outbuildings including a double-door garage – firmly locked, of course. One of the outbuildings is open but completely empty apart from a water tap. It's no Bethlehem stable with its bare concrete floors, a cobweb-encrusted window and a battered wooden door, but it is shelter with running water.

And for all I know someone could arrive at any moment and offer us shelter. This thought makes up my mind. I'll bring Lydia here. Dumping my rucksack in the dry little shed, I eye the pouring rain. The gunmetal sky shows no sign of a break, the clouds hover close to the horizon and, with a heavy sigh that I can't offer her more, I set off back to Lydia.

Worry drives my pace on the way back, although not having to carry my rucksack certainly helps and I'm back in twenty minutes, although I've been gone for a full hour altogether. I scale the hillside, scrambling up across craggy outcrops and tussocks of grass to reach the rocky overhang. Lydia is huddled where I left her and from here her white face stands out from the dark green of her waterproof. Her eyes are closed and she's motionless. A cold hand closes over my heart and I feel panic – pure, terrifying panic. It's not like me. I'm normally confident that I can manage most things, fix things, sort things out. But Lydia isn't a thing. She's never been a thing.

I finally admit as I grow closer to her that from the minute I met her I was fascinated by her, by that seemingly impervious shield around her. The solid self-containment was at odds with the warmth and interest dancing in her eyes. I suck in a breath. Please let her be all right. And then I berate myself. What does all right even mean? Is that for my convenience because I'm scared of what it might mean if she isn't? Or is it for her because I want her to be safe? Because I need her to be safe.

'Lydia,' I call in a low voice, not wanting to startle her. Again, I think it's for my benefit. For some reason, I just need the reassurance of saying her name out loud.

The pallor of her skin makes that fist closed over my

heart grip even more tightly. Shit. I have to get her back to the house. I'll break in if necessary. I can always pay for a broken window, for fuck's sake.

Her eyes flicker open. 'Tom. You came back.' Her voice sounds weak and disbelieving. The bare words hit me like a punch to the midriff, they reveal so much. I hate that she even doubted I would.

'Of course I came back.' My voice is quiet and reassuring. Did she honestly believe someone would abandon her like this? I actually hurt on her behalf. I soften my voice. 'We're a team, remember?'

'Yes.' She nods weakly, her hand scrabbling at the thermos beside her. I notice she's shivering. 'Want some coffee? I saved you some. You're soaking.'

Exasperation makes me want to shake her. She's the one that needs hot liquid inside her. Instead I say, 'I found a house. It's about a twenty-minute walk. On the other side of the valley. No one's there but they might be by the time we get back, and if not, we'll have to break in, but if we pay for the damage and explain it was an emergency, I'm sure they won't mind. Do you think you can walk there?' Stupid question because I know what her answer will be.

'Yes,' she says. Of course she does.

'You can lean on me.'

Immediately she tries to lever herself up, narrowly missing banging her head. There's dried blood on the side of her neck and a nasty graze across her cheek.

'Lydia, slow down.' I take her arm, forgetting it's the one

she was being careful with earlier, and she squeaks in pain. 'Sorry.' I back off and, typical Lydia, she lunges forward to gather up the first-aid kit.

'For fuck's sake. Let me,' I say and manoeuvre around her in the tight space to pack up the bits around her. Why does she always have to worry about doing everything herself? She's clearly in pain.

She glares at me and I regret speaking so harshly but Christ, I'm worried about her.

'Come on,' I say and watch as she slides and shuffles on her bottom over the rock and out into the rain. She turns and reaches for her rucksack.

'Leave it. I'll come back and get it later.'

'No.'

I get that she's shaken up, but seriously?

'I need my pack,' she says, her voice vibrating with tension. I can see the set of her jaw. I've got as much chance of separating her from the damn thing as of getting between a lioness and her cubs. But I try because it makes sense. 'I promise. I'll come straight back and get it.'

She shakes her head. 'I need it.'

'Lydia, why are you so stubborn?' Exasperation colours my voice. I know she's not feeling well so I try and temper my tone. 'Tell you what, why don't we take out anything you think you need. I can probably put them in my pockets.'

'I need everything,' she says, as obstinate and petulant as a toddler. I find it endearing even though it's bloody irritating. I don't understand her need to hang onto the damn thing but I understand that it's important to her and that counts for a lot. I still roll my eyes. 'I'll carry it,' she says. I can almost see her physically digging her heels into the soggy ground underfoot. 'I'm not leaving it behind.'

'Fuck's sake, woman,' I growl and grab the pack, hauling it up and swinging it so hard over my shoulder, I almost over-balance.

'Thank you,' she says so quietly that I guess she feels bad about her seemingly irrational behaviour, but if there's one thing I know about Lydia – she's not irrational. And she's certainly not stupid. It's going to be hard enough going for her to walk, let alone carry her rucksack.

I coax her slowly down the hill. It's clear she's stiffened up but, aside from a couple of early hisses, she doesn't complain once. Our pace is beyond slow and the rain continues to stream down, relentless and miserable, finding its way in through every seam of my clothing.

I guide her over the boulders, round rocks, through the rough grass and she plods along, just putting one foot in front of the other. Her face has settled into a blank mask, which worries me the most. I don't say anything because I know that she doesn't want any fuss, but I'm watching her carefully. Every now and then the pain shows on her face and she's limping. The journey requires all of my patience. If I didn't have her sodding rucksack, I'd be tempted to try and carry her, except I don't think that would ease her discomfort.

'We're nearly there,' I tell her after twenty minutes of very slow walking. I'm just trying to encourage her. We've got at least another fifteen minutes to go.

'You said that before,' she says with grim humour.

'We nearly are. See that road? It leads up to the house.'

Our progress is so slow, I think my back teeth might be ground to dust by the time we reach the road. Just the uphill bit now.

I point. 'There it is.'

'Thank fuck for that,' she whispers.

'You're doing really well, Lydia.'

We crunch our way across the gravel parking area. Still no one home but I lead her to the front door just in case.

As I knock again, to delay the moment I have to break a window, she leans limply against the porch wall.

'Have you tried a credit card in the lock?' she asks.

'Pardon?'

'It's a trick they use in the movies,' she says limply, tugging at one of the pockets of her rucksack.

'Slight complication there. They took all our cards, remember?' I'm trying not to be sarcastic because she's done in, but seriously?

'Driving licence?' She holds one up in her hand, carefully shielding the front of it.

'Smart.'

I try to take it from her because she can barely stand but she snatches it out of reach, with an almost furtive squirrelly look.

'I won't look at your picture,' I say, again hiding my exasperation.

'Okay.' She's clearly reluctant but hands over the licence.

Unfortunately, much as I try, the lock doesn't budge. I suspect there's a mortice lock on the door as well as the Yale one at the top. It's no good. Time for breaking and entering. I suppose a police cell would keep us out of reach of our hunters.

'There's a small utility room round the back. If I break one of the windows there I can climb in and let you in.'

'I'll come with you,' she says, but her eyes are glazed. There's no real force or heat there. This hopeless resignation unnerves me far more than anything else we've been through. I'm no medical expert but I'm pretty sure it's important to get her warm and dry as soon as possible.

'You'd be better off staying here,' I insist but she shivers and shakes her head. She's literally on her last legs and I'm so anxious about her keeling over that I can't bear to leave her on her own.

I can tell that she's using her absolute last reserves of energy because she actually deigns to lean on me and lets me take some of her weight.

The window I've targeted is next to a back door and I look around to pick up something to break the glass.

'Wait.' Lydia grabs my arm. A spark of light glints in her eyes. The first sign of animation I've seen in a while. She peers in the window, tilting her neck to a sharp angle as if trying to see around a corner. 'There's a cat flap.'

'I don't think either of us are going to fit through there.'

'Yes, but there's a key in the door. Move out the way,' she says and wearily gets down on her hands and knees.

'What are you doing?' I ask, as she lies down on the floor, and slides her arm though the cat flap, her left shoulder up as close to the door as she can get it. Through the window I can see her arm straining up towards the key in the lock.

'I don't think this is going to work,' I say discouragingly. Even though she can't get any wetter, I don't like the thought of her body lying on the cold wet ground like this, but she ignores me.

I just want to scoop her up off the floor and break the bloody window and get her inside.

Then I see through the window that her fingers are skimming the key. 'Bloody hell, Lydia, you're nearly there.'

She grunts and I can see her forcing herself harder against the door.

Suddenly the key is in her fingers and she's pulling it out of the lock. Gasping with the effort, she withdraws her arm from the opening and rolls onto her back, holding up the key in the rain.

'Fuck. That was amazing? How did you…'

'Used to do it all the time at home.'

'When you forgot your door key?' I remember waking my parents – just the once though. I got into so much trouble, I never did it again. 'My dad was livid when I had to wake him up to let me in.'

'They let you in; mine didn't.' Lydia's voice is so weak but matter-of-fact that I'm not sure I heard her properly. It takes a second for the words to penetrate and then she adds, 'That's how I perfected the cat-flap break-in.'

'They wouldn't let you in?' If she wasn't so obviously exhausted and her reserves hadn't run so low, I might have thought she was joking, but it's obvious that her barriers are down.

'Yeah, they were shitty parents.' Her eyes are closed as if she's unable to face me. I've got an uncomfortable glimpse of her reality and I feel a fierce need to look after her. I take the key from her and slide it into the lock. The door squeaks as it opens and it's the most wonderful sound.

'Come on, Lydia. Let's get you inside.' I crouch down beside her and help her to her feet. She doesn't resist but leans on me and follows my lead. I take her into the kitchen and guide her to a chair.

It's as if the strings holding her up have been snipped and she slumps on the table, her head resting on her arms.

Suddenly now we're out of the rain, a renewed surge of energy pours through me, which saves me from the awkwardness I'm feeling. Lydia needs looking after, and though I've never looked after anyone in my life, I want to now. There's a tenderness inside me that's alien and scary. It's not what I would choose but it's crept on me. I don't like it. Not one bit. I don't like not being in control of how *I* feel.

And yet there's that competitiveness to look after her to the very best of my ability. I have absolutely no idea what to do with this feeling except hide it and make sure she has no idea because if she did, I'm not sure what would happen, and that scares the living shit out of me.

Chapter Sixteen

LYDIA

My head is killing me and my leg is flashing bolts of pain. I grit my poor abused teeth, but I can't move or ease the pain.

Tom disappears from the kitchen and comes back a couple of seconds later. 'Excellent news. It's a combi boiler.'

'And?' I croak, forcing the word out of my throat.

'Instant hot water and I've turned the heating on.'

My head weighs a ton as I lift it to stare blearily at him. I'm running on empty.

He disappears again. Honestly, he's like a Duracell bunny on heat all of a sudden. All I want to do is sleep, even though I'm soaked through. There's a possibility I might bite my own tongue, my teeth are chattering so hard.

Tom reappears. He's only wearing jersey boxer shorts, which are so damp they cling to his junk. Even in my drowned-rat, rain-sodden state, I can't help but notice the smooth chest and vee of dark hair or the quick flashback of hot skin against mine. I avert my gaze as he picks up one of the kitchen chairs and disappears again. There's obviously a plan afoot – everything about him is purposeful and decisive. Even in my feeble state it's very attractive.

Then he's back again and it's my turn to be managed as part of his ongoing mission, whatever it is.

My body is about as compliant as a ragdoll, but he manages to get my coat off and then helps me to my feet.

'Sorry, it's upstairs. But I'll help you.'

With careful patience he helps me up to a very stylish bathroom. Pathetic as I am, even I can't fail to notice the huge walk-in shower with multiple levers and shower heads, the expensive-looking white tiles, the industrial-style shelving filled with plush towels, and the double-ended modern bath.

The chair has been plonked in the middle of the room and immediately reminds me of one of those torture scenes in a movie.

'You're not going to tie me up, are you?' I ask, a rubbish attempt at a joke.

'Not today,' says Tom with a sudden devilish grin. 'But I am going to take your clothes off.'

Okay, it seems my hormones are in a better state than my battered body because they do sit up and take notice.

Before I sit down, he undoes my trousers before pushing me into the chair. He kneels in front of me and slowly peels them down my thighs.

'Oh, Lydia,' he says and his fingers skim the mottled purple bruise running down the top of my left leg. He looks up into my face, sympathy and worry glowing in his eyes. I swallow and give him a tight smile. Thankfully he goes back to the task and manoeuvres the fabric past my knees and down my shins. The concentration on his face and the obvious care he's taking turn me inside out.

'Lydia. Lydia.' His distress is palpable as more bruises are unveiled and I have the urge to comfort him. I put a hand on his shoulder and give it a reassuring squeeze.

He undoes my boots and wriggles them off. His hands on my ice-cold feet are like little red-hot pokers as he tugs at my socks.

Then he stands up. 'Can you lift your arms up?'

I nod and move to do so, but it's too painful to raise the right one.

'I'm sorry. I'm going to have to take the scissors to your jumper and T-shirt.'

He returns with a pair of scissors and with swift snips makes short work of both.

He stands behind me and in the mirror I can see his hand hovering above my misshapen shoulder as if he daren't touch it. 'That doesn't look right.' There's a brief pause and I feel the slight brush of his hair and the gentlest kiss on my skin. I squeeze my eyes tight shut, so that the tears can't escape.

'Come on. Let's get you in the shower. You'll feel a lot better when you're warm and dry.' He's all business again, for which I'm extremely relieved. The dam could burst any second now and I could cry all over him.

Having turned the water on, checking the temperature for me, he finally deems it hot enough. At the threshold of the shower, he stands behind me and unclasps my bra and lets it drop to the floor and then he slides my pants down but in such an obviously brisk, impersonal way, I know this is nurse Tom in action. He nudges me into the shower, under the bucket head of hot water. It's bliss, pure bliss, and all I can do is stand there, limp, letting the water cascade over me, bringing blessed warmth.

'That better?' Tom comes to stand behind me. I sway a little and he steps forward, wrapping an arm around my waist, anchoring my back to his chest, holding me up. The tears I've been hanging on to finally break free to hide among the water streaming across my face. His fingers slide into my hair, separating the muddy clumps that I'd been oblivious to until now, stroking through the tangled mess. When he's done, I can't help it, an involuntary sob escapes, shuddering through my chest. Tom's hold tightens and his fingers stroke the skin at my waist.

'It's okay, Lydia,' he murmurs at my ear. 'You're safe now.'

I'm so grateful that he doesn't turn me round, that he can't see me crying properly now. He just holds me and lets me cry, embarrassed tears spilling down my face. We stand like that for a little longer and I think he might be the only thing holding me up. Numbness has taken over my body. I just want to sleep.

He wraps me up in one of those velvety soft towels, draping one over my head, too, and guides me back to the chair. He dabs at my face, smiling up at me in a reassuring, I'm-here-now way, which melts my heart even though I know I shouldn't let it, and pats me dry in that impersonal but caring way, melting my heart even more.

He's even prepared a clean T-shirt, one of his, to slip over my head, although I can only get one arm in. Once he's bandaged my leg up, like a little lost lamb, I let him take me through to the spacious double bedroom, where he peels back the pristine white fluffy feather duvet and sits me on the edge while he wraps my hair up in the towel and then pushes me back against a pile of pillows and tucks the duvet around me.

'I'll be right back,' he says, before adding with an impish grin, 'Don't go anywhere.'

I sink back into the softness, relishing the feeling of being warm and oh so comfortable.

I jerk awake to the sound of china chinking on the place mat on the bedside table next to me.

'Sorry, didn't mean to wake you.'

'I was only dozing.'

'I've made you a cup of hot sweet tea. I will never take electricity or an electric kettle for granted again.'

'Thank you.' I wrap my hands around the hot mug.

'How are you feeling?'

'A million times better and very grateful for a soft bed. Thanks for being so kind.'

'Thank you for being so brave. You make it easy. Talking of which, you need your hair drying and then sleep.'

A few seconds later, having searched through a couple of drawers, he's plugging in a hairdryer and pulling the towel from my head. I scoot forward so that he can reach the back of my head and let the hot air waft over my neck and shoulders as he rough dries it, his fingers delving in and stroking my scalp.

When I wince at one point, he slows and re-examines my head more gently. 'That's quite a lump,' he says, lines creasing his forehead. 'How many fingers am I holding up?'

I squint. I'd know if I had concussion surely, but I can tell he's worried that it's a possibility.

'Ninety-five.' My deadpan voice makes him smile and I feel happy that I've eased his concern.

'Smartarse. We need to get you to hospital.'

'Tom. I'm just a bit bumped and bruised, that's all. I don't need a doctor.' Although my shoulder is in agony, I think I'm managing to hide it quite well.

'You do need a doctor. That cut on your leg needs looking at and what if you have concussion?'

'What if I don't?'

'Do you remember what happened?'

'Yes. I tripped over a bloody rock and then slipped and went down the hill. I got wedged at the bottom and you had to rescue me. Again. Have I told you how much I hate being rescued?

'No, but I think I could surmise that.' He smiles at me. 'You're a lot more prickly than I'd given you credit for.'

I purse my mouth because he's seen more than I want him to. He has no idea how hard I work to convince everyone at work that I'm Miss Sunshine all the time.

'And I still think you need checking over. I could phone an ambulance. There's a landline in the kitchen.'

'That will take hours. I'm not an emergency. I walked here. Why don't we see how I feel in the morning? Besides, if we go to a hospital, we stand a greater chance of being caught. We're doing well.'

He sighs. 'I still think you need medical attention. My cousin's a doctor, I'm going to give her a call. Ask her advice.'

I want to be cross with him. I hate making any sort of fuss but this gentle insistence is kind of sweet.

'And after I've done that, I'll sort out some food. There's not much here. I found a sliced loaf in the freezer so at least we can have dry toast, and there's a bag of ice and one of frozen peas.'

'Would you mind bringing my rucksack?' I ask, adding an apologetic smile because the last thing I want is him delving in there.

'Sure.'

When he brings it in, it's still sopping wet, so I scramble out of bed, conscious that his T-shirt only just skims my bum. My shoulder is still killing me and I have to use my left hand. First thing I retrieve is a pair of knickers and toss them onto the bed.

'Here.' I do an awkward one-handed rummage towards the bottom of the rucksack and like a magician, pull out six sachets of instant pasta and a pack of digestive biscuits. 'All you need to do is put them in a mug and add boiling water.'

'Should I ask?' He quirks an eyebrow, clearly intrigued, but I'm not saying anything.

'No. And here. I pinched these from breakfast.' I hand him a portion pack of Marmite, five of Nutella and two mini jars of strawberry jam.

He shakes his head and looks at the bounty. 'I take it you like Nutella. I'm not sure whether to be impressed or worried.'

I shrug as I always do – except it really hurts on one side 'Just consider it useful.'

'What else have you got in there?'

'Strictly need to know,' I say with an attempt at a flippant smile, which I hope hides the quick flare of fear.

'I'll say this, you're a useful woman to know in an emergency.' He clutches everything against his stomach and starts to retreat towards the door.

'And you're a useful man.'

His face breaks into a full smile. 'Maybe we make a good team after all.' He turns and walks out of the door.

'Maybe,' I call after him, I even manage a half-hearted smile to myself because I never thought we'd get to this point, even if the circumstances are extenuating. Tom has grown on me more than I thought possible and even though I have those fluttery feelings for him, I need to remember what it was like this on that infamous weekend – the way he shut down. I can't trust that he won't do it again.

Chapter Seventeen

TOM

'Hello?' The voice holds that suspicious waver, which I guess is normal these days when you answer the phone to an unknown number. Ten times out of ten, they're sales or scam calls.

'Annette, it's me, Tom.' Thank goodness her parents have had the same landline number for twenty years and that it's an easy one to remember. Her mum gave me her mobile number without the inquisition my mum would have given.

'Tom?'

'Dereborn. Your cousin?'

'I know it's you but why are you calling me? And where from?'

'I don't have my mobile. I need some advice.'

'Oh dear God. Just let me check.'

'What?'

'That the sky hasn't fallen in.'

'Very funny.' Annette's family is very different from mine. They're very touchy-feely and supportive of each other. What she doesn't realise is that she's always been the bogeyman to me and my siblings. My super-clever cousin who went to Cambridge to do medicine has been held up as the pinnacle of success by my parents. Luckily, she's also super-nice, so when we do see her, we soften towards her, but I wouldn't say any of us have made that much effort beyond familial duty to get to know her, which now as I speak to her I regret because she doesn't hesitate for one second to help.

I explain what's happened.

'You're on a reality TV show. You?' She giggles. 'I take it the 'rents have no idea.'

'What do you think?' I ask with sigh.

'And what? You think you'll get away with it? Although, rhetorical question. I can't imagine Uncle Nigel and Aunt Barbara would be seen dead watching that "sort of rubbish".' She imitates the snobbish tones of my mother perfectly. 'What on earth possessed you?'

'Because … because I want to give up insurance and make films and this is a way of getting some capital behind me.' Maybe spending time with Lydia has made me a little more open. She's always so direct and says what she's thinking; it must have rubbed off.

I wait for the inevitable scoff.

'Tom, that's brilliant. I always remember that film you

made when I had to stay one summer … you shot it on your iPhone and spent two days editing it. You've always been creative like that. I tell my mates to follow your Insta account. Shame your dad was so anti you going to Portsmouth to do Film Production.'

I don't want to remember that. The occasion I broached it was the first time I truly understood the word 'apoplectic'. That she remembers those silly videos is a surprise. Maybe they were better than I gave them credit for. As a kid, making those was my thing. I always assumed everyone viewed life in images just like I did.

'So, my friend. I'm really worried about her.' That's an understatement. I just want to scoop her up, hold her and make her better. I've never felt the need to protect and look after someone like this and I don't know what to do with the feelings. One minute they're soaring with elation like butterflies escaping a jar, next minute they're terrifying me because they feel out of my control. What if I can't put the lid on them? I've always been good at schooling my response so that I don't give too much away.

'Where are you?' My cousin's soft voice intercepts these far too introspective thoughts.

Luckily there were a couple of letters by the front door and with my brilliant detecting skills I've deduced we're near a place called Sadgill and I tell her this.

'Did she lose consciousness?'

'I don't think so but I think she might have broken her arm or something.'

Annette asks me a dozen more questions. When I tell her that Lydia's shoulder looks a very odd shape, she makes her diagnosis.

'It sounds as if she's dislocated her shoulder. Is she with you?'

'Upstairs.'

'Can you take the phone upstairs?'

I go up to the bedroom where Lydia is lying in bed looking pale against the pillows. Against the white cotton she looks young and small and just a little fearful.

There it is again, that need to take her hand, hold it and tell her everything will be okay. I'll look after her. This time there's no holding the feelings in. Maybe I can protect myself by focusing on the here and now and compartmentalising things so that they only exist in this place, at this time. The thought reassures me and I give into my need to reassure her.

'Hey,' I say softly. 'I'm on the phone to a doctor. I need to see your shoulder.' I have to put the phone down to lift the T-shirt and I carefully avert my eyes from her breasts. I don't want to embarrass her, not when she's so vulnerable. I put Annette on speaker phone.

'Lydia, this is my cousin, Dr Annette Dereborn. Lydia Smith, Annette.'

'Hi,' says Lydia. 'Annette Dereborn? You didn't happen to read Medicine at Cambridge, did you?'

'Yes!' My cousin names her college and the years she was there and Lydia informs her they had rooms next door to each other. 'Lydia Smith. Oh my god. Of course I remember you. What a small world. Tom says you've had an accident. How you doing? No, don't answer that. You're with my cousin. The international man of mystery. If you find any juicy dirt on him, do let me know.'

Lydia flashes me a suddenly mischievous grin and mouths 'What's it worth?'

I give her a reproving look but she ignores it and smiles to herself as if she's plotting.

'Tom says you've had quite a nasty fall. What hurts the most?'

'My shoulder and my leg.'

Annette makes me describe what I can see. What I wouldn't give to have an iPhone right now and be able to snap a photo and send it.

'Definitely dislocated and it sounds as if that gash needs stitches. You need to get to a hospital. Hang on, I've looked it up. The nearest one is Kendal and a taxi there would cost about twenty quid. I can book you an Uber.'

'We can't,' says Lydia. 'I'm not going to hospital.' She gives me a recalcitrant glare. 'I thought you could just pop dislocated shoulders back in. Can't you talk Tom through it?'

Annette takes her words at face value. 'I could … but it would be—'

'I'm not going to hospital,' says Lydia, her white face tight with tension and her eyes imploring me. 'Please don't make me.' It's the first time she's ever asked me for anything.

I hear Annette huff. 'I can talk you through it but it's not like the movies where it's instant relief. The tendons, muscles around your shoulder, have been through their own trauma. It's still going to hurt for a few days and you'll have damaged the tissue around the joint. You really need an X-ray.'

'I can get an X-ray when we get back to London,' says Lydia, her mouth snapping shut with the finality of her decision.

My hands are slick with sweat on the phone receiver. I really do not want to do this.

'Fine,' says Annette, 'but this is against my better judgement.'

I put the phone down again and follow her instructions. Lydia has to lie flat with her arm out over the edge of the bed. She grits her teeth and looks away as I follow Annette's instructions.

Lydia's low moan of pain as I move her arm strikes me right to the core. I know it's dragged from her because she's the most stoic person I've ever met. I pause. I can't do this to her.

'Keep going,' she hisses through her clenched jaw. When I take her arm again, she closes her eyes and I can see her summoning all her willpower and taking slow, deep breaths. Even so, when I move the arm, a heartfelt groan escapes from her. I keep going. There's a horrible crunching sound and then a pop. Lydia screams.

'Sorry. Sorry. Oh God, are you all right?' I feel sick.

She opens her eyes and there's a slick sheen of sweat across her forehead. She nods but when I look down I can't quite believe it. The grotesque misshapen silhouette of her shoulder is miraculously back to normal. I can scarcely believe it.

'How does that feel?' I ask, almost too scared to ask.

Lydia stares up at me, unclenching her jaw with great care and takes in a shaky breath. 'Better,' she whispers. 'Still hurts. But not like … not like before.'

I cradle her face with one hand because I can't not and stare down at her. At what point did I start to care so much about her? I hate that she's in pain, that I hurt her even though I know I helped.

'All done?' asks Annette, I'd almost forgotten she was on the other end of the phone.

'All done,' I confirm, nausea still swirling in my stomach.

'Well done, Tom. Want me to tell your dad what a hero you are?' Annette's teasing holds an element of sincerity.

'No, you're good. Thank you. What about Lydia's leg?'

'It's just a cut,' says Lydia, glaring at me and shaking her head.

'I really need to see it, to see if it needs stitches. If you can't get to a hospital, you need to make sure to keep it clean. Have you got any steri strips or plasters? And have you cleaned it?'

'I washed it in the shower.'

'No, it needs to be washed with saline solution. Boil up two fifty mls of water and add half a teaspoon of salt. Clean it with that. Have you got sterile dressings? Bandage it up and don't let it get wet again.'

I tell her what there is in the first-aid kit and she congratulates me on what I've done so far.

'The biggest danger is if it gets infected. Stitches will help it heal better and close the wound so there's less chance of infection. Lydia, if there's any sign of heat around the wound and swelling, you need to see someone. In the meantime, rest and keep the leg elevated. But well done, Tom, we'll make a doctor of you yet,' she says.

'Thanks, Annette. I owe you.'

'You certainly do. You can pay me back this Saturday at the party. We'll nick a bottle and hide at the bottom of the garden away from the rellies, like we used to when we were kids.'

'Oh fuck,' I whisper.

'You will be back by then, won't you?' says Annette. 'Your life won't be worth living if you aren't.'

'Fuck, fuck, shit, piss and derision.'

'And there's the Tom I know and love,' she says and hangs up.

Lydia raises her brows. 'You going to tell me what that was about?'

'Shit. I'd forgotten. It's my mother's birthday this week and there's a royal command invitation on Saturday to their house in Berkhamsted for the annual party. Presence is mandatory.' I sink my head in my hands. 'Like Annette says, my life isn't going to be worth living if I skip it.'

'It won't be that bad,' she says. 'I'm sure your mum will forgive you.'

'Yeah,' I say vaguely. She has no idea.

'She'll get over it,' Lydia says with a reassuring smile.

'By the time she's ninety, perhaps.'

'How old is she?'

'She'll be sixty-two.'

'She's had plenty of birthdays already, then. Nothing special about this one.' Lydia's indefatigable logic makes me smile even though I don't feel like it.

Chapter Eighteen

LYDIA

There's nothing like soft cotton and clean sheets and I snuggle into them, inhaling the scent of fabric conditioner. It's only as I catch my sore leg that I come to properly, realising that I've been asleep.

To my surprise Tom is beside me, stretched out on the other side of the bed, propped up against the pillows and absorbed in reading a Jeffrey Archer novel.

Yawning, I peer over the edge of the duvet, which in my sleep I'd pulled right up over my nose. He glances towards me, enquiry in his eyes.

'How are you feeling? And points are deducted if you say fine.'

'I didn't know I had any points. My shoulder is feeling better. Still sore,' I add as his eyes narrow.' I sit up to prove my point, the duvet falling away and then I'm aware that my nipples, objecting to being removed from my cosy nest, have hardened into stiff points beneath the soft, thin fabric of his T-shirt, which I am now wearing properly. 'What time is it?' I ask, gathering up the duvet to cover myself.

I needn't have bothered, he's seen them and he takes more than a second to look up at my face, not doing a very good job of hiding his smile or the sudden flare of interest in his eyes, even though he manages to say quite deadpan, 'It's about two in the afternoon. You must be hungry.'

'Mm, a little.' I'm horribly conscious that that my nipples are tingling, hardening further, demonstrating a different kind of hunger altogether.

Shit, I remember his mouth on them, the hot wet heat of his mouth, him sucking and licking with lazy, arrogant swipes of his tongue, holding me firm and smirking whenever I writhed beneath begging him for more.

'In fact, do you know what, I'm starving,' I say in a desperate bid to defuse the growing tension coiling through my body. I fling back the covers and make a grab for the big sweatshirt in my rucksack, hastily tugging it on, grateful that I can use my right arm again, even though it's still a little tender.

'This is a lovely room,' I say, looking around as if I'm noticing it for the first time. Actually, until now, I hadn't noticed how amazing this room is. Above me is the apex of a sloping ceiling, which ends with a floor-to-ceiling triangular window opposite the end of the bed. Even though the rain is still coming down in horizontal sheets, which makes me appreciate the cosy bed even more, I can see that the view is usually spectacular.

'This place is stunning,' says Tom, thankfully following my lead and ignoring the buzz of chemistry in the air. 'Someone's spent a lot of money on it and the good news is, according to the booking sheets downstairs in the hall, it's available this week, so we've got it all to ourselves.'

'That's good news?'

'In that no one's going to turf us out.'

'See what you mean.'

'If I had my credit card and a phone, I'd book it. Would that make you feel better?' asks Tom.

'Yes, it would.'

'When we get back, I'll contact them and explain and pay.'

I stare at him. 'That's very honest of you.'

'It's the right thing to do. Besides I think they must be pretty decent people; they obviously want their guests to have all mod cons. You should see the living room, it's got an amazing panoramic view. They've even got binoculars. A wood-burning stove. A decent sized TV and Bose sound system.'

'As far as I'm concerned, this bed alone is one of the seven wonders of the world. It's so comfortable.'

'After two nights in the great outdoors, anything is going to be comfortable,' says Tom. 'I'll go make you something to eat.' He holds up a hand before I can say a word. 'Just enjoy being looked after.'

I give him a grudging smile. 'Am I really that difficult?'

'No, you're not. But you are allowed time off for good behaviour and bad accidents. It's a miracle you didn't break anything.'

'Mmm,' I say rubbing gently at the bruised tissues around my shoulder joint.

'Tom!' I call as he's about to leave. I feel a need to reassure him that I'm not going to hold him back. 'We'll just rest up tonight and then get back on the road tomorrow.'

He comes back and sits on the edge of the bed. 'We're not going anywhere tomorrow. A day's rest will do us both the power of good. I've looked it up on the map and as the crow flies we're only twelve kilometres from the motorway. If we leave early on Saturday morning, we can be at the slip road by ten and hitch a ride. There's bound to be someone heading South, if not all the way to London. We could be there by teatime and the deadline is eight p.m. That's achievable.'

'But more realistic if we leave tomorrow,' I persist.

I can see him swallow but then he shakes his head. 'You heard the doctor. A day's rest, give your leg a chance to heal.'

I sigh. My leg is throbbing at the moment, pulsing with pain. I'd only slow him down and the thought of walking for any length of time fills me with anxiety anyway. I don't want to let him down.

'Okay, but we leave really early on Saturday.'

'Deal,' he says.

Tom returns a little while later with a tray with a plate of toast and jam, the opened pack of digestives and a mug of pasta, chicken and sweetcorn. 'Those packs really aren't too bad.'

'I get them from Aldi. Cheap and cheerful.'

'What and pack them as a midnight snack in case you get hungry?' He's teasing but he has no idea how close to the truth he is.

'Thank you, this looks lovely.' It's the first time I've ever had a tray in bed and it's wonderfully decadent. I feel like I'm a film star staying in a swanky hotel with room service.

He gives me an odd look as if I'm being sarcastic or something.

'How's that leg? I ought to wash it with saline solution like Annette suggested. And I'm going to need some more dressings. We've used them all.'

'Yes, Dr Dereborn,' I say with resignation. I know he's right.

He gives me a crooked grin. 'I've always wanted to play doctors and nurses.'

I laugh. 'I bet you have. Do you want me to come back to the bathroom?'

'Not really.'

But I throw back the covers and get to my feet. My leg is throbbing and quite a bit of blood has oozed through the dressing.

Tom frowns and mutters something under his breath that I don't catch. Not that I need to, I can tell he's not happy.

'I—'

'If you tell me you're okay or that you can sort it out, I swear I will ...'

I raise an eyebrow in challenge.

'I'll think...' His face changes and there's a smirk tugging at his lips. 'I'll think of something.'

I'm glad of his ministrations when we get to the bathroom. I sit on the chair with my leg hanging at an awkward angle while he undoes the bandage and dressing. Disappearing downstairs for a minute, he returns with a bowl of water.

'Here, I made this earlier. Saline solution.' Using it he gives my leg a really good wash, apologising for hurting me every time I hiss out a breath while he's rinsing the wound.

We both look at the ugly mess. The gash is a good few inches long and the edges are ragged. 'Bugger,' I say. 'There goes my future as a leg model.'

'You need stitches.'

'Steri strips will do.' I give him a no-nonsense look. 'Look in there.' I nod towards the bathroom cabinet, beneath the sink. 'There might be a first-aid kit.'

A second later he says 'Aha!' and pulls a white packet from a big green first-aid kit on the top shelf. 'Look what I found. And fresh dressings and bandages.'

Swivelling me round he sits on the edge of the bath with

my leg in his lap. I watch him as once again he sorts me out. Honestly, the man deserves some sort of medal.

'Do you want to go back to bed?' he asks. A zing shoots through my body as we both shoot a look at the shower and it's like a bolt of electricity has arced between the pair of us. He asked me that question once before, after a shower in his flat, after a long and indulgent breakfast that consisted of more than food on his breakfast bar. I've never looked at a breakfast bar in quite the same way since.

My nipples are up again, like shouty capitals, yelling yes.

'I mean, Do you want to go downstairs? Or stay up here. I thought we could watch a film or something. They've got loads of DVDs.'

There's a faint blush that tips his ears, which is rather endearing.

'Yes. That would be good. Thank you.'

Even that weekend when it was all about unadulterated sex we were never awkward with each other. This constraint is quite weird in comparison. Maybe because now we're real people whereas that weekend we were totally anonymous. Just two people who hooked up. Unfortunately, now I know Tom Dereborn, I find him a bazillion times more attractive than the fuck buddy who knew his way around a woman's body.

The lounge is another gorgeous room. God knows how much it costs to stay here. I'll make sure I split the cost with Tom when we get back. In the meantime, he's made a fire in the squat cast-iron stove, which is glowing merrily, and lit the side lamps on the tables. I'm tucked up in a fine wool throw on the big L-shaped sofa that could seat a family of five quite comfortably, with my leg propped on a footstool. I could be on holiday.

'Don't suppose you've got a bottle of wine stashed in that rucksack of yours?' asks Tom, bringing two mugs of steaming tea through.

'Sadly no,' I say.

'Oh well, we'll have to make do.' His face is as mournful as a basset hound and I burst out laughing as we both look around at the luxurious surroundings.

'Not sure this is what counts as *fleeing for our lives.*'

He grins. 'Wonder if the other contestants are this warm and cosy.'

'I doubt it. You know, we might be the only ones still on the run. If the others didn't twig about the trackers,' I say thoughtfully. 'We're in with a good shout at winning the grand prize. We can get to London on Saturday.'

I wonder what Tom wants the money for. It must be for something important. Now I've got to know him, he doesn't strike me as someone who's going to blow that sort of money on a fast car or a speedboat.

Before I can ask him, he says, 'We're not going anywhere tonight, that's for sure.' He looks out of the window at the rain still streaming down the glass. 'Let's enjoy this place while we can. After the last two nights I think we deserve it. Especially you. How are you feeling?' His eyes soften and my heart does one of those little trips.

'Better,' I say almost in a whisper. 'The painkillers are working a treat.'

'Good,' he says a bit awkwardly, as if he doesn't know what to do now.

'Do you think we ought to film this?' I say to save him from his discomfort.

'I did a bit of filming while we were out walking this morning before you fell. They can have that, but this is for us,' says Tom and his eyes catch mine and for a moment there's a stillness in the air, but then almost as quickly he turns his back on me and crosses the room to the DVD shelf.

'Now, for the entertainment. I think it's time we rectified the deficit in your film education.' He's got an air of small-boy enthusiasm about him.

'I'm not sure I like the sound of that,' I reply with narrowed eyes. 'What are you proposing?'

'*Star Wars.*' He looks so pleased with himself I can't help but smile back. 'You can't die without seeing it.'

'I hadn't planned on dying this week. I don't think my leg's that bad.'

'It's bad enough, Lydia. As soon as we can, we'll see a doctor.'

I want to tell him to stop fussing but I know he's being kind and caring, so I keep my mouth shut. A little part of me is rather thrilled with the 'we'll see a doctor', but I don't give in to it, instead I'm all business.

'Come on then, let's see this film.'

Even though the sofa is enormous, Tom comes to sit next to me and tucks the blanket around us both.

The white lettering, which even I know is iconic, rolls up across the screen and Tom settles back into his seat with a happy sigh.

'You're so lucky,' he says cheerfully.

'Why?'

'Because this is the first time you're seeing it. It will stay with you for ever. I still remember the first time I went with my uncle. We went to a Bafta screening.'

This enthusiasm and happiness – it's a new side of Tom. He seems utterly content for a change and it makes me relax.

We watch the film and I'm relieved that he's not one of those annoying people who has to give a running commentary advising me, 'There's a good bit coming up,' 'This scene is really important' or 'Remember this bit.' I'm also relieved that I'm thoroughly enjoying it. I'm not quite sure I get why people are so nerdy about it, but it's full of action and, as I've said before, who doesn't love young Harrison Ford. Tom is happily absorbed in the story – or so I've assumed – until about three quarters of the way through when I become aware of him.

I nudge him in the ribs without turning round. 'Stop it.'

'Stop what?'

'Watching me.' Now I do turn and look at him to find his face is very serious. He's studying me intently.

'What if I like watching you?' The question hums with a thread of tension. I flush, suddenly very aware of him.

I return my concentration to the screen but it's not so easy now. I'm conscious of Tom beside me and I know he's still studying my face.

'Will you stop it?' I say without turning.

'Why?' he asks softly, and he reaches forward and tucks a strand of hair behind my ear. But then his hand slides down, his fingers brushing the sensitive skin of my neck.

I turn and look at him, our eyes lock and neither of us blink. We stare at each other, the sound of the film receding. His Adam's apple dips in his throat. I'm holding my breath because I don't want this moment to break, for reality to intrude.

My heart thuds so hard in my chest I can feel it pounding beneath my ribs and there's a warmth between my legs that if I'm honest has been on a low simmer ever since we showered together earlier. Or maybe since that first night in the tent when he made me come.

He cups my face with his hand. I'm a goner. Everything inside me turns to molten chocolate and I sigh. A sigh of consent. A sigh of hell, yes, you can do anything you like to me, with me, for me. The truth bursts inside. I want him. I never stopped wanting him. I want him with a ferocity I didn't think I was capable of.

'I never stopped thinking about you, you know,' he says, his voice raspy with desire.

'You ruined me for anyone else,' I say.

'Good.' His smile is wicked as he lowers his mouth onto mine.

His kiss is better than I remember, or maybe I just know what's coming this time and I'm revved in anticipation like a 2000cc motorbike. He coaxes my mouth open with firm, no-nonsense intent but I'm straight back at him. Giving as much as he's taking. His tongue touches mine, intimate and possessive. He's confident but so am I and I match him, pressing my lips against his, teasing his tongue in a dance for supremacy. This is what I remember. We both know what we want.

We shift so that we are lying side by side on the sofa and we pull away to look at each other.

'You're so fucking sexy, Lydia, do you know that?' he says dragging a finger down my neck between my breasts. 'Demure and confident at the same time. It's one hell of a turn-on. That dress you wore that night at the dinner. Prim at the front and sexy as fuck at the back.'

The black silk number is my all-time favourite dress. It always makes me feel like a million dollars with its high neck, three-quarter-length sleeves, flowing skirt and the dramatic slash all the way down the back. It should, it cost a fortune, but when I'm wearing it I'm confident that I fit in, that no one is going to find out I'm faking it.

'Even in this,' he says, circling the neckline of his T-shirt, 'I still want to get you naked.'

'Why don't you?' I ask, stroking his throat, my finger catching at the rough stubble.

'Because we've got all night,' he says and kisses me again, his hands sliding up under the T-shirt, skirting the undersides of my breasts. His touch lingers and teases. He's the king of slow and careful.

'What do you want me to do, Lydia?' His voice purrs in my ear as he continues the cat and mouse perusal of my skin, shying away from what he knows I want. It's torture but I'm not giving in.

'Do you really want to know?' I ask, squirming slightly against that light insinuating touch and ignoring the twinge in my shoulder.

'Yes,' he says, his voice firm, a little rough.

I give him a sultry smile.

'I want you to tell me what you want.'

A smile of approval tugs at his lips. 'You play dirty.'

'Always.' I run a hand across his firm, flat belly just above the waistband. 'You gonna tell me what you really want me to do?' I love the power this gives me over him.

His eyes are glittering as he sits up.

'Tell me,' I demand with a teasing, knowing smile.

'I want you to go down on me. I want to watch that mouth of yours on me, while you take all of me.' He pauses and then he says, 'Please, Lydia.'

Oh fuck. That breathless plea excites me so much, it

almost makes me come there and then.

I kiss him this time, my tongue circling his lips and then sucking his in, as a prelude to what is about to come. He stifles a groan. I sit up and straddle his thighs, trapping them between mine. I strip off my T-shirt. He leans forward to kiss my breasts and I let him before I pull back shaking my head, my hair falling loose down my front.

'Uh huh. That's not on the agenda.'

'It isn't?' He looks disappointed.

'Not yet,' I say and tug his T-shirt from his jeans. 'You have to help me. Take this off.'

He does as he's told, pulling it over his head, and then slumps back against the cushions, and I slide down his thighs to open up his jeans, taking my sweet time to work the zip over the swollen bulge. It's not easy one-handed, but I'm enjoying his squirms. He shifts slightly as if impatient for me to get to the good part, which makes me slow down even more. When I pull down his boxers, his dick springs free, eager and ready.

I run an experimental finger around the smooth swollen top, using the glistening drop there as lubrication. I hear Tom hiss out a breath. His eyes are slitted as he watches me and I can see the control he's exerting.

When I finally take him into my mouth he moves my hair aside so that he can see me. I give him a thorough workout, swirling my tongue around the head, sucking hard, my hand encircling his thickness, enjoying his little breathless groans. I'm relentless, never letting up, but it's such a turn-on hearing him make those incoherent noises and having complete control over him.

'Lydia, Lydia, Lydia.'

I carry on, slowing the pace. His moans are half words, quite inarticulate now.

'Lydia,' he gasps. 'You've got to stop.'

I suck harder and I feel him go rigid.

'Fuck, I'm going to come if you don't stop,' he cries out, a desperate edge to his voice.

I take my mouth away but replace it with my hand, giving him a long slow pump. 'And what's wrong with that?' I ask, knowing I'm holding all the eggs, as it were.

He closes his eyes and heaves in a ragged breath, his hips still hitching. I can feel him barely holding back. There's no way I'm letting him off the hook. I'm going to make him come, milk every drop from him.

'Because I want to come inside you,' he groans.

Warm wet heat floods between my legs at his words as he grips my arms and hauls me to my feet. He crushes me against his chest, kissing my mouth deeply as if he can't get enough of me.

'Please tell me you've got a condom in that Tardis rucksack of yours,' he says before his mouth roams over my neck, nipping at the skin in the dip of my collar bone.

'Yes,' I gasp, as his hands close over my breasts.

'Thank fuck for that.'

'In the bedroom.'

'Shit.'

Chapter Nineteen

TOM

There's a comedy moment where we both untangle ourselves from our half-removed clothes, leaving them where they fall, and then we're kissing desperately, backing out of the room towards the stairs. We bump against the bottom step and I take her hand and lead her up to the bedroom.

The scent of her consumes me as I kiss her neck, pushing aside her hair. Soft gasps punctuate the air as she breathes my name and I'm trying to hang on to sanity. It feels as if my blood is boiling and my cock is so close to bursting. The feel of her hot mouth on me has driven me to the edge and I've never wanted anyone quite the way I want her now.

The rucksack is still propped against what I'm already thinking of as her side of the bed and, thankfully without any fuss, she retrieves a couple of condoms and hands me one.

There's not much finesse as I rip into the packet as Lydia pushes down my boxers. My cock springs free and her hands are straight on me, her tight grip almost bringing me to my knees.

'Lydia,' I moan. It's too much. Too much.

She gives me a wicked grin, loosens her grip, taking the condom out of my hand. My legs shake as she takes her time, teasing and touching, slowly, slowly rolling it down my length.

'Jesus,' I manage through gritted teeth. 'Lydia, I think you're trying to kill me.' I palm her breast, focusing on the taut, tight nipple. She lets out a low groan and I pull her against me, relishing the feel of skin on skin. Her hips are jerking against mine.

I think I'm killing myself. I'm so desperate to feel her round me, the urge to race to orgasm has me in thrall.

I pull her down onto the bed and we lie side by side for a moment, our eyes locked on each other. Then, seeking her permission, I move slowly over her. She gives a tiny nod, which for some reason makes my heart leap in my chest. She's so fucking giving and open. We're both so revved but I need to check she's ready. With Lydia I don't take anything for granted. For all her efficiency and down-to-earth matter-of-factness, there's a vulnerability about her. Her eyes are wide and bright, watching me.

I slide a hand up her thigh and find she's so wet. But before I can touch her clit, she moves.

'I want you, now.'

My heart jumps again and I move over her, taking my weight on my elbows. Beneath me she spreads her legs, I lower my hips and in one fluid, hard, fast movement I slide home. The sensation of sliding into the slick, hot cocoon of her body is as much relief as pleasure.

I hear her small, shrill, desperate cry. 'Tom.' I can feel my orgasm gathering force as each thrust turns the screw higher and higher. I'm beyond anything, the pleasure is rising and rising and I need to tell her. The words spill from me, an incoherent and desperate chant, 'Lydia. Lydia. So good. So fucking good.'

I'm focused on the sweet rush of pleasure with every move compounded by Lydia's inarticulate pleas, begging for more. I grasp her hips, lost to everything but sensation, and I bury myself to the hilt. I stop to savour the moment but then momentum takes over once more and my orgasm bursts, waves of pleasure shuddering through me and I feel her spasm, gripping my cock as it pulses inside her. This woman will be the death of me.

I collapse on top of her in complete surrender as her arms clutch me to her, holding on as if for dear life. The physical connection burns bright and fierce between us and euphoria fills me. Another thought barges in: *I could hold on to Lydia for ever.* I push it away. It's just heat of the moment. Desire and lust. I don't do for ever, it's too much of a burden. There are too many conditions attached, too much expectation, and I have enough of that in my life already.

We lie there for a while, catching our breath, and despite

the tiny reservations creeping in, I'm so spent and sated that I feel as if my body could ooze through the cracks between the floorboards. Lydia's warm and soft beneath me, her hand stroking my back as if she's trying to anchor herself back to reality. I know the feeling. Conscious that I'm so much heavier than her and she has all those bruises, I move to one side and pull the duvet up over us. Just for now, I can't bear to let her go – I'll give into it and live in the present – and I pull her into my side, hooking an arm over her waist and sliding one leg between hers. I feel uncharacteristically soft. There's a tenderness inside me, a gratitude that she's given me so much. I nuzzle her neck, as much to avoid meeting her gaze as needing to stay as close as I can. There's a strange comfort in the bone-deep feeling of ease and for some reason, I realise I feel safe. Of all the emotions, gratitude and feeling secure are the two that rise to the top. I'm still puzzling over this as sleep starts to pull me into its embrace.

***

It's dark when I wake up, a half-moon shining through the big window, slicing the room with shadows. I'm snug and toasty, Tom's body, lovely and warm, is cuddled up next to mine, and I lie there enjoying the feeling of being with someone else for a change, of being part of a pair. I know it's not real and it's only temporary, but it feels good and why not relish it while I can? Things like this never last and

I'm not going to kid myself they do but for once I give myself a break and enjoy the quiet companionship of another body next to mine.

I close my eyes and catalogue the signs of Tom's presence, his breathing, the rise and fall of his chest, his heartbeat thumping inexorably, strong and steady, and the feel of his warm skin and soft hair against my neck. Normal life is a world away and I savour this out-of-reality moment, doing as I've tried to do a dozen times before with my mindfulness app, by being present.

He stirs, his hand stroking my hip with idle movements as he lifts his head.

'Hi,' he says with a smile that I can just see in the dimly lit room.

'Hi,' I respond. His fingers trace small circles just above my hipbone now.

He kisses me on the edge of my mouth. 'Did you enjoy the film?'

'What film?' I ask.

He rolls me over to face him, his hand skimming down my back before resting just above my bottom.

'We might have to watch it again then,' he says, and I know he's not talking about the film at all.

Just then my stomach gives an inelegant growl and he rolls over and kisses me just above my belly button, his stubble rasping across my skin, and I squirm, the contrast between his soft lips and the harsh graze of his chin sending pleasure and pain through me. His mouth travels down and I lie back as his hands grip my hips, holding me firm.

'I remember this,' he says and looks up at me as one hand dips between my legs. His fingers rub over my clit; it's slick and wet and all my nerve endings fire up again with needy enthusiasm. He spreads my legs wider. I can feel my inner thigh muscles complaining as they stretch to their full capacity, as I'm bared open.

He moves down and kisses my inner thighs, working up one and then down the other, still keeping my legs stretched wide. Each time the kisses get higher but he never quite gets there. I can feel the cold air and the steady tug of lust. His hands grip my hips harder as they involuntarily buck.

He grins up at me. 'Tell me what you want.'

I swallow. We've played this game before. I know he'll only be satisfied when I'm filthy, when I'm open and honest with him, telling him what I really want, but in the meantime, there's pleasure in the game.

'What do you want, Lydia?'

His use of my name this time makes me a little shy, but there's a need driving me. I'm desperate to feel his mouth on me.

He nudges my hips. 'Tell me.'

'I want you to ... touch me there.'

'Lydia,' he chastises me and stares up at me. 'I need specifics.'

'I want your tongue,' I say in a quick pant.

He tuts. 'You can do better than that.' He blows warm

air on my exposed clit and my hips twitch. I sigh and swallow. It's harder this time. More intimate. Last time it was just sex. This time ... for me it's a whole lot more.

'Lydia.' His voice is stern.

'I want you to lick me inside and suck me,' I say in a quick rush, scarcely able to believe I've said the words. It was so much easier when we were two strangers. This is so much more intimate and ... scary. Because it matters. I want him so much and I'm terrified of that hot, bright need but at the same time longing to feel his mouth on me.

'I need the words, Lydie,' he says, leaning down to blow again. The heat contrasts with the cold air and I feel myself getting wet and desperate. I can't move and it's pure torture.

He blows again.

'Fuck, Tom,' I shout out, pushed beyond my limit. 'I want you to lick my pussy and suck my clit.'

And immediately his mouth is on me and it's every bit as wonderful as I remember and exactly what I've fantasised about ever since.

My moans fill the quiet air as his tongue circles and strokes. His hold on my hips eases and I feel the hot flood as I come, gasping and shuddering. He scoots up to hold me as I sob into his shoulder as sensation drenches me.

I'm still treasuring the hot flares of pleasure firing through my lower body while Tom strokes my shoulder. 'Satisfied now?' I ask him, trying to re-establish control.

'Yes.' And then he adds, whispering in my ear, 'Are you?'

'Yes, you sod.'

'You love it really. And I love it when you finally give in, when that prim little mouth of yours talks dirty.'

He's right and it's strangely liberating. With Tom, scary as it is, I really can let go and let out a side of me that I never even knew existed before.

He flicks on the bedside light and grins at me. 'You've come over to the dark side.'

I nudge him with my arm and laugh.

'Now you've worn me out,' he says. 'I need food. I fancy a Nutella sandwich with tomato and herb pasta.'

'That's good,' I say. 'Because that's all we have.'

We dine in the kitchen and the food tastes almost quite good. Mind you, there is nothing better than Nutella. It is one of my indulgences. I once tasted it at a friend's house as a child and I vowed that when I was a grown-up, I would always have some in my cupboard. Something that I have stuck to religiously. It's still one of my favourite things.

Tom squints at the calendar opposite. The picture of the big blue lorry on the front of it is not exactly in keeping with the tasteful design of the cottage and the rest of the pictures on the walls.

'Oh God, I'm going to get so much grief for not sending my mother a card or phoning her for her birthday.'

'Surely when you explain, she'll understand,' I say as one who knows how inconsequential birthdays are in the grand scheme of things. I'd stopped placing any reliance on them by the time I was twelve.

'Not sure my father will.' Tom seems genuinely gloomy and glares down at his dinner as if that might offer some magical solution.

'I'll be thirty tomorrow,' I say, more to change the subject than anything else.

'What?' He starts as he looks up at me, incredulity etched on his face.

I shrug.

'Why didn't you say anything?'

'Who to?'

His face is a picture of bewilderment, which I don't quite get.

'But … surely you had plans. I mean, thirty's a biggie.'

'I'm not big on birthdays. My friends Eleanor and Olivia organise something every year but I've always suspected that it's more for them than for me.' I smile at the thought of the two of them and then feel a bit guilty. I should have told them I'd be away. We hadn't actually booked anything but we'd said we'd get together like always.

'Why don't you do birthdays? My friends say I'm a miserable bastard but I still celebrate.'

'It wasn't really a thing in my family.'

'What do you mean? No presents? No parties?'

I give a mirthless laugh. My parents rarely acknowledged my birthday and on the very rare occasion they did, I wished they hadn't. 'There wasn't really the money for presents. Although there were parties,' I say with an irony that is probably lost on him. For some reason I continue opening up a little more of myself to him. 'My parents' parties were infamous.'

Tom frowns. 'Not good?'

'No. They invariably got out of hand.' Tom doesn't need to know that on my seventh birthday, I slept in the garden shed because two strange men had passed out in my bed with another three on the floor. But I do volunteer with a jokey smile, 'On my ninth birthday, the police were called by the neighbours because the party was still going at five in the morning.'

'Right.' Tom nods as if that makes sense but I can tell he doesn't really understand – why should he? – and I don't really want to tell him. It's not that I'm ashamed, none of it was my fault, but I just don't want him to think differently of me. I've never felt sorry for myself and I don't want anyone else to. My past has shaped me and I think I've come out things pretty well. I'm a well-educated woman with a well-respected and high-paying job and good in the sack – although, of course, the latter stat is just between Tom and me.

Chapter Twenty

TOM

'Don't spend it all,' admonishes Lydia from the kitchen behind me as I open the front door of the house.

'I won't,' I promise. 'I'll just get some basics.' We're about to run out of her handy pasta packs and I've had enough digestive biscuits to last a lifetime, so I've volunteered to be hunter-gatherer.

'And get some footage,' she adds. I pat my pocket containing the GoPro which has been neglected for the last twenty four hours – hardly surprising.

'Now, go and elevate that leg.' Despite her usual protestations that it's fine, I really don't like the look of the gash on her leg.

'Yes, Dr Dereborn.' She gives me a cheeky wave. 'Sure you don't want to give me a final examination before you leave?'

'Don't tempt me,' I growl, thinking of her warm body and the bed we've only recently vacated as I step out into the fine drizzle that immediately seeps down the back of my neck. Once again the clouds have closed in, bringing with them a flat grey light that blurs the edges of the landscape.

Despite the dank conditions, I could almost imagine I'm on holiday – I can't remember ever feeling this relaxed. Must be all the sex. The endorphins have put a spring in my step as I stride out into the fresh air, pulling in a great lungful. My cheeriness is quite a contrast to the way I felt last time I walked this way. It's amazing the difference being warm, dry, fed and sexually satisfied can make. Especially the last. The sex is just as good as I remember it, actually even better.

I ponder this as I head down the drive to the lane at the bottom. According to the instructions left by the owners of the house, I need to turn left and walk a mile before hitting a crossroads where I take a right turn, which will lead me to the farm shop a further mile away.

Why is the sex better? And what about it is better? I'm not normally one to think about such things. I guess it's because I've got time and no other distractions as I plod along the empty road. The desperation and desire are as strong as last time, that's for sure. I can't seem to get enough of her, although she's certainly not complaining, which is doubly nice. I fancied her the first time I saw her but I realise now I know her, I fancy her even more. 'Fancy' is one of those useless non-words that you can't really define but it sums up the little frisson that fizzes in my chest cavity when she turns her head to look at me and, almost against her will, her mouth curves up even though it's obvious she doesn't mean to smile. Even now, thinking about it makes *me* smile. I like her. I mean, obviously I like her, I'm sleeping with her, but it's more than that. I genuinely like the person she is. I enjoy being with her.

My spirits are high because there's no pressure today. We can relax for another twenty-four hours before getting back on the road. I've almost forgotten why I entered the competition. I'm actually feeling quite content with life for once, although I know it's because this isn't real life. It's a break from reality where I've let myself … I was going to say let myself go, but actually perhaps it's more appropriate to say, let myself be me. Lydia is so easy to be with and the sex is the hottest, but I'm well aware this is an interlude and that we'll go back to … to what? The question hammers into my head like an axe. I'm not sure if I'm unwilling or unable to answer it. Back to what? Being friends? We were never friends in the first place, so there's no going back. We've done lovers, enemies – I think she would happily have skewered me at the beginning of this week and in Barcelona.

Could we be friends in the future? I'm starting to tie myself up in knots and I'm uncomfortable with the direction of my thoughts. Instead, I force myself to think of my screenplay and what I'd do if I had to film in these conditions. I pick up my pace and push myself to walk as fast as I can. Even though it's unlikely the hunters will find us – hopefully they're still trying to track us in Kendal – I don't want to be out in the open for too long.

It's a relief when the farm shop hoves into view and I can round up my thoughts to more practical matters. When I step over the threshold, I realise I'm in the Harrods equivalent of farm shops. The high, open-raftered barn is a positive emporium with everything from animal feed and saddlery at one end to high-end wines, a butchers' and clothes at the other. There's also a café from which emanates the rich, sinful smell of coffee. It's been nearly a whole week since I've had a decent coffee. I've got a grand total of forty pounds in my pocket, Lydia and I have pooled our resources, but much as I'm tempted, I resist the siren smell of coffee. It seems awfully decadent to splash three or four pounds on a caffeine hit.

I wander round, adding up in prices my head as I go, before I commit anything to the trendy wicker basket I've picked up. Everything is quite expensive but as I shop I decide on a menu. I'm going to cook dinner for Lydia. I pick up some chicken thighs, a lemon, an onion, some potatoes. There are still plenty of frozen peas in the freezer, so I don't bother with any more veg. I also grab the cheapest loaf of bread I can find and a tiny block of cheese, which I then put back because it's over five quid, because that's more than the chicken thighs. I spot a reduced, about-to-go-out-of-date section and splurge on bargain eggs – we can have scrambled eggs for breakfast – and pick up some duck paté, which is an absolute bargain. There's also a best-before-today pack of fondant fancies. My gran always used to get those on family birthdays.

Shit, today is Lydia's birthday. And my mother's. I'd completely forgotten. I didn't even wish Lydia happy birthday. I tot up what I've spent so far. Twelve quid. I head straight over to the wine section. Compared to everything else in the place, the wine is relatively inexpensive. For six pounds I can buy a cheap chardonnay. I pop it straight into the basket. Still not much of a thirtieth birthday celebration. I think of mine. My parents took me to a Michelin-starred restaurant and gave me a pair of diamond cufflinks. Though they were a symbol rather than a heartfelt gift. The 'correct' sort of present. I've never worn the bloody things even though they cost a fortune – I know because my dad told me the price a dozen times, so that I'd be suitably grateful. Gratitude is a big thing in our family.

I head over to a touristy gift area. I'm going to get Lydia a present. The budget isn't going to stretch to much – and she'll probably point out that it's her money as well. I'm already going to be in neck-deep shit for missing my mother's birthday, I don't want to give Lydia a reason to be pissed off with me as well. Unfortunately, it's slim pickings on the gift front. Everything is pricey and I'm mindful of Lydia's words: 'don't spend too much.' Whoever said it's the thought that counts hadn't met my family. Birthdays are a demonstration of loyalty and service, and the value of the gift and the amount of fuss you make on that one day equate directly to filial duty. In my experience, people who say, 'Don't make any fuss, don't spend too much' or 'Don't go to any trouble' don't mean it. Despite spending a small fortune on a gold locket – which my ex Natalie had dropped a dozen elephant sized hints about – I was told I hadn't made the requisite effort because I should have had it engraved with a message. As she pointed out when we split up, it was yet another example of my emotional ineptitude.

I frown – what am I going to get Lydia? Is it worth it? Given the limited options, am I setting myself up to fail? Maybe I should stick with dinner and wine…

By the time I've made my final choices there's quite a queue at the till and I realise that this place is a wet day destination for tourists in the local area. But I'm wary just in case any of these strangers might be associated with the hunters. After a lengthy wait, during which I get increasingly twitchy, I finally reach the front of the queue.

The lady at the till casts an eye over my eclectic basket.

'Hello, love. This be all?'

'Yes, thanks.'

'You on holiday?' she asks.

'Mm.' I nod. I'm hardly going to volunteer that I'm currently *fleeing for my life*. Communities round here are bound to be close-knit. Everyone probably knows everyone else. I freeze. What if she's an informant for the programme?

'Staying nearby, are you?' Her eyes are beady bright with persistence and I can't decide if she's just chatty or I really am being paranoid.

'No,' I lie. 'Just passing. Staying in Kendal,' I embellish for extra colour, which I remember is a sure sign that someone is lying.

She looks at my sopping clothing. 'Long walk from Kendal.'

I try to laugh, but it comes out as a breathy huff. 'Drove out and stopped for a walk. Thought it might clear up.'

'Good job we're not made of sugar, eh?'

I look blankly at her.

She shakes her head at my stupidity. So much for not drawing attention to myself. 'If we were we'd dissolve, love.'

'Oh, yes. Right.'

'You have a nice day, love.'

I gather everything up into my rucksack and, as I do, she turns the next person away to the other till. 'Time for my break.'

Is she going to make a phone call? I watch as she disappears through a door marked 'staff only' and I leave as quickly as I can, telling myself that I'm being totally paranoid and that not everyone can be a spy for the *Fleeing for Your Life* production.

Back in the rain I put my head down and survey the car park. There's not an orange Land Rover in sight. I take a breath and walk quickly down the road, switching on the

GoPro and talking into it before putting it on my head and heading back the way I've just come. I'm facing the traffic but every time I hear a car coming in the opposite direction, I flinch before I look round. This will probably capture some of my jumpiness. The last thing I want is the production company reneging on payment because we haven't kept our side of the bargain.

When I finally see the house at the top of the track, I allow myself a small sigh of relief. Home and almost dry. I smile to myself, already looking forward to seeing Lydia. Then, as if I've conjured her up, I look up to the bedroom window and she's standing there, waving frantically at me.

Chapter Twenty-One

LYDIA

I stand at the big triangular window in the bedroom as Tom walks down the drive, both of our twenty pound notes in his pockets

I wince slightly at the twinge in my leg, which is looking puffy and swollen today. Not that it held me back. We slept together twice last night and then again this morning, but despite intense orgasms every time, I'm still revved up, my nerve endings over-sensitive and antsy. I watch him until he disappears, a bit like a sailor's wife watching the fleet sailing out to sea. Even when I can't see him anymore, I remain by the window, not sure what to do with myself.

Then, irritated by my uncharacteristically unsettled feelings, I force myself into action, even though today I'm feeling a lot stiffer. More of my bruises have appeared and although Tom spent considerable time this morning kissing each and every one of them, I do feel as if I've been through a long spin cycle and spat out at the end. But feeling sorry for myself isn't going to get me anywhere and I decide to tidy up, because we've made ourselves so at home and suddenly it doesn't feel right.

I make the bed first and then I clean the bathroom, shooting the big walk-in shower a fond glance. Downstairs I clean up the kitchen, returning everything to its place so that no one would know we'd been here. I even hoover the lounge but that's more for something to do. Pleased that I've done everything I can to return the house to its original state, I help myself to one of the books in the bookshelf in the lounge. There's quite a selection and I pick up another Jeffrey Archer book. I've not read any of his books before and I'm quickly absorbed in a battered copy of *Not a Penny More*. The lack of sleep catches up with me and my head starts to droop. For some reason the thought that someone could look through a window while I'm sleeping makes me go upstairs. All that big open space spooks me and before I lie down on the bed, I pick up the binoculars and scan the landscape. There's a hawk circling above the hill opposite and then it drops with sudden speed to capture its prey. A second later the hawk streaks back into the air, disturbed by the heavy rumble of not one but two lorries that pass the end of the drive. The blue livery looks familiar for some reason, but I can't think why.

I lie down on the bed for a quick doze, confident that if anyone should pass and look in the windows they won't see anything amiss. The back door is locked as Tom found a spare key and left via the front door. I don't know why I'm suddenly so fearful of being caught, maybe it's because I'm on my own.

Despite knowing everything is locked up tight, my jitters have taken charge and even though I'm on the bed cushioned by the soft duvet, every time I close my eyes I think I might have heard a noise. The bedside clock ticks away with nerve-racking slowness. After an hour and a half, I give up and go to the window to see if there's any sign of Tom and I'm relieved to see him walking up the drive. I watch his long-legged, purposeful stride with his arms swinging carelessly in a carefree manner that suggests he's had a successful mission. My blood heats a little at the thought of him coming back. We've moved into this place, made ourselves completely at home and it seems totally natural. I sigh, happy, and ignore the little voice that says this is only temporary. I know that but it doesn't mean I can't enjoy it. Live in the present. Be present.

Tom is closer now and I wonder if he can see me smiling at the very sight of him and what he'd think of the thought that darts through my head, like how quickly can I get his clothes off of him? Laughing to myself, I'm about to turn away and go downstairs to meet him, when something catches my eye. I lift the binoculars.

Shit!

There's an orange Land Rover barrelling along the road below the drive. It shoots past the drive and then stops and begins to reverse. My heartrate goes into overdrive and I bang on the window to Tom, signalling frantically before racing down the stairs as quickly as my sore leg will allow to grab Tom just as he's coming through the door.

'They're coming,' I say. 'Quick. Lock the door and come upstairs.' Thank fuck, I tidied up this morning. Downstairs there is absolutely no sign that we'd been there.

Thankfully Tom grasps the enormity of the situation, locks the door, then, I'm impressed to see, slips off his muddy boots to avoid tell-tale footprints on the beige floor tiles and without question picks them up and pads up the stairs behind me to the bedroom. He eases his rucksack to the floor and stows it in behind the door and then perches on the bed next to me as we listen hard. My heart is pounding so hard, I think Tom must be able to hear it as well as our visitors on the drive.

The rumble of the Land Rover engine gets closer and closer and my chest gets tighter and tighter. I'm holding my breath so hard, my ribs ache. A car door slams, then a second.

Tom and I look at each other, our eyes wide with adrenaline-fuelled panic. The front door knocker is given an authoritative rap. I hardly dare breathe. He reaches forward and takes my hand, giving it a squeeze. I'm not sure whether it's him or me shaking, I think it might be both of us.

Then a man's voice shouts through the letterbox. 'Hello. Anyone home?'

I exchange a stricken look with Tom and he shakes his

head softly and leans close to me to whisper. 'I don't think they know we're here.'

'I hope not but I'm worried the woman at the farm shop might have called it in.'

'But you didn't tell her where you were staying, did you?' I ask in a fierce whisper.

'Course not.'

'So she wouldn't know we were here. Even if she did say she'd seen you, there must be loads of holiday cottages in the area.' I reply.

Tom holds up crossed fingers.

Two men are talking and we strain to hear them but we can't make out the words.

There's a rattle of the handle of the front door, which sends a pulse of fear through me even though I watched Tom lock the damn thing. More talking and then feet crunching on gravel.

Then it goes very quiet and we can't hear a thing. I'm not sure if that's worse. We sit in silence, tense and fearful. There's a loud, raucous shriek of grinding metal. I've no idea what it is. Tom frowns, concentrating and then shrugs. More silence. Tension pinches at my shoulders as my stomach turns somersaults.

We both jump when we hear them try the back door. They're circling the house again, obviously peering in windows. Shit! Did I pick up Tom's T-shirt from the lounge floor? My brain is suddenly incommunicado. I remember going into the living room to fold the throw and return it to the back of the sofa and finding the T-shirt I'd been wearing. I picked it up but then I put it down again and I can't for the life of me remember where. I close my eyes tight, retracing my steps and trying to picture what can be seen through the window. Fuck, I left it on the beige armchair. A bright blue T-shirt. My stomach twists in ever tighter knots.

Outside they continue to circle the house.

'Hi, Mark, it's Jordan.' The man is bellowing, obviously not a good phone connection, which is handy for us. 'Yeah … we got a tip-off. Possible sighting near Sadgill, couple walking west. Not sure who. Of course in this weather, could have been any old hikers.'

Tom grabs my hand and squeezes. It would appear the farm shop woman hadn't tipped them off. 'We're just doing a trawl of the surrounding areas, checking any isolated places. You're kidding?' His voice changes slightly, clearly talking to his companion. 'One of our lookouts had a sighting of Tansy and Rory. Heading towards the M6 slip road. They've been picked up. That's a tenner you owe me.'

There's a pause before he starts shouting again. 'Yeah, Jordan. There's no sign of anyone. Place is all locked up. We've checked the sheds and garages but it doesn't look as if anyone has been here. We'll check the rest of the places in the area. They'll have not got far. Last ones standing, so we can get all eyes on them. I'm sending the drone up to check the area and then we'll focus on the A roads and the motorway slip roads.'

We both glance towards the huge window.

'Shit,' murmurs Tom. Together we grab everything in sight before squeezing under the bed. Again I'm grateful for my instinct to tidy up this morning and to make the bed. Thankfully there's a big ottoman storage bench at the end of the bed that will obscure us from sight should they think to check the bedrooms.

It's dusty under there and I lie with my face on the floor while my heart beats double-time. Tom puts an arm around my back, his fingers stroking my bare skin where my top has ridden up, as if he's try to calm me. It's soothing but the apprehension holds me in a tight grip, the resultant tension pinching with mean fingers at every one of my muscles.

Tom's touch becomes firmer as the familiar buzzing sound gets louder. I can imagine it at the window like a fly beating the glass to get in. I close my eyes tight, willing the men to go away. The buzz dies away and I let out a tiny breath. The drone is obviously casting its lens elsewhere but we stay put. It won't be safe until we hear them leave.

Ten minutes turns into fifteen and then twenty. I need a pee but there's no way I'm risking moving or even talking. By mutual agreement neither of us has said a word. The hunters have access to all sorts of sophisticated kit, what if they have listening devices? After half an hour, Tom taps my arm and motions with his thumb. He whispers into my ear. 'I'm going to take a look.'

'Okay. Be careful.'

He inches out from under the bed and belly-crawls

across to the window. Just watching him, my head cricked at an awkward angle, makes me feel nervous.

Seconds later, he's back.

'They're using the drone to reconnoitre the surrounding area, they're standing beside the Land Rover with a monitor. Hopefully when they don't find anything they'll leave.'

'God I hope so.'

Suddenly he puts his hand to his head, he's still wearing his woolly hat encircled by the GoPro strap. 'Shit. I forgot to turn it off,' he says with a lopsided grin. 'That'll give them some footage.' He reaches up and removes the camera and hat in one swipe before switching the GoPro off.

The minute the car doors slam, I sag, all the pent-up tension oofing out of me in one popped balloon release.

'Fuck, that was close,' says Tom with an elated grin and a fist pump.

'I nearly died when I saw them and you were on the drive.' I give him a tentative grin, the relief still taking a minute to settle.

'I thought you'd had an accident or something.' There's an echo of genuine concern on his face and he nods his head towards my leg. 'You know it's bleeding again.'

'Probably me running down the stairs in a spin,' I say,

giving my leg a rueful look. Blood is seeping through the white bandage. 'Do you think they'll come back?'

'I doubt it.' Tom sighs. 'Sounds like that slip road is a no-go though. Now what do we do?'

'I don't know.'

We both sink into depressed silence. We're so close and yet so far. The prize is ours if we could just get to London in time.

Chapter Twenty-Two

LYDIA

After a lunch of scrambled eggs on toast made by Tom, we sit in the kitchen for a while. A morose mood has settled over both of us and neither of has said much. My eyes stray to the calendar and Tom's gaze follows mine. I study the page, coming back to the small square of Saturday that is tomorrow.

'Maybe they'll let us off, if you get there by yourself, if I'm injured,' I suggest. 'And anyone on the lookout would be looking for two people not one, so they'd ignore you.'

He gives me a kind but definitely an are-you-stupid look. 'Lydia, I'm not leaving you on your own. Besides I reckon they'd use any and every excuse to stop us winning.'

'You're not responsible for me, though.'

'Don't I know it,' he says and there's a touch of humour in his words. 'You're the most stubbornly independent woman I've ever met.'

'I'll take that as a compliment.'

'Actually, I think it is.'

'Aw, that's nice,' I say in teasing voice and he smirks at me.

'Behave.'

I'm smiling back at him and then I look at the calendar again and the cheesy photo above the dates, the big shiny blue cab with a grinning man standing beside it. It's hardly sexy firemen. Then I remember the blue lorries passing back and forth this morning.

I leap up, ignoring the searing pain that runs down my leg, and take the calendar from the wall, scrambling through the pages to find the back page.

'They're in Sadgill,' I say and turn to Tom.

'What?'

'I know how we can get to London, tomorrow.'

'You do?'

I point to the calendar. 'Local haulage company. I've seen loads of their lorries go past. The depot can't be that far away. We could go and ask them if we could have a lift to the nearest town.'

'What if they say no?'

'I'll go all weak and feeble on them and show them my leg. And what if they say yes?'

He looks at me consideringly and a slow smile fills his face. 'We've got nothing to lose. It's definitely worth a try. It's that or a mountain bike.'

'No, it isn't. I can't ride a bike.'

'What? You know the phrase "It's like riding a bike." It'll come back.'

'I never learned.' Keen not to get into it, I continue. 'We can rock up early tomorrow and ask. It's very difficult to say no face to face, if we put them on the spot. And we can exaggerate about my leg and needing to get home as needed.'

Tom considers my suggestion for a moment and then nods. 'Okay. We have a plan,' he says, before adding, 'Now I have a plan for the rest of the afternoon.'

We have a *Star Wars* marathon, watching the end of the first one and the whole of the second one and starting the third one. I'm so attuned to him now, I can tell that he's up to something. He keeps smiling to himself.

'Now I'm going to cook dinner.'

'Dinner?' That sounds grand. 'What do you mean?'

'I bought ingredients at the shop, I'm going to put them together.'

'Does that mean I can have a break from death by *Star Wars*?'

'Lydia Smith. You philistine.'

'It's quite a lot to take in,' I whine and pout, which is so not like me but with Tom right now I feel I can get away with it. No one has ever looked after me like this and I'm rather enjoying it, even though I know it's a luxury I can't allow myself to get used to.

'Because it's your birthday I'll allow that insult to the greatest film series ever. What would you like to watch?' He crosses to the DVD shelf. '*Pretty Woman*? *Legally Blonde*? *Love Actually*? *Sleepless in Seattle*?'

'I love that you assume I'm going to want to watch a girly film.'

'You could have more *The Empire Strikes Back*.'

'Thank you –' I shoot him an impish grin, because he got it right first time '– but I'll stick with *Pretty Woman*. Have you seen it?'

He shrugs non-committally.

I'm not going to tell him it's my all-time favourite. The perfect Cinderella story. When I was younger, before I realised that I was the only person that was going to rescue me, it was my favourite feel-good fantasy, being rescued and taken away from my life.

For the next hour and half, I lie on the sofa, wrapped in the throw, happily absorbed in the story of Vivienne and Edward and a snotty shop assistant realising she's made a big mistake. No, huge mistake. It's my favourite line in the movie and reminds me of how far I've come from the anxious to please, always scared I'd be caught out, scruffy kid that everyone teased or ignored at school.

Tom joins me for ten minutes during the last half hour.

'Something smells good. What are we having?'

'It's a surprise.'

'Can you cook?'

'Of course I can cook,' he says, sitting next to me.

'No funny stuff,' I say. 'This is one of my favourites.'

'But it was all right to disturb one of my favourites yesterday,' says Tom, kissing my neck.

I bat him away. 'You started it.'

'You shouldn't have been sitting there, sexy as hell.'

'I was watching the film,' I protest but I'm secretly pleased by the 'sexy as hell'.

'Yeah, but you were all serious and it was cute.'

I shake my head and laugh. He's talking nonsense but it's fun and I'm enjoying this relaxed interlude after this morning's stress. Tomorrow we can worry about our next move.

'Right. Dinner will be ready in ten minutes. But don't come through until I call you.'

'Okay,' I say absently with a vague wave as he returns to the kitchen, pretending that I'm not all stirred up by his presence. My hormones seem hell bent on tying themselves in knots when he so much as touches me.

'Would you like to come through?' There's a secretive smile on Tom's face as he beckons me into the kitchen. What is he up to? I'm not used to surprises … I stop dead in the doorway. I don't believe it.

'Happy Birthday, Lydia.' Tom grins at me.

A row of tealights line the centre of the table, like runway lights beckoning me in, and there's a bunch of flowers arranged in a vase, which have obviously been picked from the garden. He's also gone to the trouble of covering the table with a tablecloth and each setting is beautifully arranged, complete with place mat, cutlery, wine glass, napkin and napkin holder. There's even a little pile of presents wrapped in newspaper.

Tears prick my eyes and I gape at him.

'Tom, this is…' I sniff, which isn't terribly elegant, especially when he's made such an effort.

He looks completely nonplussed. 'Sorry, I—'

'No, no. It's lovely. Really lovely. It's just no one has ever…' I have to bite back a sob but it's no good, I can't stop the tears spilling out of my eyes.

'Hey, hey. You're not supposed to cry,' he says taking me in his arms and kissing my tear tracks.

It so beautifully romantic and sweet. I look up at him, my heart bursting. No one has ever done anything so lovely for me. There's a planet-sized lump in my throat and I really can't say a word.

He takes my hand and leads me to the chair, which is when I notice the bottle of wine in an icepack sleeve.

'I'm afraid I've pretty much blown our budget,' he says apologetically. 'But it's your birthday.'

I'd like to tell him I forgive him but I'll start blubbing again.

He hands over a folded sheet of A4 paper. On the front

there's a drawing of two people. I study them for a second and realise it's me and Tom. It's really very good. Inside the folded sheet of paper, it reads, 'Happy 30th Birthday Lydia'.

'Sorry it's home-made, but I wanted to keep the budget for other things.'

He pours us each a glass of wine, handing one to me and then lifts his to chink against it. 'To you. Happy Birthday, Lydia.'

My hands are shaking when I lift my glass. I think I might cry again. This is the nicest thing anyone has ever done for me.

'Now open your presents,' he demands.

'You didn't need to get me presents,' I say although I'm completely charmed. 'But it's so sweet that you have.' I give him a starry, watery smile. 'Oh Tom, thank you.'

His smile is so sweet. 'It's really not that much. Don't get too excited. Honestly. Remember I didn't have much money.'

'That doesn't matter,' I tell him, picking up the first parcel. 'As they always say, it's the thought that counts.'

'Mmm,' he mutters. 'But *they* don't always mean it.'

'Well, I do,' I say as severely as I can when I'm more excited than I can ever remember. Unable to savour the anticipation, I tear the newsprint wrapping paper from the first parcel, to reveal a large bar of Cadbury chocolate.

'Chocolate!' I squeal, because who doesn't love a giant-sized bar. 'Thank you.' I plant a smacking kiss on his mouth. 'If you're good, I might share it with you later.

Although you'll have to be very good,' I say playfully, 'because I do love my chocolate.'

'No!' he says with a teasing smile. 'I'd never have guessed.'

'What gave it away?' I ask, laughing.

'It might have been the I'm-about-to-have-a-spiritual-experience-here look on your face before you tucked into your Nutella on toast, or maybe you were just constipated.'

'Tom!' I remonstrate although I giggle at the face he pulls to demonstrate.

The next package is much smaller and he's watching me as I open it. This time I take more care, intrigued as to what it might be. A pair of purple hair bobbles with balls pop out, bouncing on to the table with a gentle clatter. 'Cute,' I say, picking them up and smiling because they *are* cute and I'm so going to wear them tomorrow.

'I notice sometimes you wear your hair in a ponytail. It suits you.'

Cute and thoughtful. My heart turns into a gooey mess as I vow I'm never going to part with them.

The last present is a small, oddly-shaped package that contains the ugliest fridge magnet I've ever seen, a slightly deformed woolly sheep standing on a tussock with the words 'Lake District' in neon orange letters.

'You always have to have a fridge magnet from wherever you've visited,' explains Tom earnestly, catching his lip between his teeth. 'Sorry –' his eyes crinkle in apology '– I know it's a bit damaged but the woman in the gift shop section said I could have it for 50p.'

I run my fingers over the shaggy edge of the sheep's back, studying the chip where one of its ears is missing. 'It's beautiful,' I say, and I mean it. While it might be a bit battered, it will always remind me of being here. Tom didn't have to buy me anything, but he has, and also found things that have meaning. I'm so touched, I choke up and can hardly speak.

'It's a bit crap, really,' he says, pulling another apologetic, slightly rueful face.

'No! No, it isn't.' I give him a teary smile. 'Don't you dare slag off Shaun. He's lovely. And thoughtful. And you didn't have to.'

'Shaun, eh?'

'I prefer Cyril – he looks like a Cyril – but Shaun is alliterative.' I'm babbling to hide my elation. I genuinely feel spoiled … loved, even. Although of course Tom doesn't love me … but he must like me to have bothered. *Don't get carried away, Lydia,* I tell myself. *It doesn't mean anything.*

'Now are you ready for your Cordon Bleu extravaganza?' I'm intrigued as there are some seriously lovely smells coming from the oven but no sign of much cooking apart from the solitary pan on the stove.

He leaves the table and moves to the kitchen area, switches on the kettle and as soon as the water boils, pours it into the pan and switches on one of the electric burners on the hob.

I sip my wine and watch him as he moves around the kitchen, totally at ease. My hand brushes the birthday card on the table as I put my glass down and I study the well-drawn figures. It's another piece of who Tom Dereborn is. He's talented with a pencil, as he's managed to capture us perfectly. It's the two of us drinking coffee, leaning on the wall outside the derelict cottage. I remember that morning so clearly, the brilliance of the sunshine bringing light after a long, dark night. Being with Tom in this cottage feels a bit like that. Isolated from everyone else, it feels as if the two of us can be who we really are, without any outside constraints or expectations.

After the most delicious tray-baked chicken and potatoes with frozen peas, Tom clears up.

'You need to close your eyes,' he says.

What more can he do to surprise me? I can hear him rustling about and then a match strike.

Then I hear the chink of china on the place mat as he sets a plate in front of me.

'Okay, open them.'

I do. In front of me there's a pink fondant fancy with a solitary blue candle stuck in the top.

He starts to sing 'Happy Birthday' and when he reaches the end, he says, 'Make a wish.'

I blow out the candle and promptly burst into tears

again but this time they're accompanied by full-on sobs. The last time I had my own cake with birthday candles was the year before my granny died. After she'd gone, everything in my life went to pot.

'Hey, Lydie.' Tom immediately pulls me to my feet, to cradle me in his arms. 'Shh, it's okay. Shh.' He looks down into my face with a worried expression. 'I didn't mean to upset you.'

'Sorry.' I sniff. 'You didn't. It's just no one has gone to this much trouble for me … for a long time.'

A range of emotions cross his face and, for the briefest of moments, I think I see fear in there.

'It was no trouble,' he says hurriedly. 'In my family, birthdays are a big deal. This is what we do. It's habit, really.' His smile is quick and tight, the soothing hand on my back has stilled and now he's patting me in a much more impersonal style. 'I thought it was a bit of fun, a way to while the time away before we leave tomorrow.'

Ah, yes. There it is, the reference to 'fun' and that slight withdrawal. I need to remember how good he is at that. Maybe I should come right out and ask him about it, but now doesn't feel the right time. I don't want to spoil the moment of having a real birthday cake.

'My granny always used to make me a birthday cake with candles,' I explain, with one of my trademark indifferent shrugs. 'I miss her, that's all.'

'Oh, right,' says Tom, looking ever so slightly relieved. 'My gran's still around. Though she's not a cake-baking granny. More of a bridge and afternoon sherry grandmother.'

I nod as if I know what that means. 'Right, let's tuck into this cake. Do I have to share it with you?' I paste an expression of mock horror on my face to lift the mood. I don't want Tom thinking that I think this anything more than an interlude. To make sure, I add a cheeky grin. 'Or do I get it all because I'm the birthday girl?' I snatch up the pink iced cake to make my point.

Tom's shoulders relax. 'Actually I had to buy a whole box, but they were marked down because the sell-by date is today.' With the balance regained and the status quo back – Tom and Lydie, working well as a team and nothing more – we eat our fondant fancies in silence.

'You canny shopper, you,' I say approvingly, folding up the paper cake case. 'That was bloody lovely. I'm impressed by your foraging skills. Knock-down magnets and cakes.'

'Managing the budget,' he says.

'Talking of which, are you going to tell me why you want to win the money? It must for a very good reason because…'

'Because what?' he asks with a lift of his eyebrows.

'You don't strike me as particularly materialistic. I mean you have good quality stuff.' I think of his rucksack, his walking trousers, his waterproofs and walking shoes – all probably expensive but also practical. I can tell he belongs to the get-what-you-pay-for tribe. 'But it's not flash or show-offy.'

'Thank you.'

'I'm not complimenting you,' I say sternly. 'I'm observating.'

'Observating? Is that a word?'

'My granny used to say it. It's a cross between observing and deducting,' I say with a snooty sniff that makes him smile.

'I'll tell you, if you tell me.'

'Deal. You go first.'

He picks up his wine glass and takes a sip before setting it down very precisely and lining the drink's coaster perfectly parallel to the place mat.

'Will it be any surprise to you that I don't really love insurance?'

'Are we supposed to love it?' I think about the work. I enjoy it because I'm good at it, really good at it, but I'm not passionate about it. Admittedly I've worked very hard and been determined to be as good as I possibly can but that's more about gaining status and securing my independence. I wanted to become a someone in the workplace because where else could I become a someone? No matter what career I'd fallen into, my motivation would have been the same. Work is a very important means to an end.

Tom shrugs and despite the desolation in his face, it makes me smile. I think it's something he's picked up from me.

'My dad seems to think so. My brother, sister and me all went into the industry. Dad's a bigwig – people are always impressed that we're related to him. I went into insurance because I felt I had to. And that sounds bloody pathetic but … my folks are the traditional type and when you're twenty-one and they're calling the shots, it's not that easy to rebel, especially when you're told that you'll break your father's heart, or upset him or disappoint him or all of the above.' His half-muffled laugh is bitter. 'It took me far too long to realise that the only thing that upsets Dad is when he doesn't get his own way.'

'What do you want to do?'

He looks at me, direct and unflinching. 'I want to make films. Always have. As you might have gathered, I love them. I've got a screenplay that's been accepted by a small independent production company to make full-length feature film – it's the most amazing opportunity. They can finance most of the costs but not all and if I can't raise some cash, they'll move onto the next project.'

I look at him in a new light. Tom is bold and exciting. He has a proper dream. A real passion. It shines in his voice. 'Wow,' I say. 'That's awesome.'

'It will be,' he says. 'If I can get the finances together.'

'What's the screenplay about?'

He shakes his head. 'Not yet. Why do you want the money? You don't strike me as someone who wants money for money's sake. What's your big dream?'

'It's not a big dream. It sounds very prosaic, next to what you want.'

'Spill, Lydia.'

'I grew up in my gran's house until I was five. Then she died. I inherited it but of course I wasn't legally an adult so my parents administered it on my behalf.' My gran wasn't stupid. She knew if it were left to my mum and dad, they'd have sold it and drunk the proceeds before the year was out. 'I want to restore it.'

'Has it been empty all this time?' asks Tom.

I close my eyes for a second. 'No, my parents lived there for a while.' I pause. 'They trashed the place.' I grimace, thinking of the neglect of the once beautiful home.

Tom stares at me, uncomprehendingly. 'Your parents trashed your house?'

'Yeah, like I said, they like a drink or two. They moved out when I was twenty-one and stopped paying the electricity and water bills. And I've been spending what I can to keep the place watertight and secure but this would make it habitable again.'

'You never wanted to sell it?' There's sympathy on Tom's face.

I shake my head. 'No. Stupid really but it's the last link with my gran and she wanted me to have a home. She knew it would be bad when she'd gone, and unfortunately she died very quickly.' I don't want to think about that time. I change the subject.

'Right, as you cooked, I'll wash up.' I stand up and pick up my plate, but he jumps up and takes it from me.

'Uh uh. No. The birthday girl is excused from washing

up. You go take a glass of wine and cue up the next *Star Wars* film.'

'If it's my birthday, shouldn't I get to choose?' I pout, not believing for one minute that he's going to fall for it.

He sighs. 'Go on then but you might never get this chance to catch up on the *Star Wars* universe.'

'I'll risk it,' I say and turn to take my wine back to the lounge with a cocky grin. What he doesn't know is that I have every intention of watching the next Lucas extravaganza with him.

'Big mistake, huge,' he teases.

'You *have* watched it.'

'Might have done.'

The light-hearted smile on his face as I walk away fills me with sadness. This is our last evening together. Our interlude is about to end. I don't for a minute think that back in the real world there'll be a happy ever after. This domestic bliss is as make-believe as one of his films. It's not real life, certainly not as I've ever experienced it, but we've got tonight and I'm going to enjoy it while I can.

Chapter Twenty-Three

TOM

'Tom.' Her words are husky with sleep as I lift her. 'What are you doing?'

'Taking you to bed.' My lips graze her forehead. She dozed off during the film and I didn't have the heart to wake her; she looked so serene and cosy in the low light created by the wood burner. I didn't mean to be creepy, but I've been watching her for the last half hour, piecing everything together. Tonight she's given a lot away and it's made me even more … impressed, admiring, sad for her. It sounds like her parents were a nightmare and yet she's so steady, capable and resourceful. Her genuine delight at the silly presents and the cakes has brought light into a dark space within me. She's a revelation.

'You don't need to carry me,' she says, blinking up at me.

'And give up my Han-Solo-rescuing-Leia swashbuckling fantasy? I don't think so.' I like the idea of looking after her.

'I think she rescued him just as often,' she mumbles. Her snuffly laugh as she buries her face in my chest tickles me, inside and out.

I think it's about time someone rescued Lydia for a change and treated her like a princess and I'm more than happy to look after her tonight. We're both buying into a fantasy here, away from the rest of the world. After tonight we'll be thrust back into reality and who knows what will happen? There's not going to be a fairy-tale ending, I'm sure of that. I could never give Lydia what she needs. She so self-sufficient, knows who she is and deserves better. I'm bound to let her down at some point, like I always do. I'm never quite good enough. I've not climbed the heady echelons of the insurance industry despite all the advantages my parents have given me. They're 'let down' by the fact I'm not yet a board director. I can hardly bear to think of the row there'll be when I announce I'm giving it all up to make a film.

My hands tighten on Lydia's body inadvertently. I can already hear the disappointment in Dad and Mum's voices. Lydia leans up and kisses me on the neck. I close my eyes. She'll end up being disappointed with me, too. I won't be enough in the end. I'm not going to be the successful insurance guy that she probably wants. That's why it's always easier not to get involved and to keep my emotions in check. I don't like letting my guard down because I don't want anyone to expect too much of me. I've spent my life trying to live up to my parents' expectations and it's like being on a narrow path up a mountain, one small slip and you come tumbling down and have to start all over again.

'Tom.' Lydia's fingers have slid up my nose and are stroking the lines that have formed between my eyebrows. 'I can almost hear you thinking.'

I kiss her. I don't want to talk. I just want to make her come for me, hear those breathy moans of hers and sink into the heat of her body.

When I lower her to the bed, I stroke the hair back from her face, and the soft smile she gives me makes my heart go into free-fall. This is probably our last night. I want to make it special – so that when this interlude comes to a close, we both have good memories and regret nothing. As if she can read my mind, she reaches up and pulls my head down to hers and kisses me with what feels like soft, quiet hunger.

I think she feels it too – that we're-at-the-end-of-the-line desperation.

Tonight, the sex is slow and deliberate, as if we're both trying to wring every last bit of pleasure out of every move. When I've kissed every inch of her body and she, with infinite care and a wicked sparkle in her eyes, returns the favour, I guide myself into her, millimetre by millimetre, stopping to tease and eke out every last drop of sensation. Her hips buck but I hold her tight, controlling the pace.

'Tom,' she pleads.

I shake my head. 'Slowly,' I say.

'Now,' she clutches my forearms. 'I want you.'

I grin down at her and deliberately withdraw just a fraction.

She groans and captures my mouth with another deep open-mouthed kiss.

I hold still, savouring the hot tightness of her flesh wrapped around me. The urge to drive forward is killing me but the expression of soft lust in Lydia's eyes is a heady turn-on. It makes me feel invincible.

I feel myself losing control. I have to … I have to … With a half groan, half gasp I slide home and retreat, again and again, a relentless glide. I can't stop now, the friction between our bodies sending sparkler showers of sensation shooting through me as we make the climb. I can hardly bear the feelings gathering and I'm powerless to stop the moans that come with each slow sure thrust. Lydia breathes my name and I look down at her, my jaw clenched in exquisite pain as I try to drag out each move to savour every moment. I can feel my ejaculation building, swelling, the almost painful pinch of pleasure and then I stiffen as my orgasm bursts, as I let go, pulsing into her with a burst of white-hot pleasure. 'Fuck, Lydie. Fuck. Oh fuck.'

Our eyes lock and hold with the force of a tractor beam, I can't look away even though I know I should break the connection, not make a false promise … but I can't. At this moment, Lydia is everything. The stars, the sun and everything in between and I can't have her. Swallowing regret, I kiss her on the corner of the mouth. 'Happy

Birthday.' It's a last gift to her. I'm not going to be the one to disappoint her. She deserves someone else. Someone that won't let her down. It's time for me to pull back.

———

I stand in the doorway unobserved and watch Lydia wrapping the chipped fridge magnet in her face cloth as if it's a precious jewel and then carefully tucking it into her toilet bag along with the hair bobble. My heart aches just a little. It's just a stupid fridge magnet. After that, she gives the chocolate bar a longing sniff before packing it into the front pocket on her rucksack. The whimsical gesture saddens and amuses me. I want to tell her she could have a piece now, if she wanted, but it wouldn't set the right tone. Today we're going back to reality, we need to be business-like and efficient, if we're going to get to Trafalgar Square by eight tonight.

Instead, I ask, 'All set?'

She looks up, a little startled. 'Morning.'

The calm greeting makes me feel like shit. I deliberately got out of bed before she woke this morning and showered and dressed. They say actions speak louder than words. I think I've made it clear that our time is over.

'I've made some breakfast.'

While she goes downstairs to eat, I pack up my rucksack and give the room one last look – I'm sorry to leave our safe haven. With typical efficiency, Lydia has thoughtfully stripped the bed and piled the sheets and the towels in one corner.

I stand at the window looking out over the magnificent view. For once the weather is on our side and the only clouds are distant beyond the hills and mountains. Part of me wants to stay, not have to return to London, to the job – although now the prize is within grasping distance if Lydia's plan works. There's still a chance we could be caught but the odds are in our favour.

I cast my eye around the kitchen, one last check to make sure everything is as we found it. Lydia has wiped up all the crumbs from the Nutella sandwiches she insisted on making as a packed lunch and for once I didn't argue it. After last time, I'm quite happy to let her make all the preparations she needs – even though I'm tapping my foot just a little as she slices them in half and wraps them in clingfilm.

'Let's go then.' I hold the back door open and catch a pained look on her face. I ignore it. This is how it has to be. We're a team and we're on a deadline. Despite my renewed focus, I give the house one last fond look. It's defined happiness for me as well as providing sanctuary and security for a brief spell, and with thumbscrews and pliers threatening my fingernails I might even admit it.

I am worried about Lydia's leg, which is well bandaged but she's limping. I don't say anything, namely because she hasn't, but I adapt my pace, even though I'm conscious of time. With fourteen hours to make it, every second really does count. From the Ordnance Survey map in the cottage, we've estimated that the haulage company depot is only a mile and a half away.

It's six o'clock in the morning and as we walk down the drive, neither of us says anything.

A mile and half, when you're counting every minute, is considerably further than you think it is. When the A J Evans Haulage Contractor sign looms over a drystone wall, I could punch the air with relief. It's taken us forty-five minutes, which is very slow going. Unfortunately the buildings are down a long tarmacked road, which feels unnecessarily cruel of whoever is in charge up there.

'Do you want to wait here?' I ask, nodding towards Lydia's leg. I want to run up the drive to save some time. If they say no, we're going to have to walk further.

'I think the sob story will be better if they see me hobbling up the drive,' she says.

'I still think you should see a doctor.'

She raises an eyebrow. 'How would we factor that in? I'll see one when we get back to London. There isn't time now and it's probably too risky.'

'And you don't think this is?'

'Less risky than our original plan of trying to hitch from the motorway?'

I purse my lips and together we walk up to the offices.

'Morning, you're up bright and early. Can I help you?' the woman in the portacabin greets us as she wheels her chair to the front desk, which is the closest thing to a reception desk in the somewhat shabby but immaculately tidy office. There are neat rows of filing cabinets lined up against one wall, some kind of laddered planner and a vast cork pinboard where every piece of paper is pinned in rows with orderly precision.

Suddenly, asking for a lift doesn't seem quite so straightforward now.

'I hope so,' says Lydia with her usual guileless honesty.

I glance at the woman's spotless white shirt tucked into smart black trousers and the discreet but expensive gold bracelets on her wrist. My mother would approve wholeheartedly of her understated elegance. The outfit wouldn't wow anyone on the catwalk, but it says a lot about her. I bet she runs this office with maximum efficiency. I'm aware of our rain-stained, crumpled clothes and muddy boots.

'Well, spit it out, love. I haven't got all day. I've got an empire to run.' Then she winks at Lydia. 'Run off my feet, I am.' There's an air of quiet calm which belies the words.

I smile at her as she assesses Lydia, recognising their shared type. I bet she knows exactly where everything is, doesn't like unexpected surprises, always get the job done and doesn't suffer slackers. There's only one way to approach this. The truth, the whole truth and absolutely no bullshit, which is Lydia to a T.

'I'm going to be honest with you. We're on a reality TV thing, I don't know if you've ever seen *Hunted*? It's a bit like that except we've got to get to London by 8pm tonight – we were trying to get to the M6 to hitch but I had an accident and I've hurt my leg. I can't walk that far and if we don't make it together, we're disqualified. I can't let my friend here down.'

She nods and assesses us both through shrewd eyes.

'I expect you know it's against company policy for our drivers to stop and pick up hitchers.'

I nod. 'Yes. We're both in loss adjusting and I've done a loss for a lorry hijacking. I'm well aware of the risks to drivers who make unplanned stops.'

She looks at me as if she's seeing me for the first time and nods as Lydia chips in.

'That's if they stop but ... what if they started with a passenger or two and dropped them off?'

The woman laughs and turns to me. 'Got a sharp one here,' she says, and then huffs out a sigh and catches her lower lip between her teeth, giving Lydia another one of her penetrating looks.

'Like I said, it's against company policy and I don't want to set a precedent but –' she flashes a grin '– I'm the boss, so I get to decide.'

'You're A J Evans,' I state with a responding smile. Of course she is. I bet she could run an empire.

'Aye. Antonia Jane Evans. I inherited the business from my old dad and I've doubled the fleet since then. My hubby is driving in a couple of hours and he's got an empty load, so he could take you. Only going as far as Leighton Buzzard, mind. He'll be leaving at nine. And I figure if you're wanting a favour, I could make you work for it.'

'Of course,' Lydia says plunging us straight into who knows what. Admittedly we're in for a bit of a wait so I suppose we've got nothing better to do.

'My admin lady has phoned in sick. We're doing a big presentation tomorrow and she was going to print, photocopy and bind all the documents.' She gives us a delighted grin. 'Think you can handle it?'

'Absolutely,' I say. I like her style. She's not one to take any crap and she's not above taking advantage of the situation for her own ends. Good for her. She could be Lydia's … no, not mother. Antonia has that same grab-things-by-the-scruff-of-the-neck approach. I get the impression that Lydia's parents weren't that organised. I'm intrigued by the admission that she doesn't keep in touch with them, although equally horrified that they trashed her house. I just can't imagine anyone's parents doing that. Maybe she means that they weren't able to manage the house and let it fall into disrepair, although that doesn't ring true. Knowing Lydia, she would sort things out if that were the case. Why did she let that happen to the house? It's a question I'll have to ask her later. Things are suddenly speeding up. It looks like this evening we'll be back in London. Leighton Buzzard isn't that far from London.

Two hours and a thousand photocopied pages later – or at least it feels like that – and some very nice tea and biscuits – thank you, Antonia – we're high up in the driver's cab looking down on the cars on the M6 with a very garrulous Mr Evans, who it appears is delighted to have company and is very proud of his missus.

'Runs a tight ship, does our Antonia. A few raised eyebrows when she took over but –' his shy grin is full of mischief '– by God, she put 'em in their place. Competitors don't say owt now. She don't take any nonsense.'

It's a four-hour journey, throughout which Mr Evans talks and talks and talks. He has a lively interest in just about every subject in the known universe, from the essential role of ants in the ecosystem, how to get rid of dandruff and when to prune roses, through to why there are so many UFO sightings in Area 51. Apparently it's down to the confluence of cosmic ley lines that run through that particular part of Nevada. Who knew?

Every now and then Lydia's hand sneaks into mine and gives it a squeeze when he reveals yet another one of his very interesting facts.

I have a hard time not bursting out laughing when Lydia suddenly asks completely deadpan, 'Have you ever thought about going on *Mastermind*?' Knowing Lydia, the question is kindly meant, and I feel a sudden warm glow inside. She's a really good person. When I've slept with people before I've never really worried about their character or what they're really like. Everything has been superficial. I never wanted it to be anything more. I suddenly realise that Lydia is a friend and I want her to like me as much as I like her. This revelation shakes me.

Friends are friends, not lovers. Having feelings for someone gives them control. They'll only want me if I give them what they want. My parents have always been careful with their affection. It's always earned, when we passed exams, did well at school, got our first jobs, got promoted. I'd never understood until now just how conditional it is.

Lydia nudges me in the ribs. 'That will be fine, won't it, Tom?'

I haven't heard a word of the most recent conversation, I've been too lost in the revelations suddenly exploding a bit like a volcano spewing rocks, smashing deeply held assumptions. My parents' love is based on me fulfilling their desires, not what makes me or my siblings happy.

It's a deeply sobering and depressing realisation.

Lydia repeats Mr Evans. 'He's going to drop us off at the railway station.'

'Here we go, then,' says Mr Evans as he pulls up outside Leighton Buzzard Station. 'Did you know that the Great Train Robbery happened on this line? Between here and the next stop, Cheddington.'

'Well I never,' says Lydia. 'Thanks so much for the lift.'

'No problem and give AJ Evans a shout out when you're on the telly. My missus will be made up.'

'We will,' says Lydia as we climb down from the cab. We wave goodbye as he drives off and I think my ears might just be thanking me for the cessation of a constant stream of facts.

'Do you think there's anything, he didn't know?' Lydia asks. 'He's a very nice man but I think I have a headache.'

'Hopefully next time we see him, he'll be on *Who Wants to be a Millionaire?*'

'Yeah,' Lydia says with a giggle, 'as the phone-a-friend guy.'

She starts to walk over to the station, which has the appearance of a Lego building, neat and symmetrical.

'Er, Lydia. Small problem. We don't have any train fare.'

The expression on her face is suddenly sheepish. 'Ah, well. About that… I might have a small confession,' she says, looking at the painted trim of the station as if it's the most fascinating thing to mankind.

'What sort of confession?' I ask, a little amused by the pinkness of her face.

She tugs at her earlobe. It's not something I've seen her do before. She's so cute and un-Lydia-like at this moment in time, I want to kiss her.

'Is it really so bad?' I ask.

'Not really. I mean. Well. Actually…' Her eyes slide beyond me and suddenly she straightens. 'Look! The train goes through Berkhamsted. Isn't that where your family lives?'

I nod.

She claps her hands in delight. 'Perfect. You can go and see them. Isn't it your mum's birthday party today?'

'How the hell did you remember that?'

She does one of her infamous shrugs. 'I remember stuff.

And didn't you say you were going to be in trouble if you miss it? Well, now you don't have to. It's serendipity. We can call in, stay for a few hours and still get to Trafalgar Square before 8pm.'

Her expression radiates delight. She honestly thinks she's doing me a favour.

'Your mother will be so pleased to see you.' Her earnest look makes my heart hurt. 'Do you think she'd mind one extra?'

Lydia has no idea. My mother will not be pleased to see us in this state. My presence and that of my siblings is purely so that our parents can show their friends how well their children are doing. I'm supposed to look smart and successful. I look down at our clothes. Even though we've showered and cleaned up some, our clothes are still creased and splotched with dried mud – our appearance is not saying 'young professionals on the up'.

Then I notice the stain on Lydia's trousers. Her wound is obviously weeping through the dressing and the fabric of her trousers. Shit, she really needs to see a doctor.

'No,' I lie blithely. 'The more the merrier.' I wonder for a second if I'll be struck down with this blatant lie. My mother does not do spontaneity or uninvited guests, however my doctor cousin will be there. 'And you can meet Annette, who helped put your shoulder back. She can take a proper look at that leg of yours.'

It's noticeable that Lydia neither rolls her eyes nor

makes any comment. Previously she's been insistent her leg is fine.

Suddenly we're in front of the manned ticket office.

'Two tickets to Berkhamsted,' says Lydia.

'Lydia!' I watch as she produces a sock from her rucksack and from it pulls a roll of cash. There must be over two hundred pounds in her hand.

'What the …'

She gives me a blithe smile as she hands over a couple of twenty pound notes.

I don't fucking believe it. She's had all this cash on her all this time.

'Next train is platform four at fourteen minutes past.' As the ticket guy hands over the tickets, I'm speechless – shock or rage? I can't decide which. Whichever it is, I'm mute as I follow her to the platform.

Before I can say anything, because I'm too busy seething – it's rage, I've decided – she holds up a hand. 'It was my emergency stash.'

I digest this for a couple of seconds. 'And what… What exactly … constitutes an emergency?' Yeah, I'm still a little verbally constipated right now. After everything we've been through … We could have caught a train from Kendal the very first night, we could have paid for a cab to … to anywhere.

'Well, we're so close now and we did do everything to this point under our own steam and we still could but I figured it's important for you to get to your mum's birthday celebration, so it's all right to cheat a bit. I mean if we hitched to London from here, we'd be there today. So if we spend a bit of money to do this, it's not really cheating, is it?'

I stare at her, my brain trying to catch up with her logic. Again she has that earnest look in her face, the one that suggests she's being totally honest and true to her own value system, which at this moment is totally impenetrable to me.

'Look, I know how important this is to your mum. You can't let her down.'

Shit, she means it. I feel guilty. I should have been more honest about my relationship with my parents. My mother does not deserve this blind belief in her maternal wholesomeness. Lydia has absolutely no idea and if it weren't for the damp patch on the front of her trousers, I'd tell her that we're going straight to London, but I really want Annette to take a look and persuade her she needs to go to hospital. Hopefully Lydia will listen to a medical professional, because she's certainly not listening to me.

The treat of a flat white coffee restores some of my equilibrium, even though I say for the ninth or tenth time, 'I can't believe you had all that money on you and never said anything.'

Lydia glares at me and huffs out a sigh. 'I'm not going to apologise. So you can just suck it up.'

She has the most delightful petulant expression on her face and it makes me laugh. Stubborn, funny, principled, honest and resourceful – there's nothing about her I don't like. Even though I know I shouldn't, I enfold her in my arms and pull her in for a quick kiss before resting my forehead against hers. 'You're amazing. How's that?'

'About time you recognised it,' she says and put her arms around me and hugs me back. We stand like that on the platform until the restless movement of people around us signifies that the train is coming down the track.

Chapter Twenty-Four

LYDIA

Life doesn't seem to want to go smoothly for us. Ten minutes out of Leighton Buzzard we come to an abrupt halt and there's an announcement to the effect that there's been an incident on the line and we'll be updated as soon as there is any more information.

'Fuck,' says Tom, fidgeting.

I lift my shoulders.

'You do that a lot,' he says.

'What?'

'Shrug your shoulders. Why?'

No one's ever asked me that before or even pointed it out. I want to do it again but he's pinning me to my seat with a give-me-an-answer stare.

'Why not?' I do the shrug thing. 'We can't make the train move.'

'Is it to feign indifference?' He's studying my face and frowns. 'You're not an indifferent sort of person.'

'No. It's to show that I'm not going to get worked up about things out of my control.' But a truth darts into my mind. It's also to mask my emotion. A way of not having to show my real feelings, to avoid revealing inner weakness. As a child, responding to things was a recipe for teasing, bullying and mockery so I learned to be indifferent. As an adult I've hidden my past. I never reveal the true details of my childhood. My friendships with people are guarded and although my friends from university, Eleanor and Olivia, know I had a difficult childhood, I've let them think it's merely because my parents were eccentric and I didn't get on with them.

These last few days I've shown more of myself to Tom than I've ever let anyone see. I've let down my barriers. I've enjoyed the time we spent at the house, sleeping together in the big bed, eating at the table, watching films. It's more of my life than I've shared with anyone else since my granny died.

Tonight, I'll be sleeping in my own bed back in my own space. Normally the thought of my personal bolthole fills me with satisfaction. It's my safe place, all mine, where I have complete control over every aspect of my life. If I want to leave it messy, I can – not that I ever do. Things will be where I left them. There will always be food in the cupboards. The bills will be paid. The electricity will be constant.

For the first time ever, I realise it's lonely and that I want more from life. Spending this limited time with Tom has shown me that I could be with someone, that I could share my space and that not everyone is completely selfish. The thought of going home to my empty flat is no longer as appealing as it always has been.

Suddenly I need him to know all of me, not just the bits I've let him see. Maybe I'm hitting the self-destruct button, showing him the unlovable child I was. Maybe it's a bit easier because he's pulled back. Or maybe I'm just tired of pretending it's not part of who I am. There might not be a future with Tom but there could be with someone. Maybe it's time that I let some other people in.

'When I was a kid, nearly everything was out of control,' I confess.

'Is that why you collect things?' asks Tom. 'The coffee, the pasta, the money?'

I nod and swallow ready to take the dive. 'Yeah. Stupid really, but I've never got over the fear of going hungry. Or worrying that I might not have enough money to pay for things I need.'

'Your parents didn't feed you?' Tom's horrified and I feel the familiar sense of shame.

'No, it's not that. They just forgot. They were alcoholics. Not just serious drinkers but completely addicted to alcohol. The next drink was always the most important thing. Life was very chaotic. Money went on booze before food.' I try to make light of it because I always have done but seeing Tom's face makes it so much harder. I don't want his pity. I'm a survivor. I'm me both because of and in spite of my upbringing. 'I became the master of the unlikely combinations. Tinned tomato sandwiches and peanut butter on cheese crackers.'

Tom frowns and takes my hand. 'That's awful, Lydia.'

'I survived.' I squeeze his hand, reassuring him that I'm okay. He shakes his head and brings my hand up to his mouth and presses a kiss to my palm, closing my fingers over it. He takes my hand in both of his.

'You did more than survive,' he says. 'You're amazing.'

I shrug … my usual defence.

'Don't do that. Don't shake it off. You are amazing. You never complain.'

'When I was a kid there was no point. Once my granny died, there was nothing anyone could do to help.'

'But surely … school … social workers. Someone must have noticed.'

'I was neglected but not abused. The system is overloaded. I wasn't in any "physical danger".' I trot out the phrase that I heard someone tell the head at my junior school as I sat in the corner of his office, my too-small shoes pinching my toes.

'Oh Lydia.' The sorrow in his voice triggers a quick burst of fury in me.

'I don't need pity,' I snap because I hate remembering being that defenceless child at the mercy of adults and the unkind comments of other children. I left it behind. I'm not her anymore and I don't want him to think of me like that. I need to tell him in unemotional language what it was like to show that I'm not that child anymore.

In a passionless voice, I recount the story as if it's a newspaper article, something that's remote from me. It's a way of putting distance between me and the truth.

'Apparently my mother managed to stay off the booze long enough to have and keep me. After that she and my dad went on a celebratory bender that has never stopped. As far as I know, they're still alive. How she and my dad managed to find the registry office let alone register my birth is a mystery.

'My parents were alcoholics who should never have had a child. I was a massive inconvenience which they conveniently forgot they had for a lot of the time. Luckily for me I spent most of my time with my granny until she died when I was five. I inherited her beautiful Regency terrace house, which my parents moved into. Granny would have revolved at high speed in her grave at the antics they got up to and the steep decline of the once gracious, elegant home.

'Middle-class and well-educated, my parents had enough sheen to fool the social workers who would occasionally rock up when the school flagged their concerns, when my shoes were too small, when I never had a packed lunch and when communication home went unanswered. But there are worse problems out there, and the threshold of our family issues wasn't high enough.

'So there you have it. Warts and all. Lydia Smith.' I brush over my real name. That's the final indignity and I never tell anyone. 'Now can you stop feeling sorry for me.' The fury snaps in my voice again but this is my defence mechanism. Push him away before he pushes me away. Decides he can't possibly have feelings for someone like me. My parents couldn't love me, not more than the booze, so how will anyone else?

Tom's eyes widen in surprise at my flare of anger and then his face softens before he says very firmly, 'I don't pity you. All I can do is admire you. The person you are now. You're amazing. You said you went to Cambridge. That's fucking incredible – it's an achievement in its own right but even more of one if you didn't have any parental support. You've built your life in spite of them and from here it looks like a good life. You're honest, strong, brave, resourceful – one of the best people I've ever met. You're awesome.'

I go to shrug and catch Tom's eye. 'Own it, Lydia. Say after me, yes, I'm pretty fucking amazing.'

I give him a snooty look, trying not to let the needy child that still hides inside me grab on to the compliment. I lift my chin as I retort, 'I don't need you to tell me that. I don't need your affirmation.'

'Of course you don't,' he explodes. 'I'm not telling you, you already know – it just makes me … fall a little bit more in love with you.'

Inside my chest my heart explodes, a starburst of bright

white happiness and utter surprise. Now it's my turn to stare at him wide-eyed.

'What did you say?'

'You heard me.' He sounds a tiny bit cross and that makes me even happier. 'And I've been fighting it like fuck.'

'Did you not mean to say it?' I ask, unable to resist teasing him a little.

'No,' he says, grumpily.

'Oh,' I say and look down at my lap. Disappointment floods me. Of course he didn't mean it. He doesn't want to love me. I'm not the sort of girl – daughter of alcoholics, from a less than salubrious home-life – that someone like him from a securely middle-class background falls in love with.

'Lydia...'

Now he's going to fucking apologise. I look up and glare at him.

'Lydia. I love you and it scares the shit out of me.'

My heart turns a dozen somersaults even as I frown. 'What? Why?' I half-laugh. 'I'm not that dysfunctional, am I?'

He laughs. 'No, but I am. I'm scared because the thought of relinquishing that control, giving myself up to feelings ... it fucking terrifies me.' He pulls me from the seat opposite him and I manage not to screech as the pain in my leg flares. 'Lydia. I've never felt like that with anyone before. I didn't really believe it was a real thing. But ... there's something between us. It was there that weekend. It was perfect. You were perfect. That's why I went running. I wanted to forget all about that weekend. Those feelings … I wasn't in control of them. They were in control of me. I had to put space between us. I nearly died when I saw you on that plane.'

'You saw me on the plane?' Inside I'm buzzing from his words.

'Yes. Didn't you feel me staring at you from three rows behind?'

'No.'

'And … let's just say my body never forgot you. I had a semi hard-on the whole journey back to the frigging office on the underground.'

'Did you?' I sit up, rather pleased with this admission. For some reason the physical proof of his attraction registers more than everything else he's said. It's tangible. A real thing.

'I did.'

With a sudden jerk, the train begins to move again and Tom looks anxiously out of the window. 'We'll be there in a few minutes. It's only a two-minute walk from the station.'

I take his hand. 'It will be fine. We've survived everything that's been thrown at us the last few days – dealing with serial killer foxes, wild camping and falling down mountains – what's a little family party in comparison?'

Chapter Twenty-Five

TOM

We walk in through the open gates and across the turning circle in front of the water feature. I wonder what Lydia's impression of my home is.

I've taken the three-storey Edwardian house, half brick and half rendered with generous bay windows, for granted all my life. Even mocked my mother's efforts to replace the front door after she'd bought it from the reclamation yard and spent three weeks researching which tastefully appropriate historic colour she should paint it. Now it represents the middle-class respectability and security that I've never given a second thought to. Lydia never had any of this.

I ring the doorbell. My father throws open the door and immediately glares at us.

'Tom. Where the hell have you been? And why haven't you been answering your phone?'

'Hi, Dad. This is Lydia.'

He doesn't even acknowledge her. 'You forgot your mother's birthday. No card. No call. She's very upset with you.'

Upset not worried, I note.

'Sorry, Dad.'

'It's my fault,' says Lydia. 'I had an accident and Tom very kindly looked after me. He saved my life.'

I'm not sure who's more taken aback at this, Dad or me. He actually takes a step back and looks her up and down.

'And who are you?'

'A work colleague of Tom's,' she says. 'I do hope you'll excuse our appearance but Tom was very anxious not to miss his mother's party after he'd missed her birthday.'

I can hardly look at Lydia. Her verbal dexterity and ability to read the room and her response to my dad's petty snobbery in one quick clever lie have stunned me into silence.

'Right,' he stutters. 'You'd better come in then. You'll need to get cleaned up before the party and before anyone gets here. Your mother is in the kitchen. Go straight through.'

Dad holds the door open and I slip my shoes off and drop my rucksack, with Lydia following suit, before we pad down the parquet floor towards the big kitchen, which contains every labour-saving domestic device you can think of.

The house is in full party-preparation mode. My parents

are great hosts but then it's all about appearances. Every surface is filled with cling-film-covered bowls and platters. Outside through the window I can see the gazebo has been set up to house a bar and there's a waiter out there, opening bottles of wine.

'Tom!' My mother's delight instantly fades. 'What on earth do you look like? I hope you're going to change.' Her mouth wrinkles in familiar disapproval and then she takes in Lydia and gives a pointed look at the mountains of food.

'This is Lydia.'

'I see.'

'Hello, Mrs Dereborn. Sorry to turn up unannounced but Tom has been an absolute hero and rescued me after I had the most terrible accident.' There's a newly acquired plumminess to her voice, which amuses the hell out of me. Lydia has well and truly sussed my parents.

Mum glances at me, clearly not sure what to make of this. Should she be gracious and hospitable, claiming pride in me, or berate me for being thoughtless and not thinking of her carefully planned catering portions? I want to laugh again at her blatant indecision.

Before she can say anything, my brother, William, saunters in, wearing a pair of suit trousers, a shirt and a tie.

'Tom! Look what the cat dragged in. I hear you forgot Mama's birthday. Naughty. What do you look like?' He grins maliciously. Of course he does. We've spent our formative years playing one-upmanship against each other, vying for our parents' approval.

'We've come straight here,' I say, my voice tight keeping things vague.

'New girlfriend?' he asks me, deliberately not addressing Lydia.

I want to punch him for being so rude.

'This is Lydia,' I say. 'And it's none of your business. Mum, will you excuse us while we go and get cleaned up?'

Just as I'm hoping to escape, my sister Rosie arrives wearing a suitably garden-party style dress that I know from her Instagram account she wouldn't normally been seen dead in. Real-life Rosie wears chunky leather boots, tight jeans and low cut T-shirts.

'You're here,' she says without enthusiasm.

'Rosie, do you think you could lend Tom's ... friend something a little more appropriate?' my mother requests. 'And William, find Tom a shirt and some clean trousers.' With that we're dismissed and in silence I lead Lydia upstairs to my old room, bitterly regretting that I've brought her here.

'Nice house,' says Lydia, wandering to the window of my bedroom and looking out over the back garden.

'Yeah, shame about the people.' I sink onto the edge of the king-sized bed, realising that I've never brought a woman in here before.

She doesn't say anything but comes to stand in front of me. She takes my face in her hands and leans down to kiss me.

At that moment my sister barges in without knocking, holding out a beige dress.

'Here you go. I think this will fit you.' Even on the hanger it looks like a brown paper bag and will drown Lydia's petite form, which I now realise is probably due to malnutrition as a child. This thought fills me with fury.

'Fuck off, Rosie. Stop being a cow.' Rosie steps back, surprise on her face. 'If you're not going to lend Lydia something nice, don't bother. In fact, fuck the lot of you. We're leaving.'

I stand up, pushing my hand through my hair, just as surprised as anyone else by my loss of control. Normally my siblings and I are coolly contemptuous of each other, and we never call each other out on our behaviour, but I'm incensed that Rosie thinks it's okay to drag Lydia into our competitive awfulness.

'Don't leave. I'm sorry,' says Rosie desperately. 'Please don't go.'

Now I'm surprised. She actually sounds genuine.

'Why not? What do you care?'

'Because…' She glances at Lydia. 'Welcome to the vipers' nest. Sure you want to stay? You could still leave while there's time.'

'Why, Rosie?' I persist.

'Because if you're here it dilutes the attention. If you go, it will be my fault or William's. There'll be a scene behind the scenes. You know what it's like.' Her eyes are pleading.

She's right but Lydia doesn't have to deal with this shit.

I look at her but as if she's read my mind, she says, 'We can stay, Tom,' and tucks her hand through my arm and squeezing my bicep gently, letting me know she's in this with me.

'No, Lydia. We don't need to stay. We'll go.'

Rosie swallows and looks close to tears. 'Sorry, Tom. Why don't you come with me, Lydia, and choose something from my wardrobe?'

Lydia looks from me to Rosie and back. She gives me a sad smile and squeezes my arm again. 'I think we should stay.'

'See,' says Rosie, seizing on this.

'Let's stay a while,' Lydia repeats, looking at me rather than my sister this time. 'We've got time.' She gives me a reassuring, we've-got-this nod. I smile back at her because how can I not? This woman has got my back. With her I can do this. We can stay for an hour or so, do our duty and then go into London and win our prize.

'Okay,' I say, giving Lydia a quick kiss. 'Thank you.'

'No problem,' says Lydia and follows Rosie out of the room before I can stop her. She's back two minutes later with a floaty blue number on a hanger and a hair dryer. She lays both on the bed.

I force myself not to take her in my arms. I wish I hadn't brought her here, exposed her to the family. I know she didn't have things easy but she's estranged from her parents. I'm the coward who still very much conditioned by mine, still seeking their approval. I feel very ashamed of myself. Compared to her, I've had it easy and I've not had the strength to rebel, to stand up for what I really want. I don't deserve someone like her.

'You don't have to stay, Lydia,' I say softly. 'If I were you I'd get straight on a train and get away from this shit show. We could arrange to meet up later and then go on to Trafalgar Square.'

She shakes her head, a slight smile tugging at the corner of her mouth. 'And miss all this fun? I don't think so.' Her eyes bore into mine. 'You need me. I'm not going anywhere. You're stuck with me.'

Could I love her any more in that second?

She steps forward, sliding her arms around my waist, a determined glint shining in her eyes. I realise I've said the words out loud.

'Show me,' she says lifting her mouth for a kiss.

The kiss isn't enough. I need more, more of her. I need her to eclipse the ugliness of the environment of this house. To stamp her presence here so that it will always be here for ever more. I feel raw inside and it makes me hungry. I kiss her like my life depends on it, open-mouthed, demanding. Lydia meets me head on, just like she always does. She doesn't submit, she comes out fighting, matching me in passion.

It's her that backs me up until I'm against the en-suite bathroom door. Her mouth fused to mine. I pull her tight against me, her soft breasts pressed against my chest, my hands kneading her backside. Suddenly we've gone from nought to flammable in seconds. She's tugging at my T-shirt, raking her hands restlessly up and down my back.

The door flies open and we fall through it into the bathroom, just catching ourselves. I turn Lydia so we're both facing the bathroom mirror. I want her to see herself, as I see her. Flushed, eyes diamond-bright, her chest heaving. God, she's fucking gorgeous and she's all mine. I turn her around again and push her up against the now closed door, feverish with desire and the need to create a memory with her that reminds me of who I am, who we are together. I feel that together with Lydia, I can conquer kingdoms. I want to be inside her, part of her, with her so badly I think I might explode with the feeling. I'm well and truly out of control and I do not care. 'Fuck, Lydia. I want you. So fucking much.'

'Stop talking and do something about it,' she says, her hand dropping between my legs and cupping my balls through the light fabric of my walking trousers. All thought leaves my brain.

He lifts my top, pushes down the cups of my bra and his mouth is hot against my breasts, his teeth grazing my nipple, sending shooting sparks of lust south.

'Ah,' I moan as the sensation fires through me. I'm up against the door writhing as he pleasures and tortures me, sucking hard and fast now. His hand has dropped to my crotch and is rubbing me through my jeans.

'I'm always going to want you,' he groans, pulling away from my breast, his hand grinding at the seams of my jeans. 'I can't help myself around you. There's never been anyone like you.'

'Tom.' My voice is breathy. I'm so turned on, I'm undoing his belt buckle and he's attacking my jeans' zip.

His hand slips inside my pants. 'Jesus, you're wet.'

'And you're hard.'

'So fucking hard. I'm going to explode, if I don't get inside you right now. Do you want me?'

'Yes. Oh God yes.' He turns me round and yanks down my jeans, his hand immediately finding my seam, a finger stroking my clit.

'Bend over, Lydia.' He grabs my hips and pulls them towards him. I grip the sink with both hands and look in the mirror above it. His eyes are narrowed as if he's in pain but he catches my gaze and we both look at each other.

'Watch me,' he rasps, slipping a finger inside me, then two. It's exquisite torture. The he takes them out and with the wetness, he drags them along the cleft of my bottom, his eyes boring into me.

'This is us.' I feel the push of the tip of his finger against the tight ring of muscle. I can't help the low moan that escapes as the thrill of illicit pleasure punches into me. His other hand smooths over my buttocks before his fingers push into me, rocking slightly. I gasp as he pushes a second finger in my vagina with one hand and the tip of one finger on his other hand pushes inexorably against my ring.

'I want to fuck you so badly, Lydia. Want to fill you up, every hole. Like that night at my place. God. I've never forgotten it. Those little moans of yours, so sexy, so fucking sexy. Moan for me, now.' He pushes a little hard against me, and the fingers on the other hand pump long and slow, sliding in and out, so that I can't help the low whimpers that escape.

'Tom,' I beg, watching his eyes darken, his face taut.

'I feel so fucking filthy with you, Lydia. Like I can let everything go. Why? Why is that?'

'I don't know but you talk too fucking much.' I grind my hips, desperate for more.

He chokes out a laugh and tortures me some more, his thumb finding my clit and rubbing over it, while his fingers milk me. I'm getting close, there's that burning tide rising and rising. I give him a pleading look and his grin is devilish. I drop my head. It's too much. The minute I do, his fingers still inside me.

'Uhnuh, Lydia. I want to watch you come apart. I want to see you come.'

'Not fair,' I gasp. My breath is coming in little hitches now and I push against his hand.

He starts to withdraw his fingers. My head shoots up.

He grins at me again. 'Better.'

I glare at him but his smile widens and then his fingers slide in again. The feeling is so sharp and pleasurable it's hard to keep my head up. He picks up the pace, watching me intently. My face contorts, I'm hanging by a thread but I can't look away. I whimper again, fighting it, trying to hold on, trying so hard not to let myself go, not to show myself, that ultimate moment of vulnerability, but those fingers pump against me, relentless and merciless now.

'Ahhh!' He forces me over the line and the shuddering orgasm tears through me, wave after wave of sharp pleasure, making my knees weak. Tom's smile as he holds my gaze is triumphant.

We stare at each other for a moment in the mirror. I'm a little glassy-eyed to be honest, light-headed with release, little pulses of pleasure aftershocking their way through my tender nerve endings.

Tom gently removes both hands, still watching me, and pushes his own jeans down, producing a condom and rolling it on. I feel the tip of his penis, probing and then his hands are pulling my legs wider. He uses the swollen head to tease my clit a couple of times before positioning it, his eyes holding mine and then he surges in, in one fierce warm thrust, stretching the walls of my vagina. Filling me. Oh God, it feels so good.

'Oh God, Tom.' I sigh, savouring the deliciously full sensation. My look is full of gratitude. 'Oh yes. Oh please.'

His face is strained now, concentrating as he slowly, slowly fills me but his eyes never leave my face. It's the most erotic thing I've ever experienced and I'm so turned on and holding on so tight to my breath, I can hardly breathe.

He's found a rhythm now, strong and steady. I'm having to hold on tight to the porcelain but I welcome every thrust. He's getting deeper now. Deeper and faster. His face is a tortured mask, his eyes slitted in concentration and his mouth slightly open, as he pants hard. I can hardly keep up, it's almost too much to take. Pleasure and pain battle it out. I'm not sure where one begins and the other ends.

'Fuck, Lydia. Fuuuuck.' His face twists, a silent cry on his lips and his expression one of tortured ecstasy. It fills me with so much feeling, my heart actually seems to have heated up, and then a second orgasm bursts over me, a tidal wave of pleasure and relief. Our eyes are locked in one long moment of primeval intensity that I'm not sure I'm ever going to feel again. If last night in the house felt like goodbye, this feels like death.

I'm not sure who tugs their gaze away first, but Tom pulls up my underwear and jeans before tucking himself back in and he draws me to his chest, burying his face in my hair before kissing my neck. Both of us are silent. The moment is charged with energy and it's as if neither of us dare speak for fear of disturbing it.

Chapter Twenty-Six

TOM

As I'm holding Lydia, realisation smacks me in the face. How am I ever going to let her go? Nothing has ever felt the way it does with her.

'That was quite something,' she says eventually, looking up at me – we've been standing like shell-shocked soldiers for a good few minutes. My heart rate is still jittery and erratic.

'It was,' I agree, resting my forehead against her, taking another shallow breath. There's so much I want to say to her. The words are bubbling in my throat, but they won't surface, I can't get them out. Instead, I stroke her hair and hold on tight. Just having her in my arms, with her arms wrapped around my waist, grounds and steadies me. Suddenly all the cheesy lines from movies make sense, coalescing in a bright crystal moment.

The feelings burgeoning inside me are so big and full it

feels like I'm trapped inside a balloon, feeling my way, stretching and trying to push through the outer skin. I need to put them into words but I don't have the lexicon or the experience. Love in our family has always been dealt out like cards, limited to one hand at a time, dependent on winning the last game. I don't know how to put into words the limitless depth of emotion. It's euphoric and terrifying at the same time.

I lift my hand to cup Lydia's cheeks and stare down into her face, hoping that I can share the feeling with my eyes alone.

And just like that her mouth curves and she brings her hand up to cover mine. My heart stumbles at the soft expression on her lovely face. How did I not notice before how beautiful she is, inside and out? And then suddenly it's simple.

'You're everything,' I tell her.

'Everything?' she asks and there's a question in her eyes.

'Everything. I am so gone on you, Lydia. I don't want this to be over after today.'

She swallows. 'Do you mean that?' It's the most uncertain thing I've ever heard her say and I realise that she has never been loved properly, so how can she trust the words?

'I mean it.' I kiss her slowly on the lips before lifting my head and looking into her eyes. 'I love you. You've healed something I didn't know needed healing. I never knew was there.'

To my surprise, a tear rolls down her cheek.

'Hey,' I say, swiping it away with my thumb. 'What's this?'

She gives a breathy laugh. 'That's a lovely thing to say. Thank you.'

With a sniff, she gives me a bleary smile.

'Don't cry.' My heart hurts to see her tears.

'It's nothing. I'm just happy.'

Not that it bothers me but I notice she hasn't told me she loves me.

'We should probably get ready for the party,' she says. 'Thank goodness trainers with dresses are a thing.'

'Or we could stay up here,' I tease, my heart lifting, despite noticing that she's the one that's moved on to the practical.

'You're insatiable. And I think your parents might notice that we haven't made an appearance.'

'You're no fun.'

She quirks an eyebrow. 'You weren't saying that five minutes ago.'

I kiss her, light-hearted and happy. It's not something I associate with being in this house.

'Shower time,' I say.

With a grin, she lifts my T-shirt over my head. 'Okay then.'

. . .

When Lydia sits on the edge of the bed to remove the dressing on her leg, before we get in the shower, I see how red and puffy it is. She catches my gaze.

'It's okay. Looks worse than it is,' she says with a weak smile.

'As soon as Annette gets here, she is taking a look.'

'You worry too much,' she says and distracts me by running her hand down my chest and pushing down my trousers. 'And you've got too many clothes on.' With that she strips off her bra and knickers and dashes into the bathroom. Wrestling out of my trousers I follow her.

'No funny business,' she says looking over her shoulder from beneath the stream of water, when I step into the big walk-in enclosure behind her. Her wet hair fans down her back as the water flows over her body and I want to scoop her into my arms again. I can already feel myself stiffening.

'No funny business,' I promise, even though the evidence below my waist is to the contrary. I take the expensive shampoo my mother provides in every bathroom whether me and my brother and sister are here or not and pump a good handful into my palm. Lifting my hands to the crown of her head, I begin to gently rub the soap in, taking my time, massaging her scalp.

'Mmm, that's good,' she murmurs. Her throaty appreciation, when I run my fingers through her hair to remove the soap, turns me on even more and I step closer, bringing my slick hands down across her breasts.

As my fingers touch her nipples, she goes limp and

slumps against my body, her bottom nestling into me, warm and soft against my rock-hard dick. 'I thought you said no funny business,' I tease. Despite her words, her hands cup mine, urging them on as she sighs, her head falling back against my shoulder.

Then she turns around and slides down my body and without any fuss, takes my cock into her mouth. She's a vision, water streaming down her back, her head bent, taking long slow drugging pulls along my length.

'Lydia,' I half groan, half pant. 'Oh sweet Jesus.'

She continues sucking and her mouth is so hot and tight and I can't stop watching her as I head for oblivion.

My balls tighten. There's tension in every part of my body and then my orgasm shoots like a white hot flame of pure incandescent pleasure. My knees almost give way but I haul Lydia to her feet and hold her tight, burying my face in her neck as the water pours over both of us.

'You're going to kill me,' I manage. All I want to do is close my eyes, lie down and hold her.

She gives me an insouciant grin. 'Would be a shame not to go with a bang.'

I laugh and hug her again. 'Who's incorrigible now?'

Eventually she steps out of the shower, wrapping herself in a towel.

'I need to dry my hair.'

She leaves the bathroom and I switch off the shower, momentarily feeling cold and bereft. I don't like the feeling, it's like someone's walked over my grave. An unwelcome reminder that nothing lasts for ever.

When I walk into the bedroom, there's a pair of trousers and a shirt that William must have dropped off while we were in the shower. It brings a slight blush to my cheeks. Normally I wouldn't be the least bit embarrassed – it wouldn't matter if he'd heard anything – but this is Lydia. And William is a crass idiot, he would make it tawdry. Taking the piss because that's what we do. Get in first, before the other can. If he says anything I will kill him.

'You look fierce,' says Lydia, looking at me in the mirror of the dressing table where she's sitting drying her hair into soft, glossy curls. Her towel is tucked around her chest, her shoulders bare, and I drop a kiss on her smooth, pale skin. She has a tiny freckle at the base of her neck and I go back to drop another kiss up on it.

'And you look gorgeous.' I smile at her reflection.

'You don't have to say things like that,' she says focusing on her hair, lifting her chin slightly. It's a gesture I recognise. Lydia going into battle, preparing her defences.

'I know I don't *have* to but I want to, because it's true.'

She frowns and I stroke a finger along her elegant collar bone. It's not like Lydia to be insecure.

In the mirror we make a good-looking couple. 'I noticed you as soon as I saw you at that insurance dinner. When I realised you were sitting on the same table, I swapped the place cards around.'

She turns round, her mouth dropping open. 'I didn't know that. You never said before.'

Because I hadn't wanted her to know that I'd fallen hard and fast the very first time I saw her and I've been fighting it ever since. But now my white flag is at full mast.

I shrug but give her a cocky grin. I can see that I've genuinely surprised her. 'Good move, I'd say.'

She shakes her head. 'Sure of yourself, weren't you?'

'No.' I reach out and trace a finger over her lower lip. 'Hopeful. I've never done that before.'

'Neither have I.'

We look at each other and I have another one of those moments where my heart expands with warmth and happiness.

There's a knock on the door and William shouts through it. 'Mum wants to know when you'll be ready. She wants some family time before the party starts.'

'We'll be down soon.' Family time is interrogation time. What are we all doing? Who is doing better? It's a tried and trusted Dereborn tradition.

Seeing my reluctant expression, Lydia squeezes my hand. 'I'm nearly done.'

Five minutes later, we're ready to go. In Rosie's dress she looks ethereal and elegant, not the Lydia I'm used to at all. I can't decide if I like her in it or not.

'Look at me,' she says with a laugh, flapping her frothy skirt. 'I look like an extra from *Midsummer Night's Dream*.' I laugh because while she's delicate in build she's the least fairy-like person I've ever met, which is what I like most about her. She's solid, real and persistent. She doesn't give up on things easily. Least of all me, it seems.

I hold out my arm and she hooks hers through it. 'Let's do this,' she says, squeezing my bicep. 'Just don't do a Cinderella and forget we have a deadline and a date in Trafalgar Square.'

'Not a chance.'

We leave the room and I'm conscious of her limp as we descend the stairs into the hall. Fuss or not, as soon as Annette arrives, she's on doctor duty.

Chapter Twenty-Seven

LYDIA

I always wanted a sibling – I dreamed we'd team up together against my parents. It never occurred to me that they might be used against me. As I sip the tea that Tom's mother has made for us all, I watch warily as the family circle round each other like a pride of lions waiting for the weakest prey to fall behind.

I'm wearing Rosie's dress, an expensive brand that I wouldn't normally look at, let alone wear. I'm being very careful not to spill anything down it because it's dry clean only. I really do feel like Cinderella at the ball.

People are due to start arriving in the next twenty minutes. I wish I could go outside as I'm having some sort of hot flush, every bit of me feels overheated – actually my leg is on fire – and it feels as though there's a little man with a very big hammer dancing about in my head. Probably just a stress hangover. It's been a hell of a few days.

Barbara and Nigel Dereborn are standing together, a united front, both immaculate in their smart, co-ordinating clothes. I wonder if this is by accident or design and then decide that Tom's mother wouldn't let anything in this house be coloured by accident. Everything is far too tasteful.

'So Tom, how's the new job going?' asks his father.

'Good. I went to Barcelona the other week.'

'Ah yes, the Consa-Calida fire. I hear you saved BHCA quite a packet.' Mr Dereborn senior really does have his finger on the pulse, even though he hasn't quite got his facts right. Tom *and I* saved BHCA from making a ridiculously inflated pay-out. 'Jeff Truman is leaving. I assume you'll be applying for his job.'

'I've only been there five minutes. I'm sure there are better candidates.' Tom looks at me and the corner of his mouth turns up. Is it chagrin or sharing the joke that I'm likely to be one of the other candidates, if not the sole candidate?

'Nonsense. I'll have a word.'

'Dad, you don't need to.'

'I don't *need* to,' Dereborn senior says with unnecessary sarcasm, 'but why the hell wouldn't I? Where's your ambition, Tom? William's on the board at Turnball's. We've got a reputation to keep up. You're my son. You should be aiming high, not resting on your fucking laurels.'

Barbara purses her lips. She clearly doesn't like the language, but she's right in there backing dear old Nigel up.

'He's right, Tom. You should let your father help. It's not as if you're not qualified or anything.'

'Yeah, Tom,' says William, that malicious glint back in his eye. I can't help scowling at him. He's a complete arse. I've warmed slightly to Rosie after she apologised to Tom earlier but seriously, this family is toxic. The whole environment feels worse than the one I grew up in. My parents were too out-of-it to know any different. Their neglect wasn't deliberate – just a by-product of their chaotic, disorganised, addiction-fuelled lives. These people should know better.

'And while we're on the subject –' Dereborn senior is back at it, like a battering ram, bullish and self-satisfied '– where's your mother's birthday present? Too busy to get her one, were you? Or was it that you just couldn't be bothered? It's a poor show, Tom, turning up empty-handed.' Tom's father's face is disappointment personified.

This is more than I can take.

'Actually, he's not.' Indignation makes my voice loud and a little shrill, which does nothing for the pounding in my head. But how dare they? How do they not see what a decent human being Tom is? I could go on and on about his virtues. My outburst is followed by the sort of silence that they have in films before the identity of the killer is revealed. 'He's a really good person,' I say, which sounds a bit lame, but he has so many good qualities I'm not sure where to start with them. 'You don't deserve a son like Tom.' Okay, possibly a bit strong but I need to make a point.

There's a gasp from Rosie and an indrawn breath from his mother but I can't stop now.

'The reason he wasn't around last week was because we were stuck in the middle of nowhere with no phones or access to money. Although you didn't stop long enough to let Tom tell you that. As I told you before, I had a bad accident. Tom could have left me but he didn't.' My rage has made me mildly inarticulate and repetitive. I wanted to say things in a much more erudite and cutting way, putting Mr Dereborn in his place, but I'm too choked up and emotional.

'He's kind, thoughtful, caring, supportive, loyal and kind.' I'm stumbling over my words and need an example. I'm not sure that Tom's dad has the sensitivity to appreciate a chipped sheep magnet, but Tom needs to know it counted. 'He bought me a birthday present, even though we had limited funds, because he's thoughtful. I know if he was at home and not stranded with a sick colleague, that he would have phoned his mum, bought her a present and been here, but he wasn't because he couldn't.'

Dear God, I'm putting up a woefully pathetic defence. I'm probably making things worse.

'I thought you said this woman was a work colleague.' Mr Dereborn turns his back on me and addresses Tom as if I'm of absolutely no consequence at all. What he doesn't realise is that I'm used to this, it doesn't faze me at all. What pisses me off is the fact that Tom doesn't say a word. Not one. He might as well be wearing one of those white featureless masks – there isn't a speck of emotion or feeling on his face. It's as shuttered and blank as the Sunday night at his flat he asked me to leave.

It finally dawns on me why Tom can't be emotionally available. Is it any bloody wonder, if these people were his example growing up? My fingers curl into fists at my sides, my tendons white with tension. A visceral desire to do physical harm to his dad spikes through me, raw and vicious. I've never felt anything like it before. I can understand why Tom has perfected indifferent implacability. He's had to.

'I'm the woman who actually gives a fuck about your son,' I snap. Tom's eyes widen. The shock on his face is almost amusing, except I'm too far gone with rage to find anything remotely funny.

'I don't think you know the first thing about my son,' Mr Dereborn sneers.

'What's his favourite film franchise?' I ask.

Dereborn looks outraged. 'I neither know nor care.'

'How does he drink his coffee?'

Dereborn turns away. Again. Rude.

'Tom. My study now.' With an imperious lift of his head, commanding Tom to do his bidding, he takes a couple of strides across the kitchen with short jerky steps that make him look like a puffed-up pigeon. Tom spends an agonising couple of seconds looking from me to his father and I see a vulnerability in him that I wasn't aware of.

Guilt comes tripping back in at full force. Tom is going

to kill me. I feel like something is gnawing on my intestines. I've really fucked this up. He'll never forgive me.

He's the North Pole, his face glacial.

I panic and open my mouth again. 'Don't you understand? He put aside his own priorities to help me. He's trying to win the money to make his film and he's not once complained that I've held him back. He waited a day for me to feel better and he came here to your party. You should be proud of him. Really proud. And someone wants to make his film. That's amazing.'

I've said the wrong thing. Tom's eyes flash a dozen warnings but it's too late.

'His film?' Now I know the true meaning of apoplectic. I've never seen anyone turn bright red or their veins almost burst out of their forehead but Nigel Dereborn suddenly looks possessed.

Rosie giggles not with amusement but with tense anxiety.

'My study, now,' he repeats.

Without a word, Tom follows him out of the kitchen just as the doorbell rings.

Barbara looks at her watch. 'I bet it's the Landers, they're always early.' She stomps off towards the front door.

'Well, that's set a cat among the pigeons,' drawls William, with a canary-eating smile.

'Fuck off, William,' said Rosie. 'I need a drink.' She marches off into the garden towards the bar in the gazebo.

'Welcome to the Dereborns',' says William, with a

patronising smirk. 'Tom's never brought anyone home before. You probably understand why, now.'

I glare at him. 'He's worth ten of you, that's for sure. You're a real bottom-feeder, aren't you?'

Leaving his mouth flapping like a guppy, I stalk off in the direction I'm facing. I don't want to see him, Barbara or Rosie.

I find myself in a long dark corridor with a dead end but I'm not going back into the kitchen, I might just grab a knife and chop bits off William. I know he's a product of his upbringing but I can't forgive him throwing Tom to the wolves just to keep the heat from himself.

I thought my childhood had been difficult and that having parents who cared would be all sunshine and roses. I realise now it depends on what the parents care about. Tom's obviously only care about their reputation and what people think of them, and their children are an extension of this. No wonder Tom keeps such a tight rein on his emotions. Love is a weapon around here. To be wielded to get what you want. I think he might be more damaged than I am – at least I know my own self-worth.

I lurk in the corridor for a second, not wanting to face anyone and then realise I must be outside Nigel Dereborn's study. He's bellowing at Tom.

'After everything we've done for you. And you want to turn your back on a solid career. My name will be a laughing stock in the industry. People will think you've had some sort of mental breakdown and can't hack it.'

I hear Tom respond. 'Don't be ridiculous, Dad. I'll take a year's sabbatical.'

'Sabbatical,' Nigel roars. 'I forbid it. Over my dead body.'

'Dad, calm down. Please.'

'And, what about that girl? Who the fuck is she? Going to tell me that you've knocked her up?'

'No,' says Tom.

'Well, who is she? And who's her family? What do they do?'

I wonder what Tom is going to say to this? A slight smile touches my lips.

'She's nobody,' says Tom. 'I barely know her.'

I swear my heart stops dead, the pain stabbing into my chest. I am such an idiot. Tears cloud my eyes and I have to get away. I run down the corridor, sharp flares of heat firing through my leg as I move. Turning into a room with French doors leading into the garden, I make my escape and finally stop on the other side of the expansive lawn in the shade of a large broad-leaved tree. I almost collapse on the spot my leg is hurting so much.

Hanging onto the back of a wooden bench, I stand, my chest heaving with the effort of keeping everything in. I AM NOT going to cry. My teeth are gritted so hard, they might crack at any second. I hiccough as the tears pound at the gate of my defences. I lift my chin higher and swallow the battering ram of a lump in my throat. The purple plant at the end of the garden with butterflies crowding over its buds is my sole focus as I force myself to take deep and even breaths. This is nothing new. I've been here before. What did I expect? It's my own fault for letting my barriers down. Tom's a victim of his parents' conditional love. And I'm not mad at him. It's not his fault. He's grown up having love used against him. I'm sad for him, I hadn't appreciated how damaged he is. It makes me love him just a little bit more.

I was damaged like that once, but I'm not now. I'm inured to hurt other people inflict because I don't have expectations of other people. I'm used to being let down. Except … I sigh to myself … this time is different because I allowed myself to believe. To believe that someone loved me.

Chapter Twenty-Eight

TOM

'Sabbatical,' Dad roars. 'I forbid it. Over my dead body.'

I honestly think he might have a heart attack. His eyes are bulging and his jowls, doubled with the extra weight he carries, are quivering with rage.

'Dad, calm down.' Anxiety twists my stomach as his face reddens even more. 'Please.' But he's in full patriarchal fury mode and isn't even listening. He's already moving on to the next agenda item.

'And what about that girl?'

Predictably, Lydia hadn't endeared herself with her home truths, even though her rise to my defence is a lighthouse beam in the gloom. A clear directional beacon. I've been lost for a long time.

'Who the fuck is she? Going to tell me that you've knocked her up?'

'No,' I say sullenly. By telling him the bare minimum

about her, keeping my feelings to myself, I'll protect her from his petty disapproval and manipulation. If he thinks I care about her, I know he'll interfere. He's quite capable of wrecking her career – for my own good, of course. I keep quiet, which in hindsight probably wasn't smart because Dad's hell bent on answers. He's not going to let anyone derail his son.

'Well, who is she? And who's her family? What do they do?'

There's only one way I can protect Lydia.

'She's nobody,' I say, with an indifferent shrug Lydia would be proud of, even though the outright lie pinches at my heart. *Liar. Liar. Liar.* I continue, desperate to head Dad off. 'I barely know her.'

Even as a defence mechanism, the words are a betrayal and nausea rises up my throat. Lydia deserves better. So much better. She definitely doesn't need to be tied into this warped version of love. There is no winner here. If I stay with her, I'll ultimately disappoint her. Even if I rebel against my father's wishes and make my film, it will never be good enough. Eventually Lydia will see me in the same way.

Thankfully Dad does calm down but then he moves on to stage two, reasoned, logical, wise parent.

He sits heavily in the chair behind his enormous desk as if the disappointment is too much to bear. I straighten, a Pavlovian response to the situation as the predictable lecture ensues.

'All we've ever wanted for you is for the best. Good job, good salary, good home and ... we're still waiting ... for you to settle down. At your age I was already on the board and engaged to your mother with our own home.' He shakes his head and sighs. 'Even your brother and sister have managed to get on the property ladder but you're still renting a poky apartment in a dreadful postcode. And now you're talking about giving it all up. I don't understand. What have we done wrong?'

Even though I know the anxiety twisting my gut is the result of classical conditioning, I can't stop the rising tide of guilt and sense of failure. I'm letting him down.

'You haven't done anything wrong.' God, how many times have I reassured him of this. 'I just—'

'Just what? Want to turn your back on your career for a whim? Do you know how many people would like to have a job like that? You wouldn't have it without my connections, guidance and advice. How do you think that makes me feel? That you're even considering giving it up.'

'Dad,' I say firmly and reasonably. I'm not going to back down this time. 'I'm not going to give my career up. Just take a sabbatical.'

'BCHA are hardly going to give you a sabbatical when you've just joined.' He sneers at my lack of foresight.

'I meant a personal sabbatical. I'll get another job after the film.' That's my fall-back option; I'm really hoping I can keep going making more films. There's a reason I live in a 'poky apartment' on my salary. I've been saving as much as I could for this very reason.

'And I expect you think I'll pull strings for you then, do you? Get you back in again? I'm going to have to tell my hard-won contacts that my son is just taking some time out to play, but don't worry, he's committed to his work. How the fuck is that going to look to the industry? And I can tell you what people will think. That's Nigel Dereborn's son, the dropout.' His mouth twists with bitterness as he spits out the final word and repeats it. 'Dropout.'

I've heard variations on this lecture before, when I smashed a window at school with a cricket ball, when I got a C in my Maths mock GCSE, when I wanted to go to Portsmouth, when I finished with Natalie, when William was made a director, when Rosie got married.

Love comes at a price.

But I'm not going to back down – I'm not giving up on my dream, but at the same time, I'm not going to provoke Dad any further. There's no point until I know I've definitely secured the funding.

I've had enough of chasing approval – this is why it's better to be self-contained and not allow yourself the chance to disappoint people. They will always want more. Even Lydia.

I emerge from the study with Dad on my heels just as Annette turns up.

'Annette,' my mother greets her warmly. 'How lovely to see you. And so good of you to come when I know how busy you are.'

'That's all right, Barbara. How are you?'

She greets my mother with a polite kiss on the cheek before doing the same to my father.

'Annette. How's the lifesaving business?' asks Dad. I refrain from rolling my eyes. He asks this question every time he sees her.

'Can't complain,' says Annette, with a tired smile. There are new tiny wrinkles fanning out from her eyes and deep purple smudges beneath them. I honestly think my parents believe she wafts around the wards laying a hand on fevered brows.

'Of course you can't,' says Dad with a sidelong glance my way. 'Dedicated doctor and all that.'

'Nice to see you, Tom,' says Annette giving me a hug. She gives an extra squeeze and a wink. She's much better at playing the dutiful relative than I am. 'How's Lydia?' she asks.

'You know Lydia?' asks my mother, hiding neither her surprise nor her disapproval.

Annette's smile broadens, with a just hint of mischief. 'Oh, yes, we were at Cambridge together.'

The way she says it, it sounds as if she and Lydia were

best buddies. I knew there was a reason I liked my cousin so much.

'Oh,' says my mother. 'Look, it's George and Annabel.' She darts off to the front door and I can hear her greeting them with great enthusiasm. Obviously important people. They must work with Dad.

'Any chance you could look at Lydia's leg?' I mutter while my parents' attention is diverted.

'Sure. I haven't got my medical bag with me, though. Where is she?'

I nod towards the window, through which I can see the floaty blue dress halfway down the garden near the gazebo that has been erected to house the bar.

All I want to do is get out of here. Get to London. Claim the prize and fuck off back to my flat away from everyone else. I was mad to think that I could have everything I wanted with Lydia. What the hell was I thinking?

Chapter Twenty-Nine

LYDIA

Half an hour later, I'm composed, standing – actually it's more like leaning as I grip the back of garden chair – making small talk with the couple from next door who are younger than the Dereborns and seem quite nice. The garden has really filled up now and in the mid-afternoon sunshine, it's really quite pleasant. Except as I look around the garden and the well-heeled people standing chatting with glasses of wine in hand, I realise that it's all surface and that beneath, it isn't pleasant at all.

Tom finally comes over, bringing a glass of wine for me and we move away to a spot by a magnificent rose bed. My heart turns over with that slow free-fall of love as I watch him approach. I can't help myself, even though I know that none of this has meant anything to him. I smile sadly at him. I've got my pride. I'm not going to rake over all the things he said. He must be furious with me for letting the cat out of the bag about his film.

'You can yell at me, if you like,' I offer.

'I don't need to do that,' he says, his voice so scrubbed clean of emotion it hurts. I've seen too much to ever be easy about him again. The injustice of his father's treatment is like an open wound. I want to comfort him but I have no idea where to start. Suddenly the divide between us seems wider, deeper and longer than the Grand Canyon.

'I really am sorry. I had no idea that they didn't know. They don't deserve you, you know,' I say, my voice quiet and honest.

Now, he finally looks up. 'Leave it, Lydia. You don't know anything.'

I should leave it there but I can't. Maybe it's as much for me as for him that I have to say something. I know what it's like to feel undeserving of love, to feel that you'll never be enough for anyone. It's a lonely place to be. I can't bear for him to be there.

'I do know,' I declare. 'And I promise you, you are worth being loved. For yourself.'

'And what do you base that marvellous supposition on, Ms Smith?'

My heart hurts at the way he's closed off again. Not for myself but for him. This is what love is – what they write about in songs and poems – and now I finally understand it. Love is selfless. He might not feel the same way but I need him to know that he is loved.

It's like stepping off a cliff edge when you know there is no parachute, no crash landing mat, no miracle waiting to catch you. 'Because I love you.'

Tom's face registers a brief flash of emotion before it goes blank again. 'We've been through an intense few days. I think maybe it's a bit like Stockholm Syndrome. We got close but it wasn't real. I think … that … we should leave here in the next half hour and get a train and get to Trafalgar Square.'

'Okay.' I'm not going to beg or plead. Strangely I feel quite calm. I'm not angry with him. If anything I feel liberated by saying the words out loud, by knowing that *I* can fall in love with someone. It feels like I've crossed a divide. How he feels about me is his problem. I'm not going to solve it for him but what I will do is help him achieve his goal. Suddenly, reclaiming my grandmother's house doesn't feel so important now. It won't change my life. I've changed my own life by being the person I am. The house is a symbol of a time I remember being happy, but living there again won't necessarily make me happy. I make my own happiness – it's not defined by a thing. Whereas for Tom, making that film will change his life. It will help define him. Winning the money will give him the freedom to do what he wants.

'Ah, Tom.' His parents approach us with another man in tow, the social veneer well and truly back in place. 'Do you know George? He's the chairman of the Institute of Chartered Insurers.'

The introductions are made, although I'm pointedly ignored by Nigel, treated rather like a trophy wife, albeit a slightly tarnished one, but George is one of the good guys.

'Lydia,' he says with a naughty twinkle in his eye. 'How lovely to see you. I didn't know you knew Nigel.'

'I don't,' I say with equally blithe delight. 'Tom and I work together.'

'Lucky Tom,' says George. 'Lydia's one of the highflyers at BHCA. I'm still hoping you'll join our committee one day. We could do with someone of your calibre. How many times do I have to ask you?'

Nigel suddenly warms up. 'I hear you were at Cambridge,' he says to me.

'Yes.' How the hell does he know that?

'Our niece Annette was there,' Nigel says to George. 'She's a doctor, you know.'

'Ah, talk of the devil, there she is.' Nigel bellows across the lawn, 'Annette, come join us.' When she arrives Nigel says, 'I understand you two know each other.'

Annette beams at me. 'Nice to see you again, Lydia. It's been a long time. How are you doing? How's your shoulder?'

I love her immediately, making out that we were equals at university and that she knows me.

Thankfully the Dereborns move off just then to find new victims to patronise with their largesse and hospitality.

'How's the leg?' asks Annette, catching me shifting my weight from foot to foot.

'Okay,' I say, wishing that I could sit down. It's bloody agony today. Standing on it is the complete red hot pokers experience. She gives me a sceptical look.

'Shall we go inside and I can take a look?'

I nod but as we're crossing the lawn Annette and Tom are grabbed by his parents. 'Someone you must meet.'

'Why don't I see you inside?' I say. 'I need to get my things ready. I've left my rucksack upstairs.'

'We'll see you in the front room. The door off to the right in the hallway,' says Tom.

I pack up my toiletries and lug the rucksack down the big staircase, careful not to bang it against my leg or the pristine white paintwork. Leaving it in the hall, I step into the front room. It's a library with floor-to-ceiling bookshelves and even one of those fancy ladders you see in films. With a rub at my sweaty forehead, I take a breath. I really don't feel great. My vision is a little blurry. Shit! Orange. Warning signals go off like fireworks in my brain.

Someone appears in the doorway just as I'm squinting at the big hedge surrounding the front garden. My gut twists. I can see an orange vehicle roof.

It's Annette.

'Let's take a look at this leg, then,' she says with a stern I'm-not-taking-any-shit-from-you look.

'It's fine. Honestly.' I glance back through the window, listening intently. No car doors slamming.

'Bollocks. Sit down.'

'I thought I liked you.' My words are glib but my mind

is elsewhere. Is it an orange Land Rover? I'm desperate to check.

'You do. Never bullshit a bullshitter. Now sit.'

She's too much like me to argue with. I'll get nowhere and it'll be quicker to agree.

I sit and pull up the pretty layers of the long maxi skirt.

'Fuck, Lydia. You moron.' She puts a hand out and tenderly touches the hot, puffy skin. My ankle is double its normal size and there's no definition between it or my calf. My leg is one solid column and the surface of the skin is tight and shiny.

She puts a cool hand on my forehead. 'You're burning up. I'm sorry but you need to go straight to A and E. You need antibiotics, preferably intravenous. I don't have anything on me. The nearest emergency room is Watford General.'

'Okay,' I say and I can tell I've surprised her with my instant acquiescence. 'I'll just grab my things and I'll get Tom and we'll go straight there.'

'No. Sit here. You need to keep that leg elevated. Unfortunately, I don't work in this area, so I don't know any of the medical staff there. I can't speed things up for you but if you explain at the front desk that you've got a severe infection, which could possibly result in sepsis, they'll see you quickly. We could call for an ambulance but God knows how long that will take. It's better if you get someone to drive you straight there. I'll go and find Tom and he can sort something out. He can drive his brother's car if need be.'

The minute she leaves the room I haul myself up the first few rungs on the ladder by the bookshelves. Across the street is an orange Land Rover emblazoned with the words *Fleeing for Your Life*. Two men are sitting in the front seat. They're sipping from thermos mugs.

I jump off the ladder, suppressing a small scream as pain jars my leg. It's as if Annette's diagnosis of infection has now given me permission to feel the full extent of pain. I rush out of the room. Luckily Tom meets me in the hall.

'Where's Annette?' he asks. 'Has she seen you?'

'They've found us. They're sitting in a car outside the house opposite, drinking coffee.'

'You're kidding me.'

'No, I wish I was. We need to go. How did they find us?'

'What did Annette say?'

'Annette?' I pretend it was so insignificant I've forgotten already.

'About your leg? Remember?'

'Just a bit swollen. I'll need to get some antibiotics and she hasn't got any on her. Is there any way out of the back of here? Back to the train station. We need to go now.' I look anxiously around. I don't want Annette coming back and we do need to make our escape. We're so close, we can't get caught at this stage. Neither can we give up. I can go to hospital later.

Thankfully my sense of urgency communicates itself to Tom.

'There's a gate through the garden into next door's

garden. They're on the corner, so we can get out onto a different street. They won't see us. Let's go.'

'My—'

'I'll get it,' he says.

'It's in the hall. I just need the money in the sock.'

'Bloody hell, Lydia. Are you sure?'

I muster up a smile. 'I know where you live.'

A second later we're hurrying out of the French doors at the back. Luckily this section of the garden is separate to the area where all the guests are and there's no sign of Annette. Tom leads me to a gate in the fence.

Next door's garden is nowhere near as well kept and we hurry across the uneven lawn towards a set of double gates. I'm doing my best to keep up with Tom, even though my leg is on fire, every step compounding the pain.

We stop and peer through the gates.

'We're only round the corner from the station,' he whispers and we both look upwards for drones.

'I think we're okay,' I say. We walk slowly, not wanting to draw attention to ourselves.

We turn the corner and there's the back entrance of the station. We made it. We're home and dry. My whole body sags with relief and the sudden release of tension makes me a bit wobbly as it's all that's been keeping me going.

'Shit,' says Tom and suddenly yanks me backwards.

At the end of the tunnel under the platforms, beneath the sign for the ticket office, is a familiar figure. He's on his phone and he has his back to us.

'Mark,' I say in a shocked voice. A wave of nausea overcomes me and I have to lean back against the wall. Lightheaded, I take a couple of breaths.

'Are you okay?' Tom gives my face a concerned appraisal.

'Yeah, just a bit shocked. How do you think they found us?'

'Probably staked out our homes. I should have thought of it. I don't think of this as home. For obvious reasons,' he adds with a bitter twist to his mouth. Without thinking I touch his arm.

He glances down at my hand and his mouth tightens.

'Is there any other way of getting to London from here?' I ask.

'If we could get to Chesham we could get on the underground. They probably wouldn't think of that.'

I think for a moment. I'm not giving up now.

'Presumably they have taxis here.'

'Yes, but on the front forecourt. If Mark is there, he's not alone.'

'Look at me.' With one hand I tug at my hair and the other flounce the skirt of my dress. 'They're not expecting to see a girl in a dress with curly hair. I could walk along the road under the tunnel to the front and get in a taxi and come and pick you up.'

Tom looks at me. 'It's risky.'

I think of his father. 'You want to make films, don't you? You're not going to give up now.'

341

He scowls. 'Hell, no.'

'Then it's worth the risk. We're so close.'

'Are you sure? I don't like to think of you … on your own.'

I glare at him. 'I managed to look after myself just fine before you came along.'

My heart is banging so hard as I walk through the railway tunnel along the road. I'm walking right into danger. I have a woozy moment but it's cool in the tunnel and when I put my hand on the cold stone wall, it grounds me. With gritted teeth I keep walking. When I step back into the sunlight I turn right and there is the station forecourt. Another orange Land Rover is parked on the double yellow lines. Oh for a traffic warden when you want one.

There's a line of four taxis but to get to the head of the queue I have to walk right past the passenger window of the Land Rover. I falter for a second but then remind myself that might catch attention, so I force myself to keep walking, hoping my pronounced limp isn't going to draw unwanted attention. I pin my gaze to a point beyond the vehicle. I recognise the ninja driver all in black. It's Teasedale. I only saw him once briefly. If I recognise him, he's going to know me. My hands are so clammy I want to wipe them on my skirt. I'm three steps from the car. He glances up, just as the wind tosses my hair across my face. I almost freeze. The urge to turn and run is so strong. His gaze slides off me and back down to the phone in his hand.

With my pulse doing the light fantastic I keep walking and go to the taxi driver.

'Taxi to Chesham underground please.'

He frowns. 'Is there a problem with the trains?'

'No.' I shake my head and grab the handle of the back passenger door.

'Okay,' he says, clearly puzzled. I slide in. He starts the engine.

'And can we just go to the back entrance to pick up my partner.'

'Sure,' he says with the sort of indifference that suggests if the customer is paying the money he's happy to take it, no matter how odd their request.

I sneak a quick peek at Teasedale as we drive past. He doesn't even look up. I let out the breath stuck fast in my lungs for the last thirty seconds with a small silent whoosh. Now I just have to stay conscious until we get to Trafalgar Square.

Chapter Thirty

TOM

Regret is stronger than excitement as the underground train leaves Oxford Circus station. Only two more stops to Charing Cross and we'll be home and dry, but I'm worried about Lydia. After the initial euphoria of making it to Chesham and the underground, she's become quieter and quieter. I know her well enough to know she's not a sulker; if she's got something to say, she'll say it. Maybe she's realised what I've secretly known all along: that I'm only going to disappoint her in the end. Like I've disappointed my dad, again. No matter how hard I try, or William or Rosie try, there'll always be something else we need to perfect. I don't want to be controlled like that but it's a condition of love. My parents are always quick to withdraw their praise or affection when we don't act the way we should.

I look at her. Her eyes are closed and her face is very flushed.

'Lydia, are you okay?'

'Mmm?' she asks, her eyes taking a second or two to focus on my face.

'Are you okay?'

'Mmm. Yes. Fine. Where are we?'

'Next stop is Piccadilly Circus and then Charing Cross.'

'Good,' she says. She's been distant since we left my parents' home. Not that I blame her. When she told me she loved me I took the easy way out, denied my feelings, but she'll be grateful one day. She deserves someone better – and that's so fucking easy to say but I know I'll be jealous of anyone else that gets to know her the way I do. I fucking love her but I can't risk it. Letting someone have that control, that power over me. There will always be a demand or an expectation of me.

The train pulls into Piccadilly Circus and I stare out of the window at the passengers waiting to board. As it slows I spot two broad-chested men in tight black T-shirts, earpieces and black jeans, with buzzcuts. Midge and Jonno.

They're talking to each other, and they don't look as if they're scanning the passengers, but they're about to board this carriage. I guess if they found out we left my parents they'd know we must be converging on one of the tube stations near the square.

'Lydia. We need to move.' I nudge her.

'What?' She seems fuzzy and confused.

I grab her hand and tug her though the passengers who've stood to get off. There are a few grumbles but we move into the next carriage. I push Lydia to one side of the door and stand just out of sight, so that I can keep an eye on the two men boarding the carriage we've just vacated.

Neither seem concerned with their surroundings. Both are on their phones. I glance up. Lydia is sliding down the wall.

I grab both of her forearms. 'Lydia. Lydia. What's wrong?'

'I'm fine,' she mumbles. 'J-just … tired.'

'We're nearly there,' I say and I can't help giving her a kiss on her forehead. Her skin is hot as fire. 'Lydia. You're not well.'

She straightens and focuses. 'I'm fine. Nearly there. Yes.' She gives me the ghost of a smile. 'We're going to do it.'

I nod but anxiety is gnawing a hole in the pit of my stomach. She looks terrible. How can she have deteriorated so much since we left the party? There's something seriously wrong with her. I need to get her to hospital.

The train comes to a halt and the door slides open. People pile off in front of us but I've made my mind up. We're going to Waterloo. I'm taking Lydia to Guy's and St Thomas' hospital.

'Tom.' She tugs at my sleeve. 'We've got to get off here.'

'No, we're going to the hospital. Next stop.'

'No!' She slumps sideways, virtually falling out of the

train, and I have to jump off to catch her and stop her landing on the platform.

'Lydia! What are you doing?'

'We're here.' Her words slur. 'You are going to make that film. Promise me.'

'Lydia, it doesn't matter.' I take her burning cheeks in my hand. I don't give a toss about the bloody film at this moment. She needs help.

She jerks her head back and her voice is fierce, her eyes glowing – almost demonically. 'Yes, it does. Come on. We *have* to do this.'

I shake my head. I can't do this to her. 'There'll be other opportunities,' I say and there will.

'Tom!' she hisses, her face a contorted mask of urgency. 'We're here. *I* need that money. For my gran's house. Please.'

My heart falters. I can't deny her.

'We go straight to A and E, as soon as we've…' Done whatever it is that we need to do. Funny, I've no idea what that might be. Whatever it is, I guess there'll be someone there with a camera filming.

She pushes herself up and starts to head in completely the wrong direction. I grab her hand.

'It's this way.'

We enter the ticket hall and even though she's leaning on me, Lydia is limping badly. There's a choice of exit. Trafalgar Square or The Mall. I bite my lip. What if they're waiting for us, staking the exit? That would be harsh but they've not been mucking about to date. I guess a hundred thousand pounds is a lot to give away. Although presumably they want some dramatic footage of us running into the square.

'Not going to happen,' I mutter under my breath. I need to get this over and done so that I can get Lydia to hospital. Trust her to be stubborn to the absolute last.

Daylight dazzles us as we emerge from the exit. Nelson's Column is in sight.

Lydia leans on me as we walk over to the to the pedestrian crossing. To my right I spot Jonno and Midge. They catch sight of me just as the light turns green. I stop and scoop Lydia into my arms. She's not that heavy but I'm not Superman, which results in a pathetic half-run, half-walk rather than the manly romantic gesture it would be in a rom-com. I make it across the road, stumbling slightly on the uneven pavement, my eyes fixed on the nearest fountain, aware of Lydia's grip around my neck.

'We're going to do it,' she mutters. 'We're going to do it.' A taut manic smile lights up her face – reminiscent of a scary Halloween mask. I'm so focused, I don't bother to apologise to the tourists I barge into. And suddenly we're there. At the edge of one of fountain pools with Nelson's column to our right.

I ease Lydia down, careful to hold on to her as she leans against the stone coping.

'Lydia?'

With over-bright eyes, she looks over my shoulder. 'We

made it,' she says swaying. 'We bloody did it. You can make your film.'

'And you can rebuild your house.'

'Pfft,' she snorts, or at least I think that's what it's supposed to be. It's got very little oomph. It feels like she's a leaky balloon with very little air left. 'It's just a house. I don't care anymore.'

Before I can ask what she means, Jordan and Mark materialise from the crowd, with a camera man behind them. I realise he's been filming the whole time. I hope they're bloody pleased with the footage.

'Well done, mate.' Jordan holds out a hand to shake mine. I shake my head in disbelief. He's congratulating me? 'Well played. You led us a right merry dance.'

'We need some medical ass—'

Before I can finish Lydia crumples. I just manage to catch her before she hits the deck. 'Lydia,' I cry. A hard fist clamps around my heart as I cradle her limp body. 'Lydia.' Her cheeks are two hot spots of red and there are beads of sweat across her forehead.

'Call an ambulance,' I snap at Mark, my insides like writhing snakes.

Already a crowd is gathering around us and I want to protect Lydia from their curious stares. Bloody vultures.

I lower her to the ground, my voice an agonised whisper as I say over and over again. 'Lydia. Lydia.' There's no response and, helpless, I look up at Mark, who's on the phone with his back to me.

A woman steps forward and hands me a folded fleece to go beneath Lydia's head and someone else offers a jacket to go over her. I'm not sure she needs to be kept warm but it feels like some sort of protection.

'Ambulance is on its way,' says Jordan. 'ETA five minutes.'

I hold Lydia's hand and her eyes flutter open for a second.

'Tom.' There's a faint squeeze on my fingers and her eyes close again.

I lean down but I dare not kiss her. Her breath is painfully shallow and she suddenly seems so fragile.

Mark crouches down beside me, handing me my phone and wallet.

'Well done, mate. You just won yourself a hundred grand.' I realise that Jonno is filming and I glare at him.

Can't the fucker see that Lydia needs help? I'm already on the phone dialling Annette's number.

'Tom. Are you at the hospital with Lydia?'

'What?'

'Where are you?'

'Trafalgar Square. Waiting for an ambulance. Lydia's collapsed.'

'Fucking hell. I told her to go straight to hospital.'

'What? She never told me that.'

'Fucking idiot. I told her at the house. When you'd gone, I assumed you were headed there.'

'She … never said a word.' Guilt almost strangles my vocal cords. 'I should have…'

'She should have told you her leg's badly infected. Possible sepsis. Tell the paramedics as soon as they get there. She needs pumping full of antibiotics. I told her to go straight to A and E.'

'She never said anything,' I murmur again, more to myself than Annette. Stupid. Stupid. What was she thinking? But I know exactly what she was thinking and everything changes in that one moment. Like an explosion deep below the surface, it's shock waves resonating through me. This is love. Unconditional love. There's no payment, no expectation. This is Lydia. Selfless and generous. There's no way I'm ever letting her go. She is everything.

'I wonder why?' sighs Annette. 'You'd better bloody hang on to her.'

I hear sirens growing louder and louder. 'Don't worry, I intend to.'

I see Lydia's eyelids flickering and even though I've no idea if she can hear me, I lean down to her head and whisper in her ear, 'Bloody hell, Lydia. You'd better get better quickly because I'm going to kill you and then I'm not letting you out of my sight. I love you, you crazy idiot. You're … you're everything. Remember that. Everything.' My words are choked in my throat as sheer panic constricts the vocal cords. I haven't cried for years but it seems today is the day I'm going to start again.

Chapter Thirty-One

LYDIA

'Will you just fuck off! You've got your footage, now bugger off.' My brain might be woozy but it's pretty obvious Tom is rather irate. I try to gather myself but it's impossible. It's as if I'm behind a thick plate of glass and all my senses have gone into hibernation. I give up and keep my eyes closed, aware that I'm lying down and tucked in. It's the first time I've ever given up all responsibility for myself.

Tom is still shouting and although his voice is dull in my head, I can hear every concern-filled word.

Tom. I feel a little goofy. Tom is here. Everything will be okay if Tom is here.

'Calm down, mate,' says a very reasonable voice a little distant to Tom's.

I wonder what the fuss is but it's hard to work out

among the spaced-outness of my head. I'm not sure where I am or why Tom is here.

'No, I will not calm down. Leave her alone. Just let them get her into the hospital, for fuck's sake.'

'The viewers will want to know she's all right.'

'She will be if you leave her the fuck alone. Will you switch that bloody camera off.'

It's the last thing I hear as I slip into the darkness.

There's movement and I feel myself being lifted. I open my eyes, I'm on a stretcher being lifted by two paramedics out of the white box of what I'm assuming is an ambulance. It's a new experience.

I try to say something but a garbled 'Om' is all that comes out of my mouth.

'Lydia.' He's immediately leaning over me, concern and worry etched into his features. No one would blame me for saying he's not looking his best, some might even say he's looking haggard. He takes my hand and he's not so much squeezing it as hanging on for dear life. 'It's okay, we're at the hospital. You've got a drip.' He lays his other hand so gently on my cheek, you'd think I'm made of tissue paper. His fingers are icy cold next to my hot skin and I shiver but it's because I'm touched to my very bones by his tenderness. A foolish little warm bubble loosens in my chest.

'You're going to be okay.'

Looking around, I see a cameraman, a sound man with a boom, and Mark, who's saying, 'This is good stuff. Viewers are going to love the romance.'

Tom doesn't even glance away, although his impatient growl makes it clear they're lucky they've not been punched. 'You okay?' he asks so softly, his eyes never leaving my face. I could almost believe he cares but then I remember. 'She's nobody.'

When I wake several hours later, it's dark and I'm in a small room. Tom is dozing in a chair beside me, one hand on my arm as if worried I might go somewhere. The thought makes me smile as I study his sleeping face. The grey pallor has gone but he still looks exhausted, as if he's been through an ordeal.

I guess it's been quite a day. This morning seems a lifetime ago. Like Tom said, 'We've been through an intense few days.' Amazingly, I'm feeling better – a full-blown miracle. The painful man-trap grip on my leg has eased and the paving slab on my chest lifted, making it so much easier to breathe. Aside from the physical improvement though, there's a calm inside me – a sensation of ease, though I don't really know why. Maybe it's because I'm resigned to what comes next. It's nothing new and no surprise. Tom might have put things down to Stockholm

Syndrome, and that's his prerogative, but I know what I feel is real.

'Lydia?' Tom's soft whisper pierces the quiet of the room.

'That's me,' I say.

'How are you feeling?'

'Alive. Sorry for passing out on you.'

'You should be sorry for a hell of a lot more.' He sounds angry, which I wasn't expecting, but I'm too exhausted to complain even though I want to. Seriously! What right does *he* have to be angry?

'I spoke to Annette.' He leaves the sentence hanging.

'Oh.' Why is guilt my immediate response?

There's a very severe expression on his face as he stands up and sits on the bed, leaning over me, one arm propped on the other side of my waist. My pulse takes a few missteps. I'm an idiot.

'If you'd got sepsis, you could have died. You're not stupid, you knew you were taking a risk.'

I shrug my shoulders.

Tom grasps them. 'Don't do that. It matters. You matter.'

I'm pissed off enough to rally and even though it hurts to confront it, I manage a small mocking laugh. 'No. I don't. I heard you.' My voice cracks as I hear the words again in my head. 'Y-you … t-told…' I'm back at school being laughed at, with my 'Mike' schoolbag. A nobody with nothing. I lift my chin and hold his gaze. I won't be that person again. 'You told your dad I was nobody.'

'I did.' He doesn't flinch and a tiny part of me admires his honesty even though it hurts.

I swallow back the tears and stare steadily at him.

His face softens. 'But I didn't mean it. I said it to get my father off the subject. I don't want my parents to be any part of us.'

'Because you're embarrassed by me.' I sound petulant but I can't help it. It's no more than I expected. I'm Chlamydia Smith after all. He still doesn't even know my real name – why give him any more reason to walk away?

'No, never.' Tom grabs my hands. 'You're everything, Lydia.'

I shake my head, slumping back into the hard pillows. How can I believe him? Much as I want to, I know I'm clutching at proverbial straws. 'Stockholm Syndrome, remember?'

'I didn't mean that. I was trying to protect—'

'Please don't, Tom.' I turn my head away. I'm too weary to fight back. 'Let's just leave it.'

Tom stands up, his mouth a grim line fixed above his set jaw, and he walks out of the room.

Stealth tears leak out of my eyes, but I leave them to run down my face. It's no more than I expected.

A nurse comes in to check my drip and introduces herself as she takes my temperature and pulse before checking the felt pen boundary line that has been drawn on my swollen leg.

'What's that for and who did it?' I ask.

She gives me a cautious smile. 'It's to measure how far the infection has spread and I'm pleased to say it's not moved. Dr Shadwell did it when you first came in. You were a bit out of it.'

I frown, trying to pull a memory out of my woolly brain, but there's nothing there. My last memory is of Tom picking me up and carrying me into Trafalgar Square. I remember Nelson's Column towering over me against the backdrop of the grey sky and then … nothing.

'I hear you're on some reality TV show. They were trying to film in A and E but Doctor Shadwell soon put them right.'

'Oh no,' I say, praying that they didn't manage to get any footage. I must have looked so pathetic and useless, relying on a man to carry me over the bloody finish line.

'But so romantic. Your man there got quite heated, pushing them away and then insisting you have a private room. He's quite a hottie.'

'He's…' I'm about to deny it but in the face of her appreciative grin, the words stall.

'Do you want anything to eat? You missed dinner but I can get you a sandwich or something.'

I realise I haven't eaten all day, so I nod, but I'm not that hungry.

'I'll see what I can find. It might take me a while but bear with…'

It doesn't sound promising and I wish I had my

rucksack and my digestive biscuits. See? This is why I always carry food.

She disappears and in the corridor I hear her talking to someone about finding me some food. Whoever it is offers to go for her and she thanks them. I guess she has plenty of other stuff to do.

A minute later, Mark appears in the doorway, a sheepish expression on his face.

'Hi.'

'Hi.'

'Thought I'd come and check on you.'

'It's all right. I've no plans to sue,' I say. The acute discomfort in his body language suggests he'd rather be out on a mountain in freezing rain than here.

'Good, that's good. I … em … I've got something to show you.'

'Pardon?' All sorts of things whizz through my mind. I have absolutely no idea what on earth it could be.

He takes out his phone. 'Some of the footage.' He hands it over as if it's a live bomb. 'I think you should see it.'

A tide of red has risen up his skin from the neck of his black Henley T-shirt to the tips of his ears.

I take the phone and watch. It's Tom staggering over the crossing with me in his arms, his face in a tight grimace of determination. God, this is every bit as embarrassing as I thought it was going to be. I hate my vulnerability being on show for everyone to see. I close my eyes but I can't regret it. Tom will have his money and that's worth my discomfiture.

'You need to watch,' Mark urges.

In the next moment, I see myself fainting but it's not me the camera pans in on, it's Tom's face, contorting with anguish as he cradles me before lowering me to the floor. It's when he phones someone that he turns and I watch as he breaks down. He's sobbing. It's as if my heart has been grabbed and squeezed hard and all the breath whooshes out of me. It's almost painful to watch. But there's more. I watch as Tom gathers himself and then hovers over me the whole time I'm out cold and then when he's getting out of the ambulance with me. If actions speak louder than words, then I've seen all I need.

I look up at Mark, an ember of hope burning bright.

'Why are you showing me this?'

'I'm a sucker for happy endings?'

'And?' There's more, I can tell.

He looks up at the ceiling as if choosing his words carefully. 'Tom.'

'What? Tom asked you to show me this?'

He holds out his hand, requesting the return of his phone and looks over his shoulder before nodding. 'I wasn't supposed to tell you.'

Hope leaps in my heart, as bouncy and joyful as a spring lamb.

'Do you know where he is?'

Mark gives a non-committal shrug. 'Around somewhere. We're doing a quick debrief before he goes home.'

As soon as I hand the phone back he scuttles out of the room like a small, chagrined boy rather than a six-foot man mountain.

I reflect on what I've just seen. Tom. Naked emotion on his face. There's no disguising it. In those shots, his emotions are totally obvious. Available.

Damn I need to find him. I swing my legs out of the bed and wince as my foot hits the floor. Fiery pains shoot up my leg and I have to take a moment to catch my breath. Forewarned, I take a more careful step and something tugs my hand. Bloody IV tube. I grab the rail on which the bag of solution is suspended and without thinking it through, start walking out of the room and into the corridor. I'm on a mission. I have to find Tom.

I've only taken a few steps when a voice from behind me shouts.

'What the fuck do you think you're doing?'

I know that voice. I smile and slowly turn around.

Tom is marching towards me, a paper bag clutched in one hand.

He comes right up to me, sparks of anger dancing in his eyes. He looks quite magnificent and I sigh because I've gone all gooey inside.

'Looking for you,' I tell him.

He puts his arms around my waist. 'Jesus, woman, will you just get back into bed and stop giving me heart failure?

The nurse said you wanted something to eat, so I've been out to get you something.'

Taking charge of my IV drip, he ushers me back to my room and spends an inordinate amount of time fussing over the bed, helping me in and rearranging my blankets before sitting on the bed, hemming me in.

'Why did you leave?' I ask.

'Because I needed proof. As you were brought out of the ambulance, Mark said viewers would love the romance. I wanted you to see what they'd seen.'

'You love me,' I say with wonderment, scarcely able to believe it.

'Been trying to tell you that. Although I'm still mad at myself for ballsing things up.'

'That makes two of us,' I reply, but I'm smiling at him as he traces a hand down my face, pushing my hair back from my cheek.

'No, you didn't do anything wrong, well … apart from putting your health at risk and not expecting enough from other people. From now on that stops. You deserve to be loved.'

He's right. We both deserved to be loved. Him for the person he is and not the person his parents want him to be, and me because I'm not that neglected child anymore. I'm a person in my own right.

'And so do you,' I tell him.

I realise together we're everything.

Epilogue

Two Years Later

'Shh, everyone,' bellows Nigel. 'They're about to announce the winner.'

We're in the living room of Tom's parents' house assembled for a celebration party. Even though everyone has probably seen this clip before, they do all quieten and watch the television screen.

'And the BAFTA for short film goes to ... *Love on the Run.*'

The camera picks Tom out in the audience as he rises to his feet and makes his way to the stage, then it pans to me, standing clapping hard, tears running down my face and my eyes shining with pride. I could have burst with it that night.

'Still my favourite dress,' murmurs Tom standing beside

me. I wore the black dress I was wearing when we first met – a private joke between us. He's convinced me that it was his lucky charm.

On the screen, Tom steps on stage, in a tailored tuxedo, ducking his head to the microphone. He looks as handsome as any of the movie stars there and once again I feel that same overwhelming rush of pride.

He holds up the BAFTA in his left hand and grins before launching into the expected speech, which I knew at the time he hadn't prepared because he genuinely did not expect to win that night.

Together we watch as, in time-honoured tradition, he starts thanking the cast, the production company and the crew. Next to me he winces at himself as he keeps remembering names he'd forgotten. 'I can't believe I forgot to thank Josh,' he mutters. 'Or Kit or Bella.'

'You were a little overexcited,' I tell him. 'None of them minded.'

'Shh, this is the best bit.'

I nudge him in the ribs, still a little embarrassed a week on.

'Of course there's one person without whom none of this would have been possible.' He stops and looks down from the stage at me. 'Lydia, this award is for you. For being everything to me. For supporting me, loving me and putting up with me. I love you.' He raises the BAFTA above his head towards me.

Around us there is a burst of spontaneous applause.

'You old smoothie, Tom,' says William.

'So romantic,' says Rosie.

'We brought him up well,' Barbara says smugly, linking her hand through Nigel's arm. 'More fizz, anyone? It's not every day we have a BAFTA winner in our midst.'

Nigel opens another bottle of Piper Heidsieck and starts refilling the flutes around the room. Twenty of their friends and neighbours have gathered to celebrate Tom's win.

Tom's fingers tighten on mine. The irony is not lost on either of us. Relations with his parents have been strained until very recently – funnily enough, since around the time Tom's film was longlisted. Our stock went up even more when it was nominated a month ago. After the awards were announced last week, it rose to stratospheric heights. Tonight Tom is very much top of the favourite child pile and William's much vaunted board director position has been usurped by the award-winning film director title.

Barbara comes over with one of the neighbours. 'Tom, this is Helga. Her daughter is at drama school.'

'That's nice,' says Tom, his voice as dry as year-old dust. I discreetly nudge him.

'She'd love to be in any of your future productions,' gushes Helga.

'I'll bear it in mind,' says Tom. I give his fingers an approving squeeze. He can be diplomatic when he wants to be. It's taken a long time for him to let his parents back into his life and I know he's done it for me, because having parents that care – even if they care too much about the wrong things – is better than having parents that don't care at all. I've no idea where mine are and I'm not interested in finding out. My gran's house is almost restored but I'm not moving back in. It feels like I'd be going backwards but I'm happy to see it plucked out of the mire of my parents' custodianship. I'm going to sell it and Tom and I are going to find a place that's ours.

Another neighbour comes over. 'Well done, Tom. It must be so exciting making a film.'

'Thank you,' he says graciously, catching my eye.

The movie, which was filmed in one very long month last year, had been all-consuming, with Tom working long days and nights fretting about camera angles, continuity and budgets. Although seeing the final product makes it all worth it. He handed his notice in to BCHA the December after we'd taken part in *Fleeing for your Life* and moved into my flat. Ostensibly it was to save money, but the truth was we rarely spent a night apart so it was just common sense.

The reality TV pilot was a huge hit – especially the love story – which all the tabloids picked up on. I like to think Tom and I 'made' the series. The footage of me falling down the hillside – hurrah bloody hurrah – and Tom telling the crew to bugger off in the ambulance have both gone viral. We even get recognised in the street occasionally. It's been quite a two years.

'How much longer until we can escape?' Tom whispers into my ear.

'We can't. You're the star of the show,' I tell him.

'Nah. I'm not. Come on, I've had enough adulation. Let's get out of here. I'll go first. Come out to the car and meet me.'

'You can't leave your own party.'

'Want to bet? I'm favourite child, they'll forgive me.' He winks. 'Besides, you're the only person I want to impress. Let's go.' He's like a small boy on Christmas Eve – it's quite a change from the man who could bring the portcullis down on his emotions so effectively.

We slip out to the car parked on the drive.

With the ignition switched on, Tom takes a moment before he puts the car in gear. 'Shall we go and celebrate properly?'

'What a good idea,' I say, slipping off my heels. 'Now, are you going to tell me what's in the boot of the car?' I give him an impish grin.

'You don't miss a bloody trick, do you?'

'It's a bit hard to miss an overnight bag and that my favourite knickers are missing, or that you've been fidgeting all night.'

'You're going to have to wait and see,' he says mysteriously.

When we hit the M6 going north an hour and half later, I know exactly where we're going.

It turns out Tom has booked a certain Airbnb – and this time we have the key code.

Acknowledgments

Thanks to Matt for his encyclopaedic *Star Wars* knowledge and the unabridged quote about the best characters in the series. Personally, it's still Hans Solo for me.

Especial thanks to all on Team Cassie, my editor Charlotte Ledger and everyone at One More Chapter, you've no idea how many people are involved behind the scenes to get a book out there, my agent Broo Doherty and my writing buddy squad – you know who you are.

Finally to you dear readers, I hope you enjoyed *Hot Pursuit*. I had a blast writing it.

Life is harder for some people than others and it isn't always fair, there is no level playing field and this book is for everyone who copes with difficult circumstances and still turns up with a smile on their face.

ONE MORE CHAPTER

YOUR NUMBER ONE STOP
FOR PAGETURNING BOOKS

The author and One More Chapter would like to thank everyone
who contributed to the publication of this story...

Analytics
Abigail Fryer
Maria Osa

Audio
Fionnuala Barrett
Ciara Briggs

Contracts
Sasha Duszynska
Lewis

Design
Lucy Bennett
Fiona Greenway
Liane Payne
Dean Russell

Digital Sales
Hannah Lismore
Emily Scorer

Editorial
Kate Elton
Arsalan Isa
Sarah Khan
Charlotte Ledger
Bonnie Macleod
Jennie Rothwell
Tony Russell

Harper360
Emily Gerbner
Jean Marie Kelly
emma sullivan
Sophia Walker

International Sales
Bethan Moore

Marketing & Publicity
Chloe Cummings
Emma Petfield

Operations
Melissa Okusanya
Hannah Stamp

Production
Emily Chan
Denis Manson
Simon Moore
Francesca Tuzzeo

Rights
Rachel McCarron
Hany Sheikh
Mohamed
Zoe Shine

**The HarperCollins
Distribution Team**

**The HarperCollins
Finance & Royalties
Team**

**The HarperCollins
Legal Team**

**The HarperCollins
Technology Team**

Trade Marketing
Ben Hurd

UK Sales
Laura Carpenter
Isabel Coburn
Jay Cochrane
Sabina Lewis
Holly Martin
Erin White
Harriet Williams
Leah Woods

**And every other
essential link in the
chain from delivery
drivers to booksellers
to librarians and
beyond!**

When you can't find the perfect date for the holidays, you hire him!

Hotshot lawyer Rebecca Madison is dreading the annual family Thanksgiving break where the question on everyone's lips will be *'why are you still single?'*.

When it comes to her career, she's the best of the best, hired for her take-no-prisoners approach. But when it comes to her love life…well, she hasn't found the loophole for her happily-ever-after just yet…

Available now in paperback, eBook and audio!

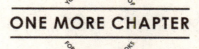

ONE MORE CHAPTER

One More Chapter is an
award-winning global
division of HarperCollins.

Sign up to our newsletter to get our
latest eBook deals and stay up to date
with our weekly Book Club!
<u>Subscribe here.</u>

Meet the team at
<u>www.onemorechapter.com</u>

Follow us!
 @OneMoreChapter_
 @OneMoreChapter
 @onemorechapterhc

Do you write unputdownable fiction?
We love to hear from new voices.
Find out how to submit your novel at
<u>www.onemorechapter.com/submissions</u>